SIREN PUBLISHING

Marisa Chenery

Lady KNIGHT

LADY KNIGHT

Marisa Chenery

EROTIC ROMANCE

Siren Publishing, Inc.
www.SirenPublishing.com

A SIREN PUBLISHING BOOK
IMPRINT: Erotic Romance

LADY KNIGHT
Copyright © 2008 by Marisa Chenery

ISBN-10: 1-60601-153-7
ISBN-13: 978-1-60601-153-9

First Publication: November 2008

Cover design by Jinger Heaston
All cover art and logo copyright © 2008 by Siren Publishing, Inc.

Printed in the U.S.A.

PUBLISHER
Siren Publishing, Inc.
www.SirenPublishing.com

DEDICATION

For my family who is always there and my father, Ray Chenery, who nurtured my love of writing.

LADY KNIGHT

Marisa Chenery
Copyright © 2008

Prologue

The sun shone brightly as Ariel walked through the meadow. The heat of the day made her regret wearing the wool homespun gown. But when she worked in the fields with the villagers she could not bring herself to wear the better quality gowns of her everyday life.

As thane of Elmstead, her father had taken great pride in administering to the villagers and serfs under him. Now all that had changed. Since her mother's death two years before, Swein of Elmstead had withdrawn from much in his life.

At ten and eight Ariel tried to take her father's place. Her father still held the moots when disputes could not be settled among the villagers. But all else, he let Ariel handle mostly by herself.

Ariel did not mind, for she had found herself more than capable of performing the job. The only thing she regretted--her father had pushed her out of his life and had practically built a wall around himself.

She pushed the thoughts of her father out of her head. Today was too beautiful to spoil with such depressing thoughts. Looking up, Ariel saw there not a cloud in the sky. The blueness of it almost took her breath away. She looked across the meadow at the myriad of brightly colored flowers that were just as spectacular as the breathtaking sight above her.

A flash of light caught her attention. Ariel watched as a Norman knight slowly walked his horse out of the forest that bordered the meadow. She knew him to be a Norman by the distinctive nasal piece attached to the helmet he wore upon his head. Ariel had only seen one other Norman knight, just before her mother died, who had been passing through. Her parents had offered him their hospitality and he had stayed the night.

Ariel had been fascinated by his broad sword and his shield, so different from that of her father's. Her father fought with a battle axe and a round shield that carried no emblem.

This Norman appeared to be very much like the other. He wore the same type of helmet and chain mail. Ariel looked lower and saw the broad sword hanging from the belt strapped around his waist. His shield hung over his saddle within easy reach. The shield bore an emblem, the same as the other knight's, but his was different. The shield had been completely painted white and in the center a gold unicorn stood on its hind legs. It almost seemed to be pawing the air as its ruby colored eye glared back at Ariel.

Her attention swept back up to the knight's face as he raised his arm and removed his helmet. Ariel felt her jaw drop open as she stared at him. His apparel may be the same, but his looks did not compare.

His dark blond hair he wore long and caught back by a leather thong so it fell to his shoulders in a tail. The other Norman had shaved the back of his head. When asked why, he had said that it was easier to control when wearing a helmet all the time.

His eyes were what intrigued her most about this Norman. At first glance they appeared to be a pale green, but at closer inspection she realized that they were actually gold. As she looked, the corners of his eyes crinkled when he smiled at her.

"I hope you found what you are looking for."

Ariel felt the heat rise to her face. She normally could talk to any person she encountered, but this knight left her speechless.

"You probably only speak English, do you not?"

Ariel continued to look at him. He thought she was one of the villagers. The rough homespun gown did nothing to make him think otherwise. Far be it for Ariel to change his opinion. She did not want to reveal herself, because if she did, courtesy would dictate she offer him her hospitality. She did not want anyone outside of the village to see what her father had become.

"Come. I would enjoy your company even if you do not understand me. I'm sure we will get our ideas across somehow."

Ariel stared at the hand he reached out with. She knew she should not take it, but for once she wanted to do something just for her. Knowing what he offered and thinking she could reveal herself if it came to be the only way, Ariel placed her hand in his so he could pull her up to sit in front of him.

He held her around her waist with one arm as he turned his horse and walked back into the forest. They did not go far for just passed the tree line a small pond sat in the center of a clearing. Surrounded by thick trees, it made a perfectly secluded spot.

Ariel looked closer at the knight's face and fought the urge to swallow. His perfectly sculptured square jaw with a slight cleft in the centre and the sharp cheekbones made him the picture of pure male essence. Ariel saw the slightly darker stubble of hair on his chin and cheeks. On some men it would have made them look shabby, but it only enhanced the male beauty of the knight. There was something about him that called out to her, to the lonely part of her. She felt alone, even though her father was still there physically.

He chuckled at her close scrutiny and lowered Ariel to the ground. When she took a step back from the horse, he dismounted and tied the reins around the nearest tree. Without turning he unbuckled his chain mail, slipped it over his head, and hung it with his sword belt over his saddle.

Ariel briefly wondered how far she should let this go. For when he turned back, he reached for her and slowly pulled her toward him. The first sensation that hit her was the all engulfing warmth that radiated from his body. She had had no idea men could be so warm. She had not been this close to her father since she was a very little girl.

When he lowered his mouth toward her, Ariel jerked her thoughts back to the knight. His lips lightly brushed hers for the first time. Ariel caught the knight's scent, a combination of horse, sweat and his own distinctive male scent.

His lips felt soft and warm, which surprised Ariel. She had expected she would not like kissing a man. She had been wrong. He increased the pressure of his lips as she tentatively slid her arms up and locked them around the back of his neck, otherwise she would have fallen.

His tongue gently licked her bottom lip. Ariel could not stop the surprised gasp that left her. He took the opportunity to slip his tongue into her mouth and gently sweep inside. It was all Ariel could do to stay afloat.

Something unknown and totally new began to build in the pit of her stomach. Ariel knew she should put a stop to this now, but the feelings sweeping through her took all her reasoning away. All that mattered was making the building pressure grow.

Ariel felt the ground rise up to meet her as the knight gently lowered her down. The weight of his body on hers felt right. With hands like magic, he stroked them down her body. Ariel arched into him as he clamped down on her breast through her gown. The heat of his mouth grew more intense as he suckled her through the coarse wool.

Ariel clawed at his back as she tried to pull him closer, seeking something she did not understand. She barely noticed her legs had been bared to the air. One of his fingers found her hot, slick opening and gently probed her, checking her readiness.

She automatically tried to clamp her legs together against his hand. He once more took her mouth until she relaxed her legs. Pushing against her inner thighs he opened them further.

His fingers began searching once again until he found her clit. He rubbed it back and forth. Ariel could not stop the moan that escaped her. Taking it as a sign of her readiness, he rose up and pulled at the fastenings of his trews. The hot, hard length of his shaft gently probed the entrance to her body.

The feel of him sent Ariel over the edge. Instinctively she raised her hips to give him better access. He slowly pushed the head of his hard length into her slick pussy. The feeling of being stretched soon gave way to pain.

At the piece of skin that barred him from sheathing himself fully, the knight pulled back and surged through it with a single stroke. At Ariel's cry of pain, he gently kissed her until the whole length of his shaft filled her. The pain started to fade as he suckled at her breast. The sensations she had felt before returned. When she rocked her hips into his the sensation increased. It was unlike anything she had felt before. With their bodies joined, Ariel felt closer to the knight. It was a closeness that she now realized had been missing from her life.

The knight began to move on her, sliding his length in and out. His pace increased and something steadily built inside her. Matching his strokes, her body tightened around his. Moaning, she let herself go as a sensation of unbelievable pleasure swept through her as her body clamped down around his hard shaft, milking him. He pumped into her once, twice then filled her with his seed.

Ariel held him close as the knight collapsed on top of her, panting. She relished the feel of his heavy body on hers. When his breathing returned to normal, he kissed her sweetly and straightened his clothes. Ariel pulled the skirt of her gown down once more feeling modest. The knight smiled down at her. He stared down at her, as if he wanted to memorize everything about her. He then pulled something off his finger and placed it in her hand.

"A gift for you in exchange for the gift you gave me. I will not soon forget our time spent together. If this was another time and place, I don't think I would be able to leave you behind."

Without another word, he donned his mail and strapped his sword around his hips. Once mounted upon his horse, he gave Ariel one last smile before he turned and disappeared into the forest.

Ariel sat on the ground and watched the sun sparkle like diamonds off the water in the pond. She looked down at her hand. On the palm of her hand sat a ring. Depicted on the gold band was the same unicorn that had been painted on the knight's shield. A single ruby eye flashed as the sun caught it. Ariel then realized what she had done. She had given herself to a man she didn't know. A man she would most likely never see again. Numb, she felt her world come crashing down around her.

Chapter 1

Elmstead, England
January 1066

Swein of Elmstead sat in his hall watching his daughter stitching near the fire. Ariel was not the same girl she had been seven months ago.

It had taken two months for the changes to break through the fog he had been living in for the past two years. He had not known how much he had come to depend on his daughter.

She had kept Elmstead together during his neglect. Ariel had taken care of the villagers, even worked along side them in the fields. But what he found to be the greatest blow was finding out his master of arms, Osbern, had started to train Ariel how to fight with a battle axe.

He had begun teaching her shortly after her mother's death and had continued to do so for the last two years. Osbern had been quick to inform him that Ariel had been afraid if the fryd was called to battle, she would have to lead Elmstead's men. She had feared her father would not be capable to do it. Osbern had even said Ariel was as skilled, if not better than, any lad her age, which Swein found shocking in itself. Now all had changed.

Swein could not help but let his eyes fall to Ariel's stomach. She was in the last stages of pregnancy. When her morning retching had soon become obvious, she had been forced to reveal her condition. .

He had watched her mother go through the same sickness in her early stages of pregnancy with Ariel. It was then he started to take back control of Elmstead. Ariel had gladly handed everything back over to him. She had been happy and relieved to have her father back. But one thing had not changed, her training with weapons continued.

Even though pregnant, Ariel trained every day for hours at a time. The training had even taken on a new twist. She had asked Osbern to teach her how to use a broad sword.

How Ariel had found out Osbern was the only one proficient enough to teach her, Swein could only guess. Osbern had once been connected to the royal court, where most of the Normans in England could be found. Osbern had learned from one of them the art of using a sword. Saxons fought with the battle axe leaving the swords to the Normans.

In the end, Ariel's request had been granted. Osbern had managed to find a sword for her and training had begun the next day. Even with her stomach large with child, she trained. Looking at her, Swein could see a strength to her body that had not been there seven months before.

Ariel must have felt him staring at her. She looked up from her stitching and gave him a slight smile. "What do you think, father? Will this hold up?" Ariel held up the small baby shift she had been working on.

"I'm sure it will hold together." Swein watched as Ariel resumed her stitching. He still found it painful to look at her.

She was so much like her mother. Blonde hair, so light, that when in the bright sunlight, it almost appeared to be white. Blue eyes that matched the color of the sky at its bluest. All were the same, even right down to the full red lips. In the last two years, as Ariel grew into a woman, the resemblance had become stronger.

There were a lot of unanswered questions hanging between Ariel and himself. They never spoke about the father of her child and he wouldn't push her. She would let him know when she was ready.

Ariel put down her stitching and stifled a yawn with her hand. "If you do not mind, Father, I'm off to bed. I just do not seem to have the same energy as before."

"You will once the child is born. You should slow down, take care of yourself. Maybe the training sessions should stop until after the birth."

"Nay, I need them right now. Don't ask me to explain for I cannot. It's just something I have to do."

Swein rose and helped Ariel to her feet. "It's your choice. I want you to know that I will be here for you."

"I know. Try to understand, you can't help me with this." Ariel placed her hand on her stomach. "This is my responsibility. This child is mine to take care of and I will not fall apart because of it."

With a kiss on her father's cheek, Ariel bid him good night and left him standing in the hall.

* * * *

The bright sunlight coming from the single window high up in the wall helped to dispel the gloom inside the hall. Two female serfs quietly cleared away the remains of the morning meal. Ariel watched the shaft of light split as each woman crossed its beam.

Now that her father had once more resumed his duties, Ariel spent more time with the running of the hall. She made sure the rushes were changed on a regular basis and chose the meals that would be served each day. In a way, Ariel felt relieved to have just the hall to worry about. She had another, larger, responsibility to see about in a few months.

She tried to think of the unknown knight every day. And not from any lovesick emotion either. She just did not want to forget what he looked like when she faced him again. And they would meet again. She would get her revenge if it was the last thing she did.

The ring he had given her hung from a gold chain that she wore around her neck, hidden beneath her clothes. She had not been able to show it to her father. What would her father think? She didn't even know the knight's name. All Ariel had was the engraved emblem on the ring. Swein would think her a fool.

His gold eyes were the other thing Ariel would not forget. No matter how long it took, she would remember the look in his eyes as he bid her good-bye. He had thought her a good bit of fun and nothing more. At least that was what she thought she had seen. When they crossed paths again, she would recognize them. She could still see the bemused look on his face. She had been nothing but sport to him. She would change that when she faced him once more.

Feeling her temper rise the more she thought of the knight, Ariel surveyed the hall. It had been built by her grandfather, the first thane of Elmstead. The sturdy timber hall had adequate space to hold a large gathering if the need arose. The tables and benches not needed on an everyday basis were stacked in one corner of the room.

The family sleeping quarters were at the back of the hall, separated by a partition. There were three chambers in total. The larger one was her father's, which he had shared with her mother when she had been alive. The other two were relatively the same in size. One had been set aside as a guest chamber and Ariel claimed the other as her own. The hall from the outside looked much like the villagers' huts except for being much larger in size.

Ariel found her thoughts interrupted when a man opened the hall door and entered with a gust of cold winter air. Ariel recognized him as one of the Earl of Essex's men. The earl was her father's liege lord.

Stepping further into the hall he came to stand before Ariel. "I bring a message to Swein, thane of Elmstead. It is of grave importance."

From his appearance he looked to have been on the road for some time. Ariel signaled one of the serfs to bring the man some ale. "My father will be here shortly. Please sit and refresh yourself while you wait. He's in the village."

Her father would undoubtedly be here any minute. When a stranger arrived at the hall, the villagers took note and usually informed Swein. Any news from the outside world was held in high regard.

The door once more opened and her father entered the hall. Spotting the messenger, he crossed the distance over to the man. "I understand you carry a message for me."

"Aye, my lord." The messenger reached into a pouch that hung from his belt and passed a piece of rolled parchment to Swein.

Ariel watched her father's face as he read the missive the Earl of Essex had written. It couldn't have been good news, for his face became more set and drawn looking the longer he read.

"Is it not good, Father?"

"Nay, I'm afraid not. King Edward has died and Harold Godwinson has been crowned king. It says the messenger will provide more information." Swein turned his attention back to the messenger and waited for him to speak.

"The earl felt it would be better if I told you in person rather than putting it to parchment. In case you had some questions."

"Tell me what you know."

"King Edward died during the night on the fifth of this month. The queen, Harold Godwinson, the Archbishop of Canterbury, and the king's friend Robert Fitzwinmark, were at his side before he passed. They were able to rouse him once before he went to his eternal rest." The man paused and looked at Swein to see if he should continue. When no questions were asked he once more took up his tale.

"When the king awoke, he spoke of a dream he had had. The earl did not hear exactly what the king spoke of, but it is said in the dream the king saw two dead monks that he had known in Normandy. The monks foretold that with all the wickedness in England, the land would be consumed with fire and war. God would only stop the punishment when a felled tree joined itself back together with no help from man, break into leaf, and bear fruit."

Swein looked at Ariel. It had been rumored that the king had promised his throne to Duke William of Normandy when the duke had come to England some years back. It had never been confirmed by the king, but it had been said the duke had taken him seriously. Now that Harold had been crowned, it would only be a matter of time before the news reached Duke William.

Ariel felt Swein watching her closely as she placed her hand protectively on her bulging belly. The messenger soon cleared his throat and looked at Swein. When he received a nod in return, he continued.

"King Edward then called Harold to his side and took his hand. He commended Queen Edith to Harold's protection. As well, he ordered Harold to serve and honor the queen, since she is his sister. Normans who resided at court were to be given the choice of either going back to their land or swear fealty to Harold. Lastly, he gave orders to where he would like to be buried at his new minister and to have his death announced everywhere without delay."

King Edward had finally chosen his successor. It could only mean one thing. King Harold's reign would not go uncontested.

Swein nodded to the messenger. "You may rest here tonight. I have no questions. You provided everything I would want to know."

"I will gladly accept your hospitality, but I must be on the road by dawn tomorrow."

Ariel moved so she stood beside her father after the messenger left the hall. "This bodes ill for England, father."

"I know. According to the earl's letter, the king was buried the morning after his death and Harold crowned king that same afternoon. It makes no difference that we don't want a foreign king, Duke William will come. There will be no peace for England."

Chapter 2

Rouen, Normandy
January 1066

The air was crisp with the sun shining brightly. It made a perfect day for a hunt. Broc St. Ceneri stood in the palace courtyard waiting, one of the many who had decided to hunt with Duke William this day. His gaze swept over the others. They were all primarily here to curry favor from the duke. By the way they acted toward one another you would never know they were almost always at each other's throat. Only on their own lands did they practice the art of war on their neighbor's castles.

Broc was not considered one of them. He was only tolerated because Duke William had taken a liking to him. It did not matter to Broc that he was not accepted. He valued his friendship with the duke above all else. Being a landless knight at the age of eight and twenty, he could not help but think he was lucky to be where he was.

A burst of laughter came from the group of men directly across from him. When they noticed Broc watching them, they turned their backs on him and continued to speak in hushed tones. Broc shook his head in amusement. They may not like him, but their wives and daughters did not share the men's opinions. Being slightly over six feet tall, and with his peculiar eye color, it made him a novelty. Those things were not the only reason why they sought him out. He couldn't claim ignorance about what his face did to women.

He accepted some of the offers from women who approached him. Mostly widows, but lately even they did not hold his attention. The face of the Saxon girl always came to mind.

Broc was always surprised to find her never far from his thoughts. She had attracted him at first sight. The stuff of her gown had made him come to the conclusion she was a peasant. He usually did not use the peasant girls as other lords did, but this time he had not been able to pass her up. She had looked so innocent with her pale blonde hair hanging down her back. When she had stared at him, it almost felt as if her eyes were gently caressing him.

He had known she had no idea what she did to him. That alone had excited him more than any experienced widow's caresses could. To have been the first man she had known had been his undoing. He had never felt such complete satisfaction from any other woman.

Duke William stepped out into the courtyard and silence descended. Broc pushed the thoughts of the girl back and smiled as William approached. Their friendship had sprung up when Broc had presented himself to the duke. He had come searching for a place in William's household. As a younger son from a not so wealthy family, there was nothing for him at home. All he could hope for was to be accepted into a rich household. The only thing he possessed worth having was his skill with the sword. William had accepted him on the spot and placed him with the knights of his court. The friendship had begun shortly after.

The duke grabbed Broc's shoulder and gave it a squeeze. "Well, my lad, are you ready for the hunt?"

"Aye, my lord." William was one of the few Broc did not have to look down on. Even at the age of eight and thirty, the duke's body was still as heavily muscled as his own. "It seems to be a perfect day."

"Right you are." Before William could continue a lone rider clattered into the courtyard. The man pulled his horse to a stop and dismounted. "I bring a message for Duke William."

The duke stepped away from Broc and walked over to the messenger. "I'm here. Tell me the news you bring."

The man gave William a slight bow. "I come from England. The holy King Edward has died. He succumbed from the illness. They crowned Harold Godwinson King of England the same day they laid King Edward to rest."

William's face went white then turned red with fury. The messenger took a step back as the duke began to lace and unlace his cloak. Without a word, William turned and went back into the palace. When he did not return for some minutes everyone assumed the hunt was to be abandoned. The other participants began to disperse as they mumbled among themselves.

Everyone had known Duke William expected to be the next King of England. Now someone else had taken the throne.

Broc knew how upset the duke must feel. It had been his tales of his time spent in England that had made Broc want to go to that country. As he made his way over to the palace, a hand reached out and pulled him to a halt. Looking behind him, Broc saw it was William FitzOsbern who had stopped him. He was the duke's seneschal and one of William's friends. Broc liked the man as much as he liked the duke.

"I will go to him, Broc. You haven't known him as long as I have. I know how to get him out of this mood. When he is ready I'm sure he will want to talk to you."

Broc nodded his head in agreement. FitzOsbern was right. He would know what to say to the duke.

* * * *

William FitzOsbern found the duke in the hall. He sat on a bench with his head against a pillar with his cloak thrown over his face. FitzOsbern entered the hall humming. At the sound of his voice, the duke looked out from under his cloak. "You might as well stop trying to hide. The news has probably spread throughout the city by now. It's time to stop grieving. It's time you do something about it. Sitting here under your cloak will not give you the throne of England."

William dropped his cloak back into place and chuckled. "You always know what to say to bring me out of my moods. So be it, my friend. I'll call the barons together."

Chapter 3

Ariel felt a hint of spring in the March air. It even smelled like spring. Birds flitted across the clear blue sky, almost as if they knew the warmth had returned to the earth.

Smiling at the bird's joyful play, Ariel made her way to where Osbern held practice lessons. It seemed to take her longer to go anywhere lately. With her belly quite large now it made her feel very clumsy.

Almost as if the baby knew she was thinking about it, Ariel felt it give her a few kicks. With a reassuring pat to her belly, she mentally told it to be patient. It would not be long now. The village healer had told her to expect the baby's arrival any day.

At the field where she knew Osbern could be found, Ariel stopped to watch two men from the village sparing with battle axes. Though farmers, the village men were trained to use the axe at a very early age. As part of the fryd they needed to know how to wage war, as well as till a field.

Her lessons had ended a few weeks before. Her father had said enough was enough. Osbern had also refused to teach her anything more until after the birth of her baby. They may have been able to stop her from handling a sword, but they could do nothing about her watching others. Ariel had come every day since her lessons had ended. She needed to learn more. A plan had begun to form in her head shortly after the messenger had arrived with his news.

Seeing Ariel, Osbern left the two men and approached her. "Must you come all the time, my lady? I thought you would have other things on your mind, what with the babe soon on its way."

"Nay. I can't wait until I can take up arms again."

Osbern shook his head at Ariel and once more turned his attention back to the two villagers.

Ariel smiled. Osbern was gruff around most people, but with her he was

always polite. He was a big man, which was not surprising. It was hard not to be when you were the master of arms. For a man in his middle years, his arms were still thick with muscle. His whole body was covered with muscle. As if that were not intimidating enough, Osbern stood well over six foot. Ariel wondered how many men would actually want to face Osbern in battle.

"Osbern, I have a request."

"What would you like, my lady?"

"After the babe is born and my lessons begin again, I would like to be fitted for armor."

"What do you mean fitted for armor?"

"You know perfectly well what I mean. I want a full sized shield, not the smaller one I have been using, chain mail and helmet, all of it."

"But why? I thought this just gave you something to do, my lady."

"Nay, it's more than that. I intend to use what you have taught me and I must be able to do it properly outfitted."

Ariel turned and left Osbern to ponder exactly what she had meant by her request.

* * * *

At barely dawn the next day Ariel found herself unable to sleep any longer. She lay in her bed and wondered what had brought her out of a deep sleep. The sensation of her stomach tightening, followed by a sharp cramp, it soon became obvious what was happening. The baby had decided it was time to make itself known.

When the pain subsided, Ariel reached for her shift and slowly donned it. About to cross the floor to her door, another pain hit her. This one felt stronger than the first. Not waiting for it to end, Ariel reached the door and opened it. "Father, I need you!" Even before the words had left her mouth, another pain hit her, followed by a gush of water.

Swein came to her chamber door, raking his fingers through his hair. He looked at the puddle of water at her feet and then back up at her face. She was sure it showed the pain she felt. "I'll get the healer. You go back to bed."

"Nay, don't leave me."

Swein put a reassuring arm about her shoulders when she looked at him with uncertainty. Gaining the attention of one of the serfs in the hall, he said, "Go to the village and get the healer. Tell her my daughter has need of her."

The woman turned and ran out of the hall. After she left, Swein gently led Ariel back to her chamber. By the time the village healer arrived, Ariel seemed to be well into the birthing process. Her father seemed surprised by how fast things were progressing. He had told her he had sat by her mother's side while she had given birth to her. According to him, it had taken most of a day for Ariel to finally be birthed.

At the sight of the thane sitting beside his daughter's bed, holding her hand the healer shook her head. "It's time for you to leave, my lord."

"Nay. I watched her come into this world and I will watch my grandchild enter it as well."

"It isn't proper." Ariel clutched tightly to her father's hand. Shrugging, the healer moved to stand at the foot of the bed. Lifting Ariel's shift to her knees, the woman reached between her legs to see how things were going. "She seems to be further along than I expected."

"That is what I thought. She woke up a few minutes before I sent for you."

"My lady must have slept through the early stages and woke up when the pains became intense. It happens sometimes." Just then Ariel let out a moan. "From the look of things, it'll not be long now."

The wait turned out to not be long at all. A few minutes later Ariel began to bear down. Swein talked calmly to her, encouraging her as she struggled to push her child into the world. When the baby finally slid out of her body, Ariel let out a grunt of satisfaction. She then lay back down on the bed and closed her eyes.

At the sound of the infant's first cries, Ariel opened her eyes. "What is it?"

"You have a fine big son, my lady." The healer wiped the baby clean and wrapped in a blanket. She placed the small bundle in Ariel's arms.

Looking down at her son, Ariel felt tears come to her eyes. He was beautiful. He had tawny blond hair and his small face was the very image of the knight's. The baby opened his eyes and Ariel stifled the gasp that rose up within her. Gold eyes stared up at her, so much like his father's.

Ariel saw Swein mark the color of her baby's eyes. There was no one in

Elmstead who had eyes such as that. "Well, Ariel, what are you going to call my fine looking grandson?"

"Colwyn. He is quite handsome, isn't he?"

"That he is. Rest now, my sweet. I'm sure there is a crowd outside the hall just waiting to hear about Colwyn."

Watching her father leave, Ariel let the healer take Colwyn from her arms and slipped into a well deserved sleep.

Chapter 4

Ariel spent the next four weeks getting to know her son and letting her body heal. To her greatest surprise she found nursing Colwyn one of the most rewarding things she had ever done. Her son became the center of her life. The love she felt for him grew stronger each day.

Hearing the baby gurgle, Ariel watched her father talk to Colwyn. Swein had the baby cradled in his arms while he showed the infant the hall.

"You pay attention, little man. One day this will be yours."

"Father, Colwyn is too young to understand what you are saying."

"He may be now, but he won't always be too young. I want him to always know what his birth right is. He must never forget."

The sting of being a bastard was what her father wanted to prevent. Swein wanted to shield Colwyn from it. Ariel had been debating with herself whether or not to tell her father about the knight. One of the reasons why she had kept silent was from embarrassment. What would her father think? She had given herself to an unknown man without giving it a second thought. He had every right to disown her. Even though she had been dressed as a peasant, she should have made her real status known to the knight.

Seeing Swein had sat down on one of the benches, Ariel went and sat down beside him. "I guess it's time we talked about Colwyn's father."

"Only if you are ready to do so. I would never force you to tell me if you weren't ready."

"I know you wouldn't." Ariel shifted until she faced her father. "You need to know. It's something I'm not proud of. The only good to come out of it is Colwyn.

"I met him in the meadow. I had just finished helping in the fields. A knight came out of the forest, a Norman knight. He was unlike any other man I had ever seen. I think it was his eyes that first drew me." Ariel could no longer look her father in the face. "I knew what the knight wanted. I just didn't stop him. He gave me this before he left."

Ariel reached into the bodice of her gown and pulled out the ring, the one she always wore around her neck. She didn't know why she kept it, but once she found herself with child she couldn't give it up. It was all she had that held a clue to the knight's identity.

Swein released Ariel's hand and reached for the ring. The ruby eye of the unicorn flashed as he moved it for a closer look. Ariel knew the emblem would be unknown to him. "He didn't tell you his name?"

"Nay. The ring is all he left as to who he is. I didn't give him my name either."

Swein dropped the ring so it hung from Ariel's neck once more. "You want to find him again, don't you?"

"Aye. At some point I do, but there is something I want to do first." Slipping off of the bench, Ariel knelt before her father. Placing her hands on his knees, she looked up at him beseechingly. "I want to go with the fryd when it's called to assemble."

He had to have been expecting this. He had to have known why she had requested armor. The armor was almost finished, waiting only for Ariel to return to her lessons.

"If you must, you must. I'll not stop you. Osbern says you have a talent for it. But I need to know one thing. What will become of Colwyn when you leave?"

"I'll only be gone two months. He can stay here with you. We can find him a wet nurse. I'll nurse him until I have to leave."

"You will not be able to continue to nurse after you come back. Your milk will have dried up."

"I know. That's one drawback. The other will be leaving you and Colwyn behind."

"Can I assume you will be leading our men?"

"If you don't mind."

Swein shook his head and chuckled. "Nay, but there is one condition. Osbern will go with you and fight by your side. I will not lose you now that we are close again. With your mother gone, you and Colwyn are all I have."

Ariel stood up and wrapped her arms around her father's neck. "I love you, father. I'll do as you wish." Looking down at Colwyn who was still cradled in Swein's arms, she found him asleep. "I see someone decided it was his bedtime. Maybe I should retire for the night as well. I start training again tomorrow. Osbern wants me to start very early."

Swein stood and gently placed Colwyn into his mother's arms. "You'll need your rest. I've told Osbern to train you as if you were a boy. It'll be a lot harder than what you have been doing in the past. I have arranged for one of the villager's daughters to come and help you with Colwyn. So I will bid you goodnight, daughter."

* * * *

Broc watched the carpenters work at the River Dives where Duke William had ordered his fleet to be built. It had taken much argument for even this to be brought about. To say the barons had not been agreeable was an understatement. The first meeting William had with his barons took place in February and had been an utter failure.

Robert Count of Mortain, Odo Bishop of Bayeux, Roger of Beaumont, Walter Gifford, Hugh of Montfort, Roger of Montgomery, William of Warren, and William FitzOsbern had all been present at the first meeting. All had thought William had a legitimate claim to England's throne. So a second meeting with the barons was suggested. It had gone a little better than the first, but not by much.

In the second meeting the duke presented his many complaints against Harold, mainly his right to his kingship. He stressed that Harold had usurped his throne. He had taken a kingdom that rightly belonged to William. But all the barons had cared about was the profit to be made in this venture. Most didn't think the profits would be worth the risk.

The main complaint of the barons was that their feudal duty did not include fighting overseas. Most thought the crossing would be too dangerous because it had never been done before. They thought England would be too strong to defeat, and the attempt to do so would ruin them all.

Broc chuckled to himself as he recalled what William FitzOsbern had told him how he had tricked the barons into supporting the duke. FitzOsbern had tricked them into making him their spokesman to the duke. Instead of supporting their complaints, FitzOsbern had addressed William in terms of servile loyalty. He had said he would provide the duke with sixty ships full of fighting men and the barons would not only cross the sea, but bring twice the number of men duty demanded. The barons of course had shouted their disagreement so uproariously the meeting had to be ended.

William then summoned the barons one by one to him, speaking to each alone. Without the support of the others, each could not win the battle of wills with the duke. In the end they each promised William a certain number of knights and foot soldiers. Most declined the offer to go with the duke, but they would be sending a son or some other relation to lead their men. One of the other promises he had wrung out of them had been to build enough ships for the crossing, which was now being built.

William had sent Broc to see how they were progressing. From the look of things, the fleet would be ready for the summer crossing. The ships themselves were based on the Normans' ancestors, the Vikings, designs, double ended with high curved sterns and sternposts. Most were decorated with dragon's heads and tails. Each had a mast and a sail since none were to be rowed. To sail them across the channel to England, a south wind needed to blow or the fleet would not move.

Chapter 5

Sweat trickled between her breasts. Ariel had not realized how hot armor could be. She had not even started her lesson yet and already she sweated.

Osbern checked her straps and the fit of her helmet before donning his armor. "Are you sure you want this, my lady?"

"Positive. I won't back out now."

With a shrug, Osbern walked to the center of the field and motioned for Ariel to follow. When she reached him, she placed her shield on her arm and raised her sword. Osbern took the first strike. Ariel moved to block it with her shield. She felt the impact all the way up her arm. Lifting her sword, she struck back at Osbern.

As the sword play continued, Ariel realized her father had been right. Wearing the armor and using the shield made it much harder. Obviously Osbern had been taking it easy on her in the past. Now his strokes came fast and furiously. With each strike Ariel could feel it vibrate through her body. Osbern was putting his full strength behind each hit.

Ariel felt her body getting more battered with each stroke of Osbern's sword. She had to do something other than just ward off his attack or he would pound her into the ground. Watching Osbern closely, she realized he may have the strength and bulk she could never match, but she had one advantage. She was smaller and could move faster than he could.

When the hit came that would take Osbern longer to recover from, Ariel knew her chance had come. Lifting her shield up high so Osbern's sword arm was slightly raised, Ariel moved to block him and with a twist of her sword she disarmed the bigger man.

Both watched as the sword landed with a thud at their feet. Ariel couldn't hide the triumph she felt. Osbern's mouth hung open in shock. His eyes seemed glued to the sword lying on the ground.

The look on Osbern's face showed surprise that someone of her size could disarm him in one stroke. "How did you do that? I never taught you that move."

"I don't really know. It just seemed like the most logical course of action to take. I'm not going to let you batter me to a pulp just so you can teach me sword play."

Osbern threw back his head and let out a roar of laughter. "Whatever you say, my lady. Just as long as you can do it again, that is what really matters. Shall we test out your new found skill?" At Ariel's nod, Osbern picked up his sword and signaled for her to come at him. The practice continued for another hour with Ariel able to disarm Osbern twice more.

* * * *

Swein came to the field halfway through the practice and could not believe his eyes. Osbern had said before Ariel's confinement that she had a talent for sword play, but what he was seeing now led him to only one conclusion, Ariel was a natural. Watching Ariel disarm Osbern was a phenomenal sight and she would only get better over time.

Ariel had always been strong for a woman, which was only natural considering the work she had done in the fields partnered with the earlier arms lessons. Now, having full training available to her, she would only get stronger.

Swein approached Ariel as she leaned on her sword panting for breath. She had just disarmed Osbern once more. "Well daughter, I think you should give poor Osbern a rest. You don't want to wear the man out. He may not be able to continue the practice sessions if you beat him too much."

Ariel looked up and smiled at her father. "Did I measure up?"

"Without question, but there is one thing. A very young man is in the hall making his displeasure known to everyone. I think you're what he wants."

Ariel saluted her father with her sword, let out a whoop, then raced toward the hall. Swein just shook his head.

"Well Osbern, do you think she will be ready?"

"Aye, my lord. She is better than any boy her age."

"I hope so. The talk going around suggests the fryd will be called this summer. If it does, I can guarantee Ariel will not be put off."

"Don't worry, my lord. I will protect the Lady Ariel until death if necessary."

"Let's hope you don't have to fulfill that promise."

* * * *

To say Ariel was sore was putting it mildly. Every muscle in her body ached. Even some she had not known she had.

Osbern, who sat at her father's left, leaned forward slightly to peer at her. It was now the evening meal and Ariel could barely lift her arm to eat.

The older man laughed as Ariel grimaced in pain. "You think you are sore now, my lady? Wait until tomorrow morning. It's always worse the next day."

"I have a hard enough time holding my baby without pain. How will I ever be able to lift a sword in the morning?"

"You will have to push past the pain. That is the way of a warrior. Besides, the exercise tomorrow will loosen and stretch your muscles. You'll feel a little better after the practice."

The conversation died off when the hall door swung open. The same messenger who had come once before from the Earl of Essex stepped through the door. It could only mean something important had happened.

Reaching the table where Swein sat eating, the messenger bowed slightly. "I have a message from the Earl of Essex to Swein of Elmstead."

"What does he send?"

"The fryd has been called to assemble by order of King Harold. As your overlord, the earl commands you to assemble all your able bodied men of your village."

"Where are we to meet?"

"Your men are to join the rest of the fryd at Bosham, near the Isle of Wight. Whoever leads your men must have them there by June."

"You may tell the earl it will be done."

The messenger once more bowed and sat down at one of the tables further down the hall.

Swein motioned to one of the serfs to provide the man with a bread trencher so he could have his meal. Ariel looked over at Swein and focused on his face, "I want to lead the men to Bosham."

"You know our men will follow you. But the earl may not like the idea of me sending my daughter in my stead."

"That's no problem. Tell him you are sending your son."

A look of wariness crossed Swein's face. "You mean to pass yourself off as a boy?"

"Aye. Every time you have had to meet with the earl you have gone to him. He has never been here before. You said so yourself, he has no interest in your family. He only cares about the rents being collected on time. I can cut my hair and bind my chest. I could pass myself off as a boy that way. I'll assume a different name and have the men use it."

Swein stared at her. Ariel hoped her father would not think her plan foolhardy. The earl was not an easy man to deal with by her father's accounts. She knew if her secret came out the earl could make her pay for her deception, but that in no way made her want to change her mind.

"If I decide to allow you to do this, I must have some promises from you first."

Ariel quickly wrapped her arms around her father's neck and kissed him on the cheek. "I'll do anything."

"Osbern will go with you. You will listen to him. He has seen battle before, whereas you haven't. I want you to only see the Earl of Essex when it can't be avoided. He will not be pleased to find out you are a woman."

"I promise, father. I'll do as you ask."

"I'm not finished yet. Do not take any undo risks with your life. You have a son. I would not like to see him grow up without his mother."

"There is no need to worry, father. Colwyn is my life. I would not like to see that happen either."

Almost as if he knew they talked about him, Colwyn let out a wail. The village girl, who had been looking after him in Ariel's chamber, came to the table.

"I think the little lord is hungry, my lady. Will you feed him now or shall I try and settle him until you're done your meal?"

"Nay, I will feed him now, Lily." Ariel stood up and took Colwyn from the girl's arms.

Lily was the girl her father had chosen to help her with the baby. She was the typical village girl. Not beautiful, but pleasant looking, friendly and eager to please.

Ariel had taken an instant liking to Lily. Even though they had been together for only one day, Ariel felt a kinship with her. The girl hadn't even batted an eye when Swein had told her what Ariel would be doing.

Entering her chamber, Ariel settled on her bed and began to nurse Colwyn. She looked up and found Lily had followed her. "You could have stayed in the hall, Lily. Did you have anything to eat yet?"

"Aye, my lady."

"Lily, if we are going to be together a lot I want you to call me by my given name. I would rather have you as a friend, not just as a servant."

"I would like that, Ariel. If there is anything else you would like me to do, I would gladly be about it."

"Nay. Why don't go home for the night? I'll be able to handle things until tomorrow." Lily gave her a quick bob then opened the chamber door and left.

She would have to work on Lily. Ariel wanted the girl to be more relaxed around her. Their stations in life should not matter. They were the same age, nine and ten. They were going to be spending a lot of time together so they should think of themselves as equals.

Looking down, Ariel watched her son nurse. His little hand lay on her breast. He looked more and more like his father with each day that passed. She would miss Colwyn when she went with the rest of the village men to fight with the fryd, but she had to do this.

Ariel had worked it all out. If the Normans attacked this summer, she wanted to be there. It was the only way she could think of seeing the knight again. Even if it came down to sneaking into the Norman camp, she would confront him.

She wanted to see his face when she raised her sword to strike. Ariel didn't want to kill him. No, she wanted to hurt him as much as he had hurt her. Now it looked as if she would be getting her wish. It was the only thing that had kept her going for the last ten months. If nothing else it would give her peace of mind.

Chapter 6

When the south wind finally started to blow, the beach became a flurry of activity. Broc could not believe the wind had at last changed for them. The fleet had been ready since mid summer. It was now September and they were ready to embark on their quest.

Broc stood beside William and watched the ships being loaded. There were three hundred and fifty in total. Three hundred would be used as transport ships, carrying horses and thirty men. The last fifty ships wouldn't carry any cargo, but would be filled with men.

"Do you think we will make the tide, Broc?"

"Aye, my lord. All seems to be moving apace." Broc saw the men hectically preparing to launch the ships. Some of the men busily loaded the supply ships, while others tried to get the skittish horses onboard still others.

"We must launch when it's high water or we will miss our chance. Maybe if I walk among them it will encourage them to work faster. Broc, will you discreetly make sure the troops are ready to board when we begin the launch?"

"Aye, my lord. They will be on the ships at the appropriate time. Have no fear."

"I know I can count on you. I will see you onboard the ship then."

The duke descended the small hill above the beach where they had been standing. As he had predicted, the men began to move faster as the duke's presence on the beach became known. Looking across the beach and away from the ships, Broc saw the troops. They were gathered together waiting for the order to board.

Broc followed the same path William had taken down the hill and headed toward the troops. He understood the duke's concerns regarding these men. Mixed in with the promised men from the barons were volunteers looking for booty. To put it bluntly, they were mercenaries. Some came from Flanders and Aquitaine, but most came from Brittany. Two thirds of the duke's army was made up of these foreign mercenaries who could be hard to control.

When the time came to board the ships, Broc discreetly moved among the troops. He didn't do much. The men seemed anxious to start the journey. Assuming everything would remain going smoothly, Broc moved further down the beach to where the duke's ship waited. Once onboard, he checked to make sure his armor was properly stowed and went to find William.

The duke stood at the rail of the ship watching the loading. Broc stopped to take a closer look at the man. The duke wore a look of determination on his face, the one he always wore when he thought of England. Broc had never met a man like William before. That he was intelligent, there was no doubt. He also had strength of will most men could not match, and that strength would give William the throne of England. In a way, Broc felt sorry for Harold. But the man had brought this on himself when he had been crowned king.

William motioned Broc over when he caught sight of him. "Did everything go all right?"

"Aye, my lord. The chance of booty is the stronger pull at the moment."

"Let's hope it does not change too quickly." The duke grabbed the side of the ship as it began to sway. Now that all had been loaded, the anchor had been raised and the ship began to move into the River Dives.

William smiled at Broc. "It has begun. I shall take back what is mine. Don't worry, Broc, you will receive some of the booty. You have my promise right here, you can have any piece of land you wish. I'll need friends such as you to watch over my kingdom."

Broc felt speechless. He had not expected to be given any land. It was his dream, one he had not really believed he would ever attain.

With no further speech between them, Broc stood silently beside William and watched the other ships slowly take their positions behind the duke's vessel.

* * * *

The wind seemed to be with them, but their good fortune changed halfway through the journey. Slowly the wind shifted until it began to blow in a westerly direction. Shortly after that the wind began to blow in earnest and ended up being their undoing. Much to their disappointment they did not see the shores of England that day. For some, they would never be able to see it. A few of the ships became wrecked on the shore or lost at sea. The survivors came into St. Valery, the closest land, exhausted, frightened and looking for someone to blame for the mishap.

With the ships anchored off shore, and the men once again on land, they tried to reassure the troops. Many deserted. Then the rain came and the wind once more went back to blowing to the north. Spirits fell and grumbling could be heard. The duke went to many of the men to ease their worries.

As camps were set up, William seemed to be everywhere. His presence alone held the remainder of the troops together. Broc watched William with awe. After the wait of four weeks at the River Dives and now this misfortune, a lesser man would have given up. Not the duke. To hide the lack of supplies, William increased daily rations given to each man. And to cover the number of men who had died on the shore, he ordered the burials to be done in secret.

Nothing could be done now but wait for the south wind to come again, and to pray the wait would not be for long. Winter was fast approaching. If the wind did not shift soon, the crossing would have to wait until next spring.

* * * *

That very same day, Harold dispersed the fryd. He had kept them six weeks beyond their feudal duty and now had run out of provisions. Ariel couldn't have been happier to be going home. She had not expected to still be at Bosham. She missed Colwyn to distraction. The separation had been harder on her than she had first thought it would be.

The first couple of days she had been in pain, physically. Ariel had been glad she had to bind her chest so tightly. As her milk accumulated the pressure had turned to pain. When the milk finally stopped coming, Ariel couldn't help but feel she had lost one of the ties she had with her son.

She knew he was being well cared for back home. Lily had turned out to be just as attentive to Colwyn as Ariel herself. The girl had even found the wet nurse needed in her absence, another girl from the village whom Lily knew. The wet nurse had a son of her own and seemed to have enough milk to nurse both babies. The weeks of inactivity had not helped to take Ariel's mind off of Colwyn either. Osbern had tried his best to distract her. He tried to fill her days with sword play and tales of the battlefield.

Most of the fryd remained inactive. They practiced arms, but Ariel spent more time than others on it. She had even managed to catch King Harold's eye when he had walked among the fryd one day. She stood out for being the only one who used a sword instead of a battle axe.

Harold had stopped to watch her practice. Osbern had bent down to pick up his sword when Ariel sensed the small crowd that stood a few feet away. Seeing the king among the spectators, she bowed to him.

Harold stepped out of the crowd and walked over to Ariel. "What's your name, boy?"

"I'm Wulf of Elmstead, sire." Ariel had chosen her new name with the idea of trying to keep it short and easy to remember. The men from the village now always used her male name, even when away from the rest of the fryd, so she was quite used to it.

The king looked her up and down before he spoke again. "You look young to have the skill you do."

"I'm ten and seven, sire."

"That old? I would have taken you for younger." Harold paused once more, as if he thought something over in his mind. "You have great potential. I shall see you again before too long, Wulf of Elmstead." With that said Harold left Ariel to wonder what he had meant by those words.

Now the fryd had been released and Ariel would never find out. The king had not returned to their camp. Ariel glanced at her men, and at Osbern's nod, she turned to start the long trek back to Elmstead. About to mount her horse, a hand reached out and held her back.

"I told you I would see you again, Wulf of Elmstead."

Ariel turned and found the king standing beside her. He was tall, almost as tall as the knight. Being in his early forties, he made a fine looking man. She had heard a lot about him since joining the fryd. Harold was known to be generous and kind to men of goodwill. But he could not tolerate any man with evil intent. He was reputed to be even tempered and able to bear contradiction without retaliation, a trait any good king should have.

Ariel believed all the things said of the king. For here he stood before her, smiling with genuine warmth. "Aye, you did, sire."

"I want you to send your men back to Elmstead. I'm going back to London and I want you to accompany me." Ariel opened her mouth to respond, but Harold held up his hand. "I know what you will ask. Why? Well, it's quite simple. You have skills I would like readily at hand. How would you like to become one of my house carls?"

"I would be honored, sire."

"Good. Once we reach London I will have you put through the tests. I know you will pass." As Osbern moved to stand beside Ariel, the king nodded. "You may come with the boy. Both of you may travel with my house carls once your men have started for home. We will talk further once we are in London." Harold clapped Ariel on the shoulder and left her standing with her head spinning.

Ariel looked at Osbern as she felt a full display of emotions run across her face. He leaned closer to her and spoke quietly. "Sorry, my girl. You have to go. He may have said it nicely, but that was an order." Seeing her worried expression, Osbern must have understood what troubled her. "Before the men leave, write a missive to your father. He will help you figure out what to do about Colwyn. Right now, cheer up. The king has honored you. If you pass the tests, you'll be the youngest member of the house carls. You will be making history by being the only woman among them. Now go write that missive. We can't keep the king waiting.

Chapter 7

The march to London turned out to be an uneventful one. But Ariel wouldn't have noticed even if a boulder had been dropped on top of her. All she could think of was, with each step, she was getting farther away from Colwyn.

Not knowing how this new role in life would turn out, Ariel had asked her father to help bring Colwyn to London. She could not stand to be separated from her son for much longer. As it stood now, he probably wouldn't even recognize her. She had been away from Elmstead for the whole summer instead of the two months she had planned on.

The first impression Ariel had when she entered London was the utter size of the city, and then the smell. Ariel had never seen so many people living together in one single place, which also explained why the city smelled so bad. In some places Ariel had to cover nose or she would have gagged.

Osbern who rode beside her, laughed at her attempt to block out the foul odor. "It's something you will have to get used to."

"How? The smell seems to be everywhere."

"Only during the summer months. When winter sets in, it does go away."

Ariel shrugged at the older man. She thought that highly unlikely. The smell was just too strong. They rode the rest of the way in silence. Regardless of the smell, Ariel could not stop herself from drinking in all the new sights. All too soon they arrived at the king's residence.

It was the biggest hall Ariel had ever seen. She thought Elmstead's hall was large, but this took her breath away. Made out of wood with a thatched roof just as other halls, its size alone suggested it belonged to a king.

Ariel dismounted with the rest of the group, nervously adjusting her cloak. She watched as a woman stepped out of the hall. Upon seeing the king, she ran up to him and threw her arms around his neck. When the woman passionately kissed him, Ariel realized who she was.

She was the king's lover, Edith Svanneshals, or swan throat. Harold had not made her his wife, even though they had been together for twenty years and Edith had given him three sons. It was said Edith was content though. She would never leave the king, even without the offer of marriage some thought she should demand. But it was also said Harold loved her with all of his heart.

When the embrace ended, the couple turned and went into the hall. Ariel envied them. She wanted to have what they shared. She could not help wondering what it would feel like to have someone love her that much. With that thought, the knight's face came to the forefront of her mind.

The past month Ariel had been having disturbing dreams about the knight. They were so intense she swore she could feel his body pressed to hers. She could even smell his scent on her skin after she awoke. It was when she woke up that Ariel felt the most agitated. The burning in her loins left her aching for much more than what a dream lover could give her. Now that she knew first hand the pleasure that could be had between a man and a woman, her body seemed to crave it. Ariel ceased her musing as a large man approached her and Osbern. She recognized him as one of the king's house carls.

"You two are to come with me. We stay in a separate barracks. You'll be sharing a room." His words were gruff and none too friendly.

As the big man turned to lead them away, Ariel looked over at Osbern. With a shrug he followed the other man. Apparently he also didn't understand the man's animosity toward them any more than Ariel did.

The barracks had its own small hall with chambers situated at the back. Their small chamber only had two cots and a chest at the end of each one. It was nothing special, but it would serve its purpose. Ariel chose one of the cots and sat down. She undid her cloak and pulled it off as she looked down at her tunic and trews. With mud crusted to her boots and up her legs, she wished for a bath along with the much needed change of clothes, but that would not be something she could indulge in.

Osbern cleared his throat. "I'll watch the door, lass, if you want to clean up."

"You don't mind?"

"Nay. I'm sure the king will call you to him soon. You need to clean up. I'll be in the hall, close to the door. Let me know when you're finished."

After Osbern closed the door, Ariel reached for her pack and pulled out a fresh tunic and trews. She hoped the king did not leave her waiting for long. Ariel needed to know what he had planned for her. Arrangements had to be made.

* * * *

The call did not come that day or the next. It so happened that the king had been brought to bed with a crippling pain in his leg. Nobody knew what had brought on the attack. Talk of the king did not last long though, greater fears preoccupied people's minds. The news reached the court three days after the king had become ill. An invader had come to the shores of England.

It was not Duke William, who they had waited for all summer, but another. The least expected man had come to try and take Harold's throne. King Harald Hardrada of Norway had landed two hundred and thirty miles away in Northumbria and burned the town of Scarborough to the ground. They had waited all summer with nothing happening. Now with the fryd dispersed and winter about to set in, they had thought themselves safe.

The king ordered the house carls to prepare to march and confront the invaders. The hall where Osbern and Ariel stayed was thrown into an uproar. As the men prepared to march the following dawn, they piled their armor and needed belongings in the hall. Ariel had no idea what she and Osbern were supposed to do. She had not yet spoken to the king and the tests had not yet begun. Not being a member of the house carls, Ariel figured when they marched she would be left behind.

"What has you so deep in thought, Wulf of Elmstead?"

At the sound of the king's voice, Ariel shot to her feet and bowed. Osbern quickly followed suit.

"I was wondering what would happen to me when the others march out, sire."

"You will be coming with us."

"But, sire, I haven't completed the tests. By rights, I am not a member of the house carls."

Harold smiled. "Invaders have come to our land. I need every available man I can get. The house carls are only three thousand strong, but I'm sure King Harald Hardrada brought much more than that. I've seen you fight. You would have no problem passing the tests. I decree you are now officially a house carl."

Ariel stood with her mouth open, unable to speak. When she had left Elmstead it had never occurred to her she would go so far. "Thank you, sire."

"Thanks are not necessary. Just don't let me down. I expect you and your man here to be ready to march at dawn."

"You can count on me, sire. We will be prepared."

Ariel and Osbern bowed once more as the king turned and left the hall. Once again alone they set off at a run to their chamber. If they were to leave at dawn there was much that needed to be done.

Chapter 8

Sweat broke out all over Ariel's body and her hands grew so damp the handle of her sword kept slipping. She didn't know if she could go through with this, even though Osbern had reminded her that she had the skill and was capable of coming out of this without a single wound. Right now all Ariel could see were the Norsemen on the other side of the bridge preparing to meet them in battle.

They had marched to Tadcaster, one hundred and ninety miles from London. There, they received news of the Norsemen's whereabouts. The Norse had headed to York after their first victory. It had made sense when it became known that Harold's brother, Tostig, was among the invaders. King Edward had been the one to banish Tostig for some grievance. With the banishment he had been stripped of the title of Earl of York and all that went with it. So it made sense that he would have marched on that city.

The new earl, Morkere, who was ten and six, along with his brother Edwin, collected what men they could. The battle did not last long, only about an hour, but it had been a thorough victory. The Norsemen won and took over York. Once inside they demanded hostages. Tostig and Harald had then left leaving orders for the hostages to be taken to Stamford Bridge. So at this bridge the battle lines had been drawn between the English and the Norsemen.

Sensing Ariel's nervousness, Osbern moved closer. "What you are feeling is natural, especially when it's your first battle you are facing. Once in the middle of it, it will pass. Let your instincts take over, don't think. I'll be at your side." Ariel gave the older man a wavering smile and once more wiped the palm of her hand on her trews.

The waiting would soon be over. Talks were taking place between the king a huge Norseman and a slightly smaller man. As the news filtered back to Ariel, she found out the identities of the two other men. The large man turned out to be King Harald Hardrada himself and the other Tostig. From her vantage point Ariel could see the men talking, but could not hear what they said to each other. After a short exchange, Harold rode back to his army. The king dismounted and the battle began in earnest.

The Norse held the York side of the bridge and the hilly ground on the opposite bank. The fighting began on the York side. As Ariel moved to engage the enemy, she made a silent vow that she would survive this day. She'd be damned if she'd leave her son an orphan.

Osbern had been right. After she settled into the hacking and slashing motions as she swung her sword, Ariel blocked out everything else around her. The smell of blood, the anguished cries of the wounded and the dying, didn't bother her. She fought so many opponents that she soon had their blood on her face and caked on her arms.

The Norsemen were slowly beaten back across the bridge and into the river. The water became choked with bodies. One large Norseman remained on the bridge and defended it single handedly. Hard as they might, the English couldn't move him. He alone killed forty men before an Englishman drifted under the bridge in a small boat, unseen, and speared him up through the chinks in the wooden deck. With the Norseman now eliminated, the English charged the bridge and battle began on the other side.

Ariel crossed the bridge with Osbern still at her side when King Harald went berserk. She watched in awe as the big man charged out, flailing about him, holding his weapon in both hands. The spectacle didn't last long though. The Norse king ended being brought down with an arrow to his throat.

At the end of the battle, the Norse were defeated. It had lasted from morning until dusk. Watching the last spurts of fighting die down, Ariel stood panting. When awareness set in, she smelled all the blood around her. Pitiful wails of the wounded drifted on the wind. Looking down, Ariel found herself to be covered in blood. It seeped from small nicks on her hands and from a slight wound on her forearm. Ariel had felt nothing during the battle, but as her system returned to normal, they began to sting. Reaching up to remove her helmet, she found her hair stiff with dried blood.

It took all her willpower to swallow the bile that rose to the back of her throat. She would not disgrace herself by throwing up the contents of her stomach on the battlefield. But looking at the dead lying scattered around her and floating in the river almost defeated her.

Someone gave her shoulder a reassuring squeeze. Ariel looked up to find Osbern still at her side. She realized now he had kept his promise. He had not left her alone in the sea of carnage that had just taken place. Ariel saw Osbern was also covered in blood.

"You didn't leave me."

"Nay, not that you needed my help." Osbern looked to see that they would not be overheard before he spoke again. "I must say, lass, you have lived up to surpass my expectations. Look at you, hardly a wound on you. If only your father could have seen you fight this day. You have done him proud."

"I have my teacher to thank." Ariel raised her sword to salute Osbern. Finding it covered in blood she stopped in mid-motion and swallowed hard. Osbern chuckled.

"You're blooded now, lass. The next battle you fight it won't hit you so hard."

"If you say so. Right now I need to wash up before I make a spectacle of myself."

Osbern draped his arm around Ariel's shoulders and turned her. "It will get easier. You are a true warrior now, lass. I think a goblet of good mead is in order. Let's go back to camp."

Ariel let Osbern lead her across the bridge. It would take quite a few goblets of mead to make this day unremarkable.

Chapter 9

Broc watched, enthralled, as she slowly came closer. Her scent wafted over him when she stood in front of him. She smelled like sunshine, flowers, and her own woman scent. The smell of it made his body harden even more.

With shaking hands he pushed his fingers through her hair. It felt like silk. The sun turned it almost white as she pressed her cheek into his palm. Closing his eyes, Broc slowly lowered his head until their lips met. Feeling hers soften under his, he increased the pressure. Knowing what he wanted, she parted her lips. Her taste almost undid him. He didn't think he would ever get enough of her.

His body ached for the feel of her. Releasing her hair, Broc slid his hands down her back and pulled her closer, bringing her body flush against his. She had to know how much he wanted her. The evidence of his arousal nestled against her belly, hard and throbbing.

He broke off the kiss and looked into her blue eyes. She smiled. Taking his hand she placed it on her left breast. Her heart beat just as fast as his. Then she did the unexpected. She silently mouthed the words, I love you.

Broc bolted upright on his cot with his body covered in sweat and with an erection so hard he knew he would be uncomfortable for most of the day. The same dream had plagued him for the last month. And he always woke up just as she spoke those words. The Saxon girl had become so much a part of him she now lived in his dreams. Why she stood out in his mind so strongly, he couldn't really explain. Making love to her had somehow bonded her to him. Broc hated to admit that she had become his obsession, but there was no denying that she had. That didn't sit well with him.

Running his fingers through his hair, Broc stood and stretched. While dressing he came to the only logical solution to his problem. He had to go back to his Saxon girl. She had given him her virginity, how could he not think of her but his? And to be certain he saw her again he planned to ask for Elmstead to be his after William won his throne.

Last night the south wind finally started to blow once more. After being stranded at St. Valery for two weeks their chance at England had come again. This evening the fleet would sail. By God's will, Broc would see the Saxon girl again.

With the darkening sky the Normans set sail for England. The duke led the way in his ship called the Mora, a gift from his wife Matilda. The light on the masthead was the beacon for the rest of the fleet to follow. Broc, along with William FitzOsbern, were one of the few who sailed on the Mora with the duke.

Once underway the men not needed to sail the ships settled down to sleep on the deck. Tomorrow they would reach England. There was nothing to do but wait.

With the coming dawn it became clear events had transpired during the night. The Mora was alone with nothing in sight. No coast of England, no other ships of the fleet. The duke ordered the sail lowered and brought the Mora to a stop. Acting as if everything was as it should be, he decided to break his fast.

As time passed the men began to worry, but the duke showed none of their discomfort. When a sail finally was spotted off in the distance a cheer went up. Broc felt himself relax. He spotted another ship behind the first, then another and another. Obviously the Mora had out sailed the rest of the fleet. Maybe they would make it to England after all.

By the time the duke had finished eating, the other ships had caught up with them. The Mora once more got underway and a short while later land came in sight. They had made the crossing virtually unscathed. Only two ships had disappeared during the night.

At seeing such a large fleet of warriors, the people of Pevensey ran and hid. Some of the Normans leapt ashore prepared to do battle as others urged the horses to jump overboard. With all confidence, William gained the shore. A gasp of horror went up through the men as the duke slipped and fell forward. He landed with both hands on the ground. Realizing most of the troops would consider this an evil omen William calmly got up and brushed his hands clean.

"By God's splendor, I've seized the soil of England in both my hands." A cheer went up. The duke managed to turn the tide on a potentially bad situation with guile, making it seem a minimal occurrence.

Finding no opposition, the Normans plundered Pevensey for food and claimed it as their own. They built a fort inside the old Roman walls. After a few days of rest the duke decided to move further inland. William divided his army. Some of the troops went by ships and the knights rode while the foot soldiers marched. Whichever way they traveled, William's men left death and destruction all the way to Hastings.

Chapter 10

Four days after the Norman's landing Harold received the news at York. The messenger arrived during the feast celebrating the defeat of the Norse. Gathering the house carls, along with the fryd who had fought at Stamford Bridge, the king marched for London.

Messages were sent to Duke William telling him he had no right to England's throne. In reply, the duke held firm to his belief that Edward had promised him the throne. Left with no other choice, Harold sent a last message to William. He would march at once and he would be marching to battle. With the final message sent Harold could be overheard saying, "May the Lord now decide between William and me, and may he pronounce which of us has the right."

Harold led the army out of London and marched towards Hastings. Other men were expected to join the army there, coming from Kent and Sussex, meeting up with the king at an ancient apple tree. The tree grew at a junction of tracks outside of Hastings. There, Harold set up his battle headquarters.

Ariel once more found herself standing in a line facing a battlefield with ever faithful Osbern at her side. She was nervous, but not as badly as she had been when she had faced the Norse. This time she knew what to expect. The only difference from the last battle would be she now had to face the countrymen of the knight. The blood that ran through their veins also ran through her son's. For all Ariel knew the knight could be among the men on the other side of the field.

Ariel knew the English would be fighting on foot. Unlike the Normans, they never fought on horseback or used archers. But the numbers looked to be on their side. Where William had around eight thousand men, Harold had slightly more.

The knights on the Norman side dismounted and donned their chain mail. Remounting, they prepared for battle. Ariel stiffened as a lone rider left the Norman lines. She could not believe what she saw next. The man started to sing as he threw his sword up in the air. He caught it as it came down and continued to canter his horse across the valley to the English lines. When he reached them he killed three men before being brought down.

After that spectacle the real business of waging war began. The Norman archers stepped forward. In response, the English doubled their front ranks, to form a wall of overlapping shields. The archers loosed their missiles at fifty paces.

Ariel felt the impact of the arrows without having to be in the front rank. Not all the missiles hit the shields, some found their mark. Men around her dropped to the ground screaming. She blocked out the sound and withdrew her sword from its sheath.

After the archers, the Norman infantry advanced. The English made their first move by throwing spears at the new wave of men. Behind the infantry came the mounted knights. The house carls came forward to swing battle axes. With the sword as her choice of weapon, Ariel was not among the house carls when they first engaged the enemy. They had never fought men on horses before and she would be more of a hindrance than a help.

It soon became obvious the knights had never met men in battle swinging axes. At the last minute they broke away. In their retreat, they ended up riding down the infantry and archers. Those who did not end up under the horses' hooves they put to flight. At a marshy section at the bottom of the valley some of the horsemen fell in, causing the right wing of the English to break ranks and rush down their hill to attack.

The Normans then broke ranks. Some were heard to shout that the duke was among the knights who had gone down and was now dead. This in turn caused most to retreat. William stopped their retreat by yanking off his helmet and riding to the front of his men. He shouted and threatened them with his sword. That seemed to work as their mad flight came to an abrupt halt. William then rode out and cut off the isolated English who had broken rank. The Norman's used the opportunity to slaughter them on and around a little hillock in the lower part of the valley.

A few of the men near Ariel muttered that the Norman's confusion should have been used against them, but the order to attack never came. All stood firm and never advanced. Even near the end they did not retreat as a whole.

The shield wall began to shrink in length as men fell and were not replaced. When the mounted knights started to come in at the sides, Ariel finally faced the enemy. Letting the rhythm of slashing and hacking take over, Ariel saw nothing except for each target as it presented itself. Even when a hail of arrows fell, it didn't register.

That soon ended. The knights kept coming. With each swing, Ariel's arm grew increasingly tired. A pain ripped through her left shoulder, bringing her out of her trance like state. Ariel had to look, she couldn't stop herself. Blood welled out of the sword cut that ran across the whole width of her left shoulder. She watched fascinated as it soaked the sleeve of her tunic and began to drip down her hand.

As she looked down, Ariel found something else—something she never thought she would see. It was Osbern. An arrow stuck out of his chest. Without looking, she knew she would find his eyes staring, lifeless. As her legs gave out, once more oblivious to what went on around her, Ariel knelt down beside Osbern. Her hand shook as she reached out and gently closed his eyes. A wail of despair welled up in her throat. Little did she know that her cry had caught the attention of one of the Norman knights.

* * * *

Broc pulled his mount up short at the sound. Looking around him, he found the source of the noise. A Saxon warrior, no, taking a closer look he realized a young boy, was bent over the body of a dead man.

The boy's size made Broc wonder who had allowed him to fight. The way he was bent over, kept his face hidden. The very pale blond hair sticking out from under the boy's helmet drew him. He walked his horse closer. Just before he reached him, the young man looked directly at Broc. If he had not been holding onto his horse's reins, Broc would have fallen to the ground. The strikingly familiar face took his breath away. It was the face of the girl, the one who had haunted his dreams for the last year. The one he had not been able to forget.

As Broc loomed above, the boy screamed with rage and attacked him. That he was mounted seemed to be no deterrent for the boy. Broc quickly lowered his shield and blocked the sword before it could do any damage to his horse. That must have been all the strength the boy had left in him. Thwarted, he lowered his head as if he expected Broc to deliver a death blow.

When he did no such thing, the boy looked up at him. Broc watched as his gaze landed on his shield. The boy stiffened then jerked his eyes up to Broc's face. A look of recognition flashed across the boy's face before he quickly hid it.

Waiting to see what the boy would do next, Broc watched him. When the boy seemed about to run, Broc dismounted and grabbed the boy by his left arm. At his cry of pain, Broc noticed the wound for the first time. From the amount of blood on his sleeve and the boy's hand, he realized the wound would be deep.

Broc had a decision to make. He could either let the boy go or take him as his prisoner. If he released him and the wound was not taken care of soon, the boy could die from loss of blood. Looking at the face that so reminded him of the girl, Broc knew he wouldn't be able to leave the boy behind.

Not knowing if he would be understood, Broc spoke to the young man. "You'll come with me. I'm sure you will be worth something to someone."

"I'll go nowhere with you, Norman. I would rather be dead."

Chapter 11

"You understand me?" Broc almost released the boy's arm at the sound of his voice.

"Of course. My father is a thane, he provided me with the education I need for my station."

"Is that your father?"

The boy looked down at the body of the large man who lay near him. At the reminder of the dead man, he seemed to have to compose himself before he could reply. "Nay, my father is at home. This was Osbern. He came with me to fight."

"He must have meant much to you." Broc loosened his grip a little seeing the boy's eyes go glassy with unshed tears.

"Osbern taught me everything I know about arms. He has been with my family for years. Why should you care?"

"What's your name boy? If I'm to ransom you I need to know who to contact."

The boy seemed to debate with himself whether or not to tell him anything. In the end, he took a deep breath and said, "I'm Wulf of Elmstead."

Broc felt all the air empty out of his lungs, as if someone had punched him in the stomach. *Could the girl be this boy's sister?* The resemblance was too close to be a coincidence.

"Do you have a sister, Wulf?"

"Nay. I'm an only child."

The sounds of battle had slowly been dying away as they spoke, which could only mean one thing. One side had become the victor. Too many Norman knights could be seen on the Saxon side of the field. It looked as if William had won himself a throne.

Gripping the boy's arm tighter, Broc started to pull him away from

Osbern's body.

"Wait. I can't leave my friend like this. He deserves to be properly buried." When Broc did not slow his pace, he started to dig his heels into the ground. "I'll not leave him. Stop whatever your name is."

"My name is Broc St. Ceneri. Don't worry. Your friend will be taken care of. From now on you will do as I say. Until I receive your ransom you are my prisoner." Feeling the fight go out of the boy, Broc continued. "The first thing we need to do is take care of your shoulder. It would be a pity to have you die before the gold arrives."

* * * *

After he had dragged her away from the battlefield, Broc left Ariel with one of the Norman monks who turned out to be a healer. He silently lifted the sleeve of her tunic and began to clean her wound. Wincing slightly as the water seeped into the cut, Ariel looked around for Broc. He was nowhere to be seen.

With her arm taken care of, one of the Norman foot soldiers led her to the small shelter that had been set up for prisoners. Ariel appeared not to be the only one who had been captured, escaping death on the field. Three other men shared the tent like structure with her. From them Ariel learned how the battle had been won. Even now, hours after hearing it told, she felt her stomach churn.

Harold had been shot in the eye with an arrow. Probably around the same time poor Osbern had met his end. Some Norman knights took advantage of his blindness. They rode in on Harold and hacked him to pieces. One stabbed him in the chest, another cut off his head, and another disemboweled him. As if that was not bad enough, one knight cut off one of his legs at the thigh and carried it away with him.

Ariel doubted she would sleep or find a good night of rest after hearing how that good man had died. He hadn't deserved that type of death. *What kind of God would allow something so inglorious to take place?*

Blocking out the bloody scene from her mind, Ariel pulled her blanket closer around her, the only item given her to take the chill out of the air. Outside a huge fire burned and sounds of festivity could be heard.

She was so cold even though her wound felt on fire. Shivers racked her body. Turning onto her side, Ariel pulled her legs up to her chest. A single tear slid down her cheek. For the first time since leaving her home she was alone. Alone and scared. Her wound was bad. Bad enough for her body to now be wracked with wound fever.

If she didn't get help she could die. With Osbern gone she had no one. No one except Broc St. Ceneri, but the chances of him coming for her, she couldn't count on. He had not returned to see her since leaving her with the healer.

Closing her eyes, Ariel let sleep claim her. Too weak to fight the darkness that rose up to take her over, Ariel sank down into it and her pain went away.

* * * *

Broc waited patiently while William finished talking to two commanders of his army. He was not happy. What had been done to Harold's body had not been ordered by William. The man, who had cut off his leg and carried it away, had been dismissed from the army.

Two men stood before William as he gave his last order. "I want you to find someone who will be able to identify Harold's body. He should have a proper burial. That will be all for now." Bowing, they left Broc alone with the new King of England.

"What can I do for you, my friend?"

"What makes you think I want something? Maybe I thought you would like to join me in having a goblet of wine."

"You want something. Since the battled ended everyone who feels they are entitled to the share of the wealth has come to remind me of their service during the fighting. Why shouldn't I hear what my friend wants from the spoils? Pour us each some wine and tell me what you would like."

Going over to the small table sitting in the corner of the tent, Broc poured two goblets of the wine inside the pitcher. Handing one to William, he settled his big frame into one of the camp chairs in front of the table that took up most of the space in the room.

"It's true, I want something. Do you remember before we came to England you said I could have some land? If you're still inclined to grant me lands, I would like to make a request."

"If it is land you want, you may have it."

"I'd like Elmstead for my own."

Pulling one of his maps of England open, William scanned its surface. "Are you sure this is the land you want? It's not very large. I hold you in higher regard than the others. I'll give you a bigger grant."

Broc shook his head. "Nay, I want Elmstead. I've seen it and it is all I want."

William smiled knowingly. "That is where you met the girl, is it not?"

"Aye, and as luck would have it, the prisoner I took for ransom is the thane's son."

"I wondered why you took a prisoner. You usually don't take many, if at all, during battle." William closely studied his friend's face. "There is something more you have not told me."

Broc smiled. William never missed anything. "You know me so well. All right, I saved the boy's life because he looks a lot like the girl. I think they must be brother and sister. Although the boy is a thane's son and the sister a peasant."

"She is probably a bastard. That doesn't bother you, her having peasant blood as well as being illegitimate?"

"Nay, it does not." Some of the barons had trouble dealing with William because of the peasant blood in his veins. Even though his father had been a duke, men could not forget that his mother's father was a tanner. The added stigma of being a bastard on top of it did not help either.

The new king sat back and formed a steeple with his fingers before him. He appeared to be thinking something over before he spoke once again. "If I give you this land, when would you leave to take possession?"

"With the dawn." At the shocked look on William's face, Broc quickly pushed on. "I have served you faithfully. All you need to do is summon me and I'll come in your time of need. This is something I must do. The girl haunts my dreams. She's never far from my mind. She is an obsession I cannot shake. Besides, you know your friendship with me has not been highly looked upon."

"I'm not blind. I see how the others shun you. Fine, the lands are yours on one condition. You spend Christ mass at court. I will not break my friendship with you just because the others feel they will lose out on some profit."

Standing, Broc bowed before his king. "I thank you, sire. I will take the boy with me. I'm still your man and always will be."

With a nod of his head, William acknowledged his words. Giving him another bow, Broc turned and left King William on his own.

* * * *

The dawn broke crisp and clear, a perfect day for traveling. Broc pulled his heavy cloak more closely around him. He had not slept well that night, the boy dominated his dreams. Dreams he found disturbing.

He would be making love to the girl, and then the scene would change. The girl would turn into Wulf. What bothered Broc the most was even though he knew it was the boy he could not stop himself from making love to him. Broc had never had any of those feelings towards a man before. Ever. *So why did he dream of the boy?*

Crossing the camp, Broc saw most of the Saxon dead had been cleared away. William had chosen to camp where Harold had held his position on the ridge during the battle. Last night room had to be made by dragging the dead aside. When the small tent came into view, Broc steeled himself to face Wulf.

Entering the tent, Broc noted the three other Saxons who sat at the opposite side of the tent away from Wulf. They barely glanced at Broc as he passed them to awaken the boy.

"Wulf, wake up." Getting no response Broc grabbed his shoulder and gave him a shake. The boy moaned. Rolling Wulf gently onto his back, Broc sucked in his breath. He could feel the heat coming off the boy's body. Placing his hand on Wulf's forehead and flushed cheeks, Broc felt the fire burning within him.

Pulling the left sleeve of Wulf's tunic up, Broc gently unwound the bandage that covered his shoulder. The wound was bright red with infection. With a curse, Broc inspected the discarded dressing. Just as he had thought, the healer had neglected to apply a poultice to keep the infection away.

The boy must have started to suffer sometime during the night. Gently probing the wound brought puss to the surface. Wulf moaned in pain. Broc felt his temper rise, anger at the healer for not doing his duty properly. Even though the boy was Saxon, he did not deserve to die this way. But most of his anger was directed at the three others that had listened to the boy moan in pain and did nothing.

Rising to his feet, Broc walked over to the older men. Hands formed into fists, he stood before them. "Why did you let the boy suffer? If you could not help him, why did you not call for someone?"

One of the men stood up to face the knight. "He deserves to die."

"Why?"

"He failed in his duty. The least he could do is die from the wound."

Broc thrust the urge away to punch the man in the face. "What exactly did he fail at?"

"To protect the king. That boy over there is one of the king's house carls. He should have died with the king instead of being taken for ransom. Most of the others died proudly beside their liege."

Unable to contain his anger any longer, Broc went back to Wulf's side. Wrapped in a blanket the boy still shivered. Broc knew what had to be done to save him. He had to get him home.

* * * *

With that decision in mind, Broc picked up Wulf and carried him out of the tent. A few of the soldiers stared at Broc as he passed through the camp. So intent on reaching his own tent, Broc walked right past William who stood outside his own.

Broc turned at the sound of another's footsteps behind him. Seeing it was William, he gently placed the boy on his cot and looked up at his visitor.

"I could use your help. If you do not mind."

William stepped over to the cot and looked down at the boy. "He looks in rough shape. Is this the prisoner you took?"

"Aye. It seems I should have kept a closer eye on him. The healer did nothing to the wound but bandage it. I will not let him die."

William raised a brow at his friend's stricken tone. "He reminds you of the girl that much?"

"Aye." Broc softly pushed the pale blond hair from Wulf's brow. "Aye, he does. But right now I must start the fight to save him. Can you take off his tunic while I go to the healer for the medicines I'll need?"

"Go, I'll help. He looks so young. He deserves to live a little longer."

* * * *

Broc ran out of the tent to get what he needed. William took a closer look at the boy. He was very young. Not even a hint of a beard could been seen on his cheeks. But William had to admit the boy was handsome. Some would even call him beautiful. If Broc's girl looked similar, then she would indeed be something a man would not forget.

Turning back to the task at hand, William grabbed the hem of the tunic and lifted. Underneath he encountered white strips of material that completely swathed the boy's chest. William stopped and stared. All was obviously not what they seemed to be. Reaching down to the space between Wulf's legs, William confirmed his suspicions.

When the girl stiffened in protest, he looked up to find two beautiful blue eyes staring back at him. "What's your real name?"

She answered barely above a whisper. "Ariel."

"You are her. The girl Broc met in Elmstead?"

"Aye. Please don't tell him."

"But why? He has not been able to get you off his mind."

"There is more at stake than my telling him who I am."

It did not take much deducing on William's part to figure out why the girl wanted her secret kept. "A child. He left you with child."

Ariel tried to prop herself up. "He must never know. He gave up that right when he walked away. He didn't even bother to find out my name." Ariel slumped back down on the cot. Her face had gone white from having to hold herself up. "Who are you?"

"William, your new king." At Ariel's shocked look, the king chuckled. "Broc is my friend, but I'll not tell your secret. You will have to decide what to do about the child. You see, I just gave Elmstead to Broc. He will be living with you, closer than you would like I suppose."

"How could you? My father never fought against you."

William shook his head at the girl's misconception before he continued. "I can because I'm now king. Broc asked for Elmstead, so I gave it to him. You're lucky, he's a good man. He won't evict you off the land. In fact, I would strongly urge you to tell him who you are, then marry Broc. That way you will not lose your home."

Ariel shook her head. As the last of her strength ran out, her eyes fluttered shut and she slipped into unconsciousness.

Chapter 12

The first drops of rain started to fall shortly before darkness fell. Broc kicked his horse into a canter. There definitely would be no stopping for rest. The rain would not help the boy's condition.

Upon his return from the healer's tent, Broc had been a little surprised by what he had found. William had been sitting on the cot with Wulf cradled against his chest. It almost seemed as if he was protecting the boy. Since the king had refused to release Wulf, Broc had had to work on the boy's shoulder while in his arms. William had watched him intently the whole time. Even William's parting words had seemed strange. He had said there was more to the boy than met the eye. He then advised Broc to look deeper, whatever that meant.

The rain that had started as a light shower now came down in buckets. He had to keep Wulf warm. Broc undid his cloak and wrapped himself along with the boy in it. If only the rain had waited. The day wore on and the rain showed no sign of letting up. There was nothing to do but push on. Darkness fell. The thick clouds from the rain covered the moon's brightness, obscuring most of the light it would have shed. Broc knew he had to reach Elmstead or Wulf's chances of survival would be slim to none.

A few miles from their destination, Broc pulled his horse off the road. The rain had lightened to a drizzle and dawn had started to inch over the horizon. Wulf now thrashed in his arms and kept calling for someone named Colwyn.

Heat washed over him when Broc pulled the wet blanket off of Wulf. As he had expected, the fever had increased. The boy's face looked even more flushed and he was becoming delirious. Broc cradled him on his lap and as gently as he could, pulled the bandage from the wound. The infection had grown worse. Puss ran out of the wound at the slightest probing.

He quickly applied a poultice and re-bandaged the wound. Broc knew he did not have much time left. He felt lightheaded from lack of sleep. Somehow he settled the boy once more in a manageable position on top of the horse. Looking down at the boy, Broc scanned his face.

The features were so fine they could almost be a woman's. He resembled the girl so much Broc had to stop himself from doing the unthinkable. The urge to kiss the pink, slightly pouting lips seemed almost too much of a temptation. He shook his head. It must be lack of sleep making him think this way. It had to be.

An hour later they galloped through the village of Elmstead. Broc did not pull up until he clattered into the yard of the thane's dwelling. Even though the hour was still early, a few villagers could be seen milling about. Broc shouted to one of them. "I need the thane. Tell him it's urgent."

A man who stood closest to the hall rushed inside. He reappeared a few minutes later with an older man. Broc studied him as he approached. Despite his years, the man would still be considered good looking. His body still had a warrior's build. His hair was blond, but not quite as blond as his son. When he came closer, Broc noticed his eyes were grey. He assumed Wulf must resemble his mother more in looks rather than his father.

The thane came to stand beside the horse. "I am Swein, the thane. What's so urgent?"

Broc reached down and placed the boy in the older man's arms. He then watched the blanket fall away from Wulf's face. Swein turned white. He clasped the boy close to his chest and spun around to return to the hall. Quickly dismounting, Broc gave his horse's reins to a villager then followed Swein into the hall.

Wulf had been laid out on a table, and it had not taken the thane long to find the wound. Without looking up, Swein spoke. "How did this happen? I know you are a Norman. Did your Duke William finally arrive?"

Broc pulled his helmet off and placed it at Wulf's feet before coming to stand at the opposite side of the table. "Aye, he did. He is now King of England. Harold is dead."

The older man still did not look up. "So what is to happen to us Saxons? Are we to lose everything? Our respect? Our way of life? Our lands?"

"I don't know what the king has in mind for England. All I do know is he gave Elmstead to me."

Swein's head snapped up to look at the Norman who stood on the other side of the table. His eyes seemed to become riveted onto Broc's face. "What is your name?"

"I'm Broc St. Ceneri."

"Well, Broc St. Ceneri, we will discuss who owns Elmstead later. Right now I have to save my son."

Broc tried to reassure the thane. "I have done everything I could for Wulf. I don't think it was enough. Bringing him home seemed the best thing I could do for him."

"I am grateful for that mercy. Our healer will take over now." Reaching down, the thane lifted his son off the table. Before he could walk away Broc stopped him.

"Wait. I would like to help, with Wulf that is."

"You have done enough already." Swein turned to Broc and spoke with anger in his voice. "If it had not been for you Normans, I would not have my child brought home half dead. And why are you alone with my son? Where is Osbern? He would never leave Wulf's side without a fight."

Broc shook his head. "He died during the battle. He protected your son until the end."

Swein's face grew grim as he nodded. "Well I hope he did not die in vain. I now have to mourn the loss of a friend. God help you if I have to mourn the loss of my child."

"Then let me help. I wouldn't like to see the boy die."

Swein looked at Broc. He must have seen something on Broc's face that made him nod once again. "Fine, I'll let you know when you can be of service. Get some rest first. I will have one of the serfs show you to a chamber."

Broc felt something akin to panic as he watched the thane take his son to one of the chambers at the back of the hall. He actually found himself taking a step forward to follow before he pulled himself back.

The thane was right, he needed to sleep. In his need to hurry he had not slept at all in the last twenty-four hours. If he wanted to be of any help at all he had to get some rest.

* * * *

The pain was almost unbearable. It would be so easy to sink back down into the blackness, but something or someone beckoned. Ariel tried to ignore the voice as she felt herself starting to sink back down into the void. The voice became more persistent.

Why would it not leave her be? The blackness was her friend. The pain went away while it embraced her.

Still the voice called.

This time Ariel followed the sound to the surface. If she answered it maybe it would leave her alone. Her eyes fluttered open. A face hung above her. Blinking, Ariel let her eyes adjust to the brightness of the room. The face smiled. She almost wished she had not opened her eyes. It was Broc's face she saw, very close to her own.

"Come on, Wulf. Stay with us for awhile."

Ariel let out a groan. "What...what? Where am I?" Her voice sounded rough to her ears.

"At home in Elmstead."

Looking around the room she found herself in her own bed, in her own chamber. She closed her eyes in contentment. She was home. But then reality set in. Broc was at Elmstead. Her eyes snapped open. "I must see my father." Pushing herself up, Ariel tried to get off the bed, but her body failed her before she could lift herself very far.

Broc gently pushed her back down on the bed. "Where do you think you are going? Your fever has just broken. I'll get your father."

As soon as Broc left the room, Ariel scanned her chamber. Someone had removed all of her gowns, for they no longer hung on the pegs along the back of the wall. In their place hung tunics and trews. She felt herself relax. Her father must have realized Broc knew her only as a boy.

The chamber door opened and Swein walked in. Seeing Ariel awake, he rushed to her side, knelt down and grabbed her hand to place a kiss on it. "I praise God the fever has passed. You had me worried, my girl. Especially after the Norman said you had not awoken for the last few days."

Worry marked Ariel's face. "The Norman is Colwyn's father."

"Aye, I know. You only have to look at his face to reach that conclusion."

"Where is Colwyn? Broc must not see him. He hasn't recognized me. I'm not going to tell him I'm really a woman."

"I figured that much when he called you Wulf. Have no fear about him seeing your boy. While the Norman slept, I moved Colwyn into one of the new huts in the village. Lily is with him." Ariel let herself relax at that bit of news.

"I want to see him. He probably will not remember me since I've been gone so long. Nothing went as planned."

"How were you to know the king would choose you to be one of his house carls. I must say I am proud of you. A house carl. I'm sure Osbern felt the same."

Ariel felt tears come to her eyes at the mention of her friend's name. Over the last few months they had formed a bond and Ariel would miss him greatly. "I'm sorry father, about Osbern. If I had not wanted to fight with the fryd, he would still be alive."

Swein patted his daughter's hand. "Now don't go blaming yourself for Osbern's death. He would not want that. As for Colwyn, he may not recognize you, but he's still young. Though there is one problem with you being able to see him."

Ariel stiffened. "What could possibly stand in the way of my seeing my son?"

"The Norman is in the guest chamber right beside yours. He also refuses to leave your side."

Ariel felt herself slipping into sleep. She had used up most of her energy by talking to her father. Sleep would help her body heal itself, but she had so much more she needed to say to her father.

Seeing Ariel's eyes flutter shut, Swein released her hand and stood up. He bent down and kissed her cheek. "Sleep, Ariel. I will figure out a way to bring Colwyn to you. All you have to worry about is letting your wound heal. Once you are up and about you'll see Colwyn as much as you want at the hut."

Her father's words were the last Ariel heard before sleep finally claimed her.

Chapter 13

Broc could not remember the last time he had been so exhausted. It was late, very late, but sleep eluded him. Being at Elmstead once again brought memories of the girl back in a rush, so vivid he could almost taste her. He could almost feel her body pressed against his own. Just thinking of her made his body ache. There would be no ignoring the pressure in his trews as his cock swelled.

He gave himself a mental shake. Those thoughts had to stop, he had to sleep. A sound coming from the direction of the hall distracted him from his wayward thoughts. Broc wondered who could be moving about at this hour. He had thought the last of the inhabitants had retired hours ago.

Broc opened his chamber door and saw a lone woman cross the length of the room. She headed toward the chambers with a bundle cradled in her arms. Peering closer he realized she held a baby. A blanket covered the child's face obscuring it from view. Judging from the woman's dress, Broc guessed her to be from the village.

He watched the woman enter Wulf's chamber. Broc had to wonder if the boy had already sired a child. Thinking it unlikely, Broc shook his head to himself. Wulf was too young. He was not even old enough to grow a beard. Besides it had never been mentioned, Wulf having a child.

Whoever the woman and child were, Broc would find out. But it could wait until the morning. He had to get some sleep. For tomorrow he would start taking over the reins of Elmstead. The people had to know he now controlled Elmstead and not their one time thane.

* * * *

Ariel opened her eyes at the sound of her chamber door opening and being closed quietly. At the sight of Lily with Colwyn in her arms, she painfully raised herself into a sitting position.

Lily came and sat down on the edge of the bed. "Are you sure you're strong enough for this? You just came out of the fever."

Ariel smiled. "I will manage. Nothing is going to stop me from holding my son. It has been too long."

Lily nodded her head and gently placed the sleeping baby into Ariel's arms. When she pulled the blanket away from her son's face, Ariel found him still asleep. She felt tears come to her eyes at the sight of him.

The similarity between father and son hit her first. The other was how much he had grown. Colwyn was not the tiny baby she had left behind four months before. Sadness washed over her, she had missed so much. She had missed his first smile, his first laugh, his first attempt at crawling.

Placing a kiss on the sleeping baby's forehead, Ariel wondered if he would hate her when he grew up. She had chosen to wage war instead of staying with him. How could she blame him if he did?

Tears still shimmered in Ariel's eyes as she looked at Lily. "I've missed too much of his life. I should have stayed in Elmstead."

Lily squeezed Ariel's hand briefly. "Don't say that. Aye, you missed some things, but you have years to make up for your absence."

Ariel pushed back her tears. "True. It is one thing that is making it easier to bear." She once more looked down at her sleeping son. "What's he like?"

Lily smiled and gently stroked back the hair that had fallen over Colwyn's forehead. "He's a happy baby. Only cries when he's hungry or tired. He smiles all the time. Don't worry, Ariel. He will take to you very quickly."

Ariel let out a sigh. "Well I plan to spend a lot of time with Colwyn, even if I have to live in a hut with him."

Lily shook her head. "You'll not have to do that. While you were gone your father had a smaller hall built for you and Colwyn."

That surprised Ariel. She hadn't expected her father to do that. "Truly? He had not mentioned it before my leaving."

"He wanted it to be a surprise. But I figure it's a blessing now. We will be able to keep Colwyn away from the Norman there."

Ariel had to agree with Lily. "Aye, but Broc has been given Elmstead. I have no idea what he has planned for father and me. For all I know he may send us away."

Sheepishly, Lily looked at Ariel. "Then maybe it would be better if you told him who you really are. He would not want to have his own son homeless."

Ariel shook her head vehemently. "Nay, I will not tell him. He hasn't recognized me yet. I can only assume what we shared together must not have meant all that much to him. So what would be the point in telling him who I am? I meant nothing to him."

* * * *

Silence fell in the hall when Broc entered. Obviously the inhabitants of Elmstead had heard of the change in ownership. And from the looks on their faces it did not sit well with them.

He chose to ignore the scathing looks sent his way and went to sit next to the thane. The older man acknowledged him with a nod of his head.

Once seated, a female serf placed some fresh baked bread and a couple of wedges of yellow cheese in front of him. She then placed a tankard of ale next to the food. Tasting the fare given him, Broc found it to be delicious, even the ale was good.

Out of the corner of his eye, Broc noticed the thane watching him. "The food is very good."

"I'm glad it meets with your high standards."

Apparently Swein was not happy with his presence as lord here either. "I know you are not pleased with my being here. Let's just make the best of the situation."

Still being barely civil, Swein answered the Norman. "Fine with me, but there is one thing I need to know. What is to happen to my son and myself?"

"I'll not expect you to leave Elmstead, if that is what worries you. You know this land better than I. I would like you to help me with the running of it."

"What of my son?" It seemed Swein was still not satisfied with his answer.

Broc remained silent as he thought of the best way to word what he wanted to say. "I understand Wulf is very talented with the sword. Talented enough for him to have been chosen as a house carl. I would like to further his education in arms. I will make Wulf my squire and when I feel he has learned what he needs to know, I'll knight him."

Swein did a double take, as if he didn't think Broc was serious in his offer."But why would you do that? Wulf is a Saxon, your enemy."

Broc shook his head at Swein's statement. "Nay, he is not. Neither are you. I feel it would be a waste of talent if Wulf did not reach his full potential. Do you think he'll accept my offer?"

Swein took a few minutes to answer his query. "Aye, Wulf will do it. But I suggest you ask him yourself whether or not he'll become your squire."

"I'll do that." Broc rose after he finished his meal. "Now I think I will go to the village and have a look around. It's time the people of Elmstead got to know me better."

* * * *

The village of Elmstead was small, but it sported its own mill and salt-house. There were beehives as well. The honey collected from them was used to make mead that the thane and his family used. The villagers kept goats and sheep as well as farming the land.

Broc felt the villagers' eyes on him as he walked by their homes. He did not stop and talk to any of them. Even if they understood him, they probably would not speak to him. He was the outsider and they would not let him soon forget it.

Two newer looking huts sat at the edge of the village. Broc figured there would not be much more to see beyond them. Just as he decided to go and inspect the fields, he noticed a woman sat on a chair in front of one of the huts with a baby on her lap.

She seemed familiar. Broc was soon able to see that this woman had been in the hall last night the closer he got to her. Maybe he would get some answers from her.

Occupied with the baby on her lap, she didn't notice him until he stood before her. When she did, his presence seemed to startle her. A baby blanket was draped over the back of her chair. She reached for it and casually covered the baby with it.

Broc watched the girl cover the baby. Now that he had a better look at her face, he saw how young she was. She had the typical Saxon looks, blond hair and blue eyes. Her gown was made of rough homespun. The blanket wrapped around the baby had been made of much finer stuff. Broc wondered how she came by it.

"Can I do something for you, my lord?" The girl spoke in perfect French.

"What's your name?" Broc was surprised and pleased the girl understood him.

"Lily, my lord."

Now that he knew he could communicate with the girl, Broc started to ask her some questions. Maybe she had the answers he sought. "Do you live here alone with your child?"

She seemed leery of him as she hesitantly answered him. "Aye, my lord."

"What happened to your man?"

"He died last winter. He took sick and never recovered."

Broc could not help but think it was very convenient, or the girl was not telling him the truth. "It must be hard for you, to be alone."

"My family lives in the village. The thane and his son look out for me as well."

"The thane must be a good man."

"Aye, he is. He always looks out for us in the village. We are his people."

The jab at his taking over Elmstead was unmistakable. "I'm sure he does. Do you know if the thane has a daughter as well as a son?"

"I don't know what you mean, my lord?" Lily looked up at him with a slightly confused expression on her face. Broc figured she had no idea where he was going with his line of questioning.

"I came to Elmstead over a year ago and I met a girl. I think she lived in the village. She looked a lot like Wulf. It made me think maybe Wulf had a sister."

"Nay, my lord. The thane only has one child. Just one." The way Lily stressed that the thane only had the one child, Broc had to think she was trying to tell him something. Maybe the thane did have an illegitimate daughter stashed away somewhere that the villagers wished to protect.

"I thank you for taking the time to speak with me. Since I'm to take the thane's place, we will see more of each other." Broc then left Lily at the hut and made his way toward the fields.

Chapter 14

The move did not go as smoothly as expected. Ariel still could not believe the arrogance of the man. When he had found out about the new hall Broc had refused to let her leave.

That morning everything had gone according to plan. That is until Broc had come to see how she was doing. He had not missed seeing the serfs had collected up her belongings leaving her chamber virtually empty.

"What's going on here, Wulf?"

"Since you have taken over as thane of Elmstead, Father and I are moving to the new hall he had built for me while I was away. Father and I need not be under foot, the hall is yours."

Broc sat down beside her on the bed and signaled the serfs to leave them. Once alone, he turned and smiled at her. "Before you go I would like to ask you something."

"All right." Ariel held her breath.

"How would you like to be my squire?" At Ariel's questioning look, Broc quickly added, "I forgot Saxons don't have knights. As my squire, you would serve me at table and in my chamber. You would help maintain my coat of mail and sword. In return I will teach you how to fight on horseback and anything else you need to know. When you have learned all that I can to teach you, I'll knight you."

Ariel felt her jaw drop open. Broc had just offered her something she never hoped to attain--knighthood. Now with the Normans ruling England, the Saxon order would not stay the same. If she became a knight, her father and son would never have to worry if they were forced to leave Elmstead. She could attach herself to some lord's household and provide for them. The only part of Broc's offer she felt reluctant about was serving Broc in his bedchamber. But if it would help her reach her goal she would manage somehow to get through it.

"I accept. How long would I have to train before you knight me? Being a house carl that should give me some standing in the training."

Broc chuckled at her show of enthusiasm. "Let's first see how fast you learn. But if you pick it up quickly enough, probably in a few months."

"When can we start?"

"Wait until your shoulder heals."Broc said with a laugh. "If we start too early you could do more damage than good."

"I could start with the other duties, the ones that don't include arms training."

"All right. If you feel up to it you can serve me in the hall and bedchamber." Broc stood and started toward the door. He stopped before he reached it. "I'll tell your father you will not be moving with him."

"What do you mean?" Ariel had a bad feeling about this. She could see her well conceived plans falling apart.

"As my squire you will stay with me at all times. I have to know where you will be. I will send the serfs back to finish packing your belongings."

Now very confused, Ariel asked "If I won't be going with my father, then where will I be moving to?"

"A squire sleeps on a pallet in his master's bedchamber. I may have need of you in the middle of the night. It makes things easier. So you will be moving into my chamber."

Ariel wondered who it would be easier for. It sure as hell would be difficult for her. Watching Broc's retreating back, she wondered how she would be able to keep her secret from him. They would be practically living on top of one another. She would have to talk to her father. He would know what to do.

* * * *

Swein did not give her the answers Ariel wished to hear. Her father had put it quite simply, if she wanted to be a knight she would have to work through the hard parts.

Once all her clothes had been moved into Broc's chamber which had at one time belonged to her parents, she had been allowed to go see her father. Broc only stipulated that she return by the evening meal. Using her free time she went to see Colwyn.

The new hall was a smaller version of the main building. Ariel found it to be cozy and wished she could stay with her family there. But until Broc knighted her, she would try to spend most of her free time with her small family.

Colwyn had been a little leery of her at first. This was understandable, considering how long she had been away from him. As an outgoing child it had only taken a few minutes of being around Ariel before he had reached out for her. She would never forget that moment. Holding her son close, Ariel made a vow to never leave him behind again.

Mother and child played together until Colwyn grew sleepy. Ariel picked him up and cradled him in her arms. She gently rocked him until he fell asleep. Noticing her charge had fallen asleep, Lily reached out her arms to take Colwyn. With a kiss across his cheek, Ariel passed him to Lily.

Ariel felt her father gaze at her. There was wistfulness to his expression. She knew what he was thinking. The first time she had caught him staring at her so, she had asked what was on his mind. He told her he didn't know if he had done the right thing by letting her go off to fight. She had changed, and it wasn't because her hair was now shorter and she dressed as a man either. Inside she seemed changed. Ariel had quickly reassured him that the changes in her had been for the good not the bad. She was happy with the way she was now.

Ariel stood up and stretched. She winced at the pain in her shoulder. It was mending, but she would carry a scar there to her grave. Her first battle scar would always be a reminder of what she had done.

"Well daughter, now that you have a slight reprieve from the new lord, what would you like to do?"

Since waking from her fevered sleep one thing had been on her mind. "I want to have a bath. I can't very well have one with Broc around. That particular indulgence I greatly missed while away."Her father laughed. "A bath it is then."

* * * *

She was in heaven. Her father had arranged for a large wooden tub to be dragged into the hall. It now sat in front of a roaring fire. Since he had left the hall and Lily was watching Colwyn, Ariel had decided not to use the privacy screen. She was alone and did not expect anyone to bother her.

She had washed her hair and body and decided a good long soak would be in order. It felt glorious. What she enjoyed even more was having the bindings removed from around her chest. She had to tie them so tight, she felt as if they were steel bands. She never could take a deep breath while wearing them.

Ariel let herself sink under the water. Coming back up to the surface her body clenched at the sight that met her eyes. Broc stood with his back toward her. He faced the hearth watching the flames.

Ariel quickly pressed her body against the side of the tub, shielding her body from Broc's line of sight. "What are you doing here? I thought you wouldn't need me until later."

Broc turned at the sound of her voice. "I came to see your father."

"He's not here. So if you do not mind, I would like to finish my bath." Ariel hoped Broc would leave without too much preamble. The water had started to cool and she would soon be forced to get out of the tub.

"Continue your bathing. When you're finished we'll both go and look for your father. What I want to talk to him about concerns you as well."

Now what was she going to do? She could not very well tell him to leave. She was supposed to be a man. "If you go look for him I'll meet you later."

"Nay, that won't be necessary."

She was in trouble now. There had to be something she could say to make him leave her alone, but nothing readily came to mind. Stuck, she found herself unable to do anything except stare up at him.

"Well? Continue with your bath. You have only just recently recovered from wound fever. It won't do you any good to sit in a cold bath." When Ariel made no move to comply, Broc stepped closer to the tub. "Must I remove you myself?"

Broc was just about to reach for her when something stopped him. He seemed to take in her wet hair, which she had slicked back off of her face. His gaze then moved to her cheekbones and chin He seemed to hover over her lips before his gaze moved onto her eyes. Ariel felt her breath catch. Surely Broc saw her for the woman she was now.

He continued to stare at her with what Ariel slowly recognized as longing. He bent closer to her. His eyes became focused on her lips. His breathing grew quicker. Transfixed, Ariel watched him lower his head until his lips came within mere inches of hers. Her involuntary sharp intake of breath effectively broke the spell. Broc jerked himself upright and took a quick step back.

Ariel could not believe what Broc had almost done. It only made her body ache for his. When he quickly moved away, Ariel felt the loss. Even though she knew very little of men, she could tell he had not been unaffected by the encounter. His breath still came in shallow, rapid puffs, same as hers did. Her body throbbed with desire.

They stared into each other's eyes, the silence hanging between them. Neither one moved. Broc finally broke the mounting tension surrounding them. He mumbled something about maybe it would be best if he went in search of her father after all. Turning from her he practically ran out of the hall.

Now alone, Ariel stepped out of the tub and quickly dried her body. She bound her chest and donned a fresh tunic and trews. It wasn't hard to figure out Broc had thought he had almost kissed a man. He couldn't get away from her fast enough. His mind may have perceived her as male, but his body knew she was all female. Lily had been right, Broc could not be very observant.

As it turned out Broc was not with her father and couldn't be found anywhere around Elmstead. Ariel guessed he needed to be alone to recover from their brief encounter. She had to admit she didn't feel quite herself either. The mere thought of that almost kiss made her heart beat faster.

* * * *

The evening meal came and went and still Broc did not return.

Since Ariel was not going to have to act the part of a servant this night, she sat with her father before the hearth drinking ale. Even though she told herself there was no need to worry, Ariel's eyes kept drifting to the door. *Where could he be?* It had been hours since he had last been seen.

Swein seemed to pick up on Ariel's anxiousness. He raised a brow in her direction when he caught her looking at the door for the tenth time in as many minutes. "All right, what happened?"

Ariel jumped at the sound of her father's voice. "Nothing."

"Come on now. Your Norman has been gone most of the day and you look like you lost your best friend."

"He's not my Norman. Why should I care where he goes?"

The look Swein gave her said he did not believe her. "Maybe you do because you still have feelings for him. He must feel something for you. Lily told me he asked if I had a daughter. She said he looked like he didn't want to believe her when she told him I had only one child. So what happened between you two?"

Reluctantly, Ariel answered her father's question. "He walked in on me while I bathed." Seeing Swein's face light up, Ariel narrowed her eyes at him. She could not believe it. *Did he want Broc to find out her secret?* "Stop looking so happy, he didn't see anything. I thought you had agreed with me that I would stay being Wulf around Broc."

"I had, but now I've come to know him better. Maybe you should tell him."

That was all Ariel needed to hear from her father. Now she had to worry where his loyalties would be. "Are you telling me if I don't tell him, you will?"

"Nay. You are and always will be my daughter. I would never betray you. I only feel if he finds out on his own he could make it go badly for you. What if he decides since you lied to him he can't trust you? He could very well try to take Colwyn from you. It is within his rights."

"All the more reason to keep Colwyn away from Broc. I will not take that chance."

"Fine, it's your decision. Now tell me what made him run off?"

After a couple of deep breaths and a sip of ale, Ariel told her father the rest of the tale. "As I said before, he didn't see anything. I tried to make him leave at first, but for some reason he decided he would wait until I finished. All I could do was stare at him like a fool. Then something came over him, something that caused him to almost do something else. Let's just say he left in a very great hurry."

Swein let out a roar of laughter. "So he wanted to kiss you. No wonder the poor man ran. He thought he almost kissed another man. That would be enough to have any male question his masculinity, and that also explains where he went."

"Then where is he?"

"If that happened to me at Broc's age, I would go in search of a willing woman to prove I was still a man."

Ariel's reaction to her father's words had her reaching for her tankard of ale. She finished what remained in two large gulps and got up to get more. She couldn't stand the thought of Broc with another. No matter what she said, she had started to care for him. And she didn't like it one bit

* * * *

She tried to ignore the sounds coming from the hall. All Ariel wanted to do was sleep. After talking with her father, she had had a little too much ale. So far she had only managed to sleep a few hours, which hadn't done much to stop her head from spinning.

The noises from the hall came closer. Ariel had already figured out who had finally come back when the chamber door slammed open. Broc practically fell into the room. It looked as if he had downed too much ale as well, and he was not alone. Two women clung to his arms. Trying not to be noticed, Ariel lay completely still and hoped they would assume she slept. But that was not to be, Broc had other plans for her it seemed. Seeing the slight form curled up on the pallet in the corner of the chamber, he made his way over to Ariel. Realizing she had been spotted, Ariel tightly closed her eyes.

"You were right, my lord. He is a fine looking lad." Ariel opened her eyes to find one of the women bending over her. The woman reached out and brushed her knuckles across her cheek. "His cheeks are as soft as a babe's bottom."

Pushing herself up and out of the woman's reach, Ariel glared up at Broc. "What are they doing here?"

Broc stepped closer. The other woman continued to cling to him. "As you are my squire, I figured I would further your education. I thought it was time you became better acquainted with the opposite sex. This nice lady has agreed to initiate you."

Ariel felt all the blood drain out of her face. "And why is the other one here?"

"I decided to sample some of this fine lady's charms." Broc lowered his head and gave the woman on his arm a kiss. To Ariel the kiss seemed never to end. Seeing the woman's hand run up and down Broc's thigh, Ariel felt the bile rise up to the back of her throat.

She had to leave. Getting to her feet she tried to move past the woman who had been meant for her. She reached out and pulled Ariel to a stop. "Where are you going? There's no reason to be shy. I will be gentle with you." The woman's hand snaked out and grabbed Ariel's bottom.

Ariel shoved the woman off of her and took a step back. "I'm not interested." Noticing Broc had finally ended the kiss, she directed her next words at him. "Since you'll be entertaining tonight I will leave you alone. I have no intention of taking part in any of this."

Roughly brushing past the woman, Ariel almost made it to the chamber door. Broc stopped her before she could cross the threshold. "I didn't give you permission to leave."

Ariel swung around to face Broc. "You cannot make me stay."

"Oh, but I can."

"Why? Why is it so important I stay?"

"I don't have to give you a reason. You are my squire. You must do what I say without question. If you leave, I won't knight you."

She had no choice, she needed that knighthood. With England under Norman rule it was essential. "Fine, I'll stay." The other woman assumed it meant Ariel would accept her advances, but she soon backed off when Ariel scowled at her. "I'll stay, but I will sleep alone. And you, Broc St. Ceneri, can go to hell as far as I am concerned."

Chapter 15

Hell, utter and absolute hell, was where Ariel found herself in and she didn't think she could make it through the night. After making her point very clear to Broc, she returned to her pallet. To make her rejection even more complete, Ariel curled up on her side so she faced the wall.

One of the women laughed. "Maybe this one is still a little boy. What do you say, my lord, are you man enough for the two of us?"

"Now I can't leave one of you ladies wanting. It would not be polite." The women's breathy laughter filled the room.

With her back to the bed, Ariel couldn't see what was taking place. If only she could have blocked out the sounds emanating from the bed. She tried pulling the blanket over her head, even stuck her fingers in her ears, but nothing helped.

When the women began to moan in pleasure, sleep became impossible. Having to hear the women was bad enough, but the moans they elicited from Broc affected Ariel far more. They reminded her of her first time with a man, with that very man on the bed. She wanted to rage at Broc. Yell at him, *How could you do this to me? How could he betray her like this?* She had not wanted another man in that way, much less two at the same time.

But then her body turned traitor. She had been able to ignore the sounds the women made, but Broc's moans were something else entirely. She remembered when he had made those sounds at her touch, when their two bodies had joined as one. Remembered the feel of the hot, hard length of him moving inside her. Wetness pooled between her legs.

Finally the sounds of passion gave way to silence. All became quiet once more. Ariel prayed they would sleep. But once again fate did not go her way. The noises started up again after a short interval. The only option she had left to her was to lay there and wait for it to end.

Before the night ended, Ariel vowed to make Broc pay for his behavior.

As for her being his squire, a few changes had to take place. She would accept his lessons of warfare, but being his servant was now out of the question.

* * * *

Pain shot through his head the moment he opened his eyes. Groaning, he shut them once more. Broc usually didn't drink heavily, but last night had been an exception. He had tried to forget the memory of Wulf's face, how it looked when he had wanted to kiss the boy. It hadn't helped. It only left him with a pounding head.

Opening his eyes, Broc realized it was still very early. Something had brought him out of the deep sleep he had been in. As he turned his head to look about the room, he saw he didn't sleep alone. Two women lay on either side of him. Lifting the blankets slightly, he found them both to be naked.

He couldn't remember much from the night before, but what he did remember sickened him. Bad enough he had tried to force Wulf into taking one of the women, but what made it even worse he had taken both of them to his bed. That was something he had thought he was not capable of doing. A sound came from the far corner of the chamber. Broc looked across the room. Wulf lay curled into a ball on his pallet. He was dreaming. The small sounds coming from him had awakened Broc.

Gently as he possibly could, Broc climbed out of the bed. Looking over his shoulder, he checked to make sure the women had not been disturbed. He saw they hadn't awakened. He pulled on one of his longer tunics and moved to where the boy slept.

Broc grew more disgusted with himself the longer he looked at Wulf. He not only lay curled up into a tight ball, but one of his hands still covered his ear. He had been in the chamber the whole time. Flashes of himself telling the boy he couldn't leave almost made Broc ill. *How could I have done that to Wulf?* But Broc already knew why. His damn pride demanded he prove he was still a man. Wulf whimpered in his sleep once more. Hoping to comfort the boy, Broc reached out and brushed the hair away from Wulf's eyes. That turned out to be a mistake.

* * * *

The feel of someone touching her brought Ariel instantly awake. She had thought the woman had taken the hint to leave her alone. When her eyes focused on the face before her, her body clenched. She then did what she had wanted to do all night long. Pulling back her arm with her hand fisted, Ariel punched Broc square on the jaw. Not suspecting the blow, it knocked Broc onto his backside. Ariel watched those gold eyes of his widen in surprise. Ariel rubbed her bruised knuckles.

"I deserved that."

Ariel surged to her feet and looked down at Broc. "Aye, you did. How could you?"

"I don't know. I've never done anything like that before, I apologize."

"You can't actually expect an apology will help. If this is how you Normans act, you can keep your knighthood. I'll have none of it." Ariel had to get away from Broc. Her body started to do terrible things to her just at the mere sight of him. Anger waged war with desire. His moans of pleasure still echoed in her head. Stepping around Broc who sat on the floor, Ariel moved past him to leave. Once again he held her back. This time Broc had a hold on one of her ankles.

"Wait, don't go."

"I refuse to stay and you can't make me. I'm not your squire anymore, so release me."

In one graceful move Broc surged to his feet. Before Ariel could move away, her arm became held in what felt like a band of steel. As he started to pull her out of the chamber, Ariel fought Broc every step he took. It didn't do any good. He just dragged her behind him. He didn't stop until they stood in front of the hearth in the hall. Seeing no one was about yet, Broc pulled her until Ariel stood facing him.

"I did not release you. As far as I am concerned, you still are my squire."

"And I told you I don't want the knighthood. I will not serve a man I can't respect."

Broc closed his eyes as if Ariel's words had brought him pain. "I can understand your feelings. But I want to continue your training."

Ariel shook her head. "Why is it so important you knight me?"

Broc could only shrug. "I don't honestly know. It's something I feel I must do."

Silently Ariel thought over her next words. "If I decide I want to continue I want some changes made."

"Such as?"

"I will not serve you at the hall nor will I sleep in your chamber. All I want is the training in arms. The king's house carls has to mean something."

Broc paused then answered. "Agreed."

"I'm not finished yet. My father told me you are going to court for Christ mass. When you come back, I want you to knight me."

"That depends if I deem you ready."

"Oh, I will be ready. I'm a fast learner. Do you agree?" Ariel held her breath, hoping she had not gone too far.

Broc once more took the time to think over what she had said before answering. "Aye, I agree. We'll start your training when your shoulder is healed."

Ariel shook her head. "I want to start tomorrow. It's better."

"Fine. If I see you in pain, I will stop the training session."

"Agreed. Now if I have your permission, I would like to get some sleep." Before she could move, Broc held her back.

"I agreed to you not sleeping in my chamber, but not to you leaving the hall. Go to your old chamber. I'll have your belongings put back later."

Ariel wanted to scream at Broc. She did not want to be even that close to him. But it seemed she would not have much of a choice, especially if she wanted to become a knight. Nodding her head in acceptance, Ariel spun on her heel and left Broc alone to watch her retreating back.

* * * *

Returning to his chamber Broc started to rid it of any evidence of last night's activities. He still could not believe what he had done. It sickened him. The sooner he put this behind him the better.

The two women still slept stretched out across the bed. Broc had no idea who they were. He didn't even remember meeting them. All he wanted to do now was get them, as quickly as possible, out of his bed and the hall.

From what Broc could remember about last night, he knew they had not been virgins. If anything they were the opposite. Their clothes could by no means be mistaken for the silks and fine linens of a lady. They were also strewn all over the chamber floor.

Without further ado, Broc walked over to the bed and shook each woman awake. "Get dressed. It's time for you both to leave."

They both grumbled at being awakened so early, but at Broc's commanding tone did as he ordered. The women must have also realized any advances made in his direction would be rebuffed. Neither one of them made a move to touch him. Once they had donned their clothing Broc ushered them out of the hall. He closed the door behind the two leaving the women to find their own way home.

* * * *

After having slept for a few hours, Ariel went to her father's hall. Broc had not been around, which suited her just fine. She couldn't trust herself not to do him bodily harm. Once Ariel crossed the threshold of the new hall, she felt herself relax. Here she could truly be herself, a daughter, a mother, a woman. All the people who cared about her most in the world dwelled here.

Colwyn sat on her father's lap, both intent on the other so they did not see her until she was half way across the room. The baby saw her first. He wiggled his little body until he could reach out his arms to Ariel.

Rushing over, Ariel scooped her son up and swung him around in a circle then clutched him to her chest. It was exactly what she needed to make her feel better. When Colwyn stared up at her, she could not resist the urge to place a big kiss on his small mouth.

"So what happened to your Norman? Did he come home?"

"Aye, he did." Ariel swung Colwyn onto her hip and sat next to Swein. She really didn't want to tell him what had happened last night, but Elmstead was small. Most of the villagers probably already knew about the two strange women who had come out of the Norman's hall this morning. Her father would find out sooner or later. She thought it best if he heard it from her.

"He didn't come back alone."

"What do you mean by not alone? Did he come back with soldiers?"

"Nay. He had not one, but two women with him."

Swein's mouth opened and then shut before he spoke again. "You slept in his chamber. Please tell me he told you to leave."

Ariel looked down. "Sorry, I can't do that. One of the women had been meant for me. I refused, so he took both to his bed instead. He then ordered me to remain, even though I did not participate."

Her father's rage came unexpectedly. Ariel almost didn't make it off the bench before Swein stood up and sent it swiftly flying. His face turned red and he clenched his hands into fists at his sides.

"Where is that bastard? I'll kill him for this. How dare he? Just because he's Norman and we're Saxon it does not mean he can treat us without any respect!"

Swein's last words came out in a bellow. Lily, who must have been in another chamber, came into the hall to see what had upset the thane. Ariel shook her head at Lily and passed Colwyn to her. The girl must have realized she would be better off leaving because she returned to her chamber without saying a word.

Ariel turned and found her father pacing as he grumbled to himself. "Calm down, father. You can do nothing about what happened."

"Aye, I bloody well can."

"Tell me what exactly? Broc still thinks I'm male. You can't very well take drastic action. He will become suspicious."

Ariel's words brought Swein to a halt. He looked at her with a scowl on his face. "Something has to be done."

The double meaning of what her father spoke of was not lost on Ariel. She knew what he was asking, but it was out of the question. "Sorry, father. I will not be the one to tell him."

Ariel closed the gap between them and wrapped her arm around her father's waist. The feel of Swein's arms holding her calmed her like nothing else could.

"As for the other, I think Broc already regrets what he has done. So much so, I wrung a few concessions out of him."

"Are you sure they're enough, Ariel? I know you have feelings for the Norman, no matter what you tell me. It must have hurt you, his seeking out others while you are near him."

"Don't concern yourself, father. There is nothing I need from Broc except for one thing. All I want from him is the knighthood."

Chapter 16

Dressed in full battle armor and with hesitant steps, Ariel walked toward the lone figure standing in the middle of the practice field. The chain mail hung heavily across her shoulders and her sword hung at her side. She wore her helmet and carried her shield on her left arm. Ariel was ready for her first lesson.

The dawn air swirled cool and crisp around her. The nip of cold told of winter soon to come. Sunlight reflected off the frost that coated the grass. Ariel stopped a few feet away from Broc. Slight currents of tension drifted between them from what had taken place in his chamber the other night. After their conversation the morning before, Ariel had not spoken to the man standing before her. She had stayed with her father and Colwyn well into the night. It had been late and no one had been about, including Broc, when she had returned, something she had counted on.

Now facing him again, all that had gone on that night came rushing back. Her father had guessed right. She still carried feelings for Broc and he had hurt her, badly. Badly enough that she would never willingly reveal her true self to him, no matter what occurred.

Broc made a small movement as he shifted his weight. The sound of a sword being drawn from its scabbard drew Ariel's attention. She looked from the sword to Broc's face. He already wore his helmet. His gold eyes stared at her intently as a small smile played across his lips.

"I can tell by the look on your face you still feel some anger toward me for the other night. Well here is your chance, Wulf. Try and give me the thrashing you think I deserve."

From the cocksure look on his face, Ariel assumed Broc thought she would not be able to best him. He was going to be in for a surprise.

As Ariel's first blow landed, Broc's expression turned to one of surprise just as she had predicted it would. She then proceeded to show him how he had sorely underestimated his opponent. With glee, Ariel pushed Broc across the field with each of her hits. She may look quite small for a man, but for a woman she was strong. Her slim body was deceiving, which had been Broc's first mistake. Ariel knew he thought he could overpower her just by his sheer size. But Ariel was more agile and didn't completely rely on brute strength to best her opponent.

Ariel had to admit she played with Broc, a sort of retribution for the other night. But he did deserve what he got. The look of shock that had flitted across his features at her first hit was well worth it.

When an opportunity came to end their match, Ariel took it. She had gotten what she had wanted from him. With a lunge and a quick twist of her wrist, Ariel sent Broc's sword skidding across the field.

Her shout of victory echoed around the open space. Ariel removed her helmet and wiped the sweat from her brow. Broc was a good swordsman, but she was better. She wondered how he would feel if he knew he had just been bested by a woman.

Retrieving his sword, Broc moved to stand before Ariel. "How...how did you do that?"

Ariel couldn't take the smile off her face. "I don't really know. I just find myself able to do it."

"Why didn't you tell me before you are a natural?"

"Well I did tell you I learned quickly."

Broc shook his head. "If this demonstration you have given me is any indication, you'll be more than ready by Christ mass to be knighted."

Thrilled, Ariel felt like jumping up and down, but she managed to keep her emotions under control. "Good. Then let's continue."

Broc held up his hand. "Wait one moment. How is your shoulder? Are you in pain?"

"I'm fine." To prove it, Ariel lifted her left arm and gave it a little shake.

Broc laughed. "All right, have it your way. But if I see you favoring that side at any time, I will call the lesson to a halt."

"Agreed. It won't be necessary though."

Not saying another word, Broc stalked across the field. Ariel watched him head toward the stables. She sheathed her sword and ran to catch up with him.

* * * *

Late that afternoon Broc finally called the lesson to a halt. Even though Wulf would not admit it, he was in some pain. The boy had not shown any outward sign of the strain it must have taken to hold his shield for so long, but Broc noticed the flinches he gave near the end. He had to give Wulf credit, he tried his hardest to hide what he felt.

Through most of the lesson, Broc had a hard time not showing his emotions to Wulf. The boy was unbelievable. What should have taken months to teach another man, Wulf picked up in a matter hours. The boy may not have the bulk behind his sword arm, but he was able to out maneuver any man Broc's size, which gave Wulf a distinct advantage.

The boy had already gone to the main hall to change, Broc slowly followed. The evening meal would be ready in a short while. After his exertions on the field he needed to have a big meal. They had only stopped briefly once during the lesson to quickly eat some bread and cheese.

The hall was deserted except for the serfs who had the task of preparing the meal. Wulf appeared to still be in his chamber. Broc entered his chamber and started to shuck off his chain mail. It soon became apparent that the wall separating the two chambers was not very thick. The sounds of Wulf moving around on the other side could mutely be heard. For some unknown reason Broc moved to lean against the wall, listening. The sounds coming from the other chamber comforted him.

The unnatural urges Broc had for Wulf still seemed to be with him. Even after that debacle of the night with the two women. *Why would it not go away?* It bothered him more than he would like to admit.

The sound of a chamber door being slammed shut brought Broc out of his musing. Quickly finishing up, he went back into the hall. He couldn't see Wulf anywhere. Broc felt a little disappointed. He had thought the boy would stay and share the evening meal with him, but apparently Wulf had made other plans for the evening.

On impulse, Broc retrieved his cloak from his chamber and made his way to the smaller hall. He caught sight of Wulf slowly walking through the village. The villagers shouted a greeting as the boy went by. Obviously Wulf was held in high regard.

As predicted, Wulf went to the other hall. The girl named Lily stood outside at the front of the building. She held her child in her arms. Broc slowed his pace and stopped several yards away, watching. With some surprise, he watched Wulf rush up to the girl and take the child from her. Laughing, the boy held the baby up and spun around. The child's shouts of glee drifted over to where Broc stood. Fascinated, he found himself unable to look away.

Something akin to loneliness washed over Broc when Wulf cuddled the baby close to him for a kiss. He felt left out. Almost as if he belonged up there with them, not standing off by himself. The child had to be the boy's. No other explanation would account for Wulf's behavior. Something about the scene bothered Broc though. Wulf showered the baby with attention, but none of it he directed toward the girl, the baby's mother.

That led Broc to think Lily had lied to him at their first meeting. She had said the child's father was not around. She had to have some reason for withholding the truth from him. And Wulf had to be doing the same. But why? Now that he thought about it, every time he had seen the child the baby's face had been hidden from view. Broc didn't even know the sex of the child. Something was just not right. He had a feeling if he saw the child's face it would all be explained.

Broc felt eyes on him and realized he had been spotted. Wulf came stomping toward him. The girl and baby could no longer be seen. From the look on the boy's face, Broc could tell he had upset Wulf with his presence.

"What are you doing here, my lord?" Wulf said in barely contained irritation.

"I just wondered where you had gone. The evening meal is not too far off."

"I plan to eat with my father that is if you have no objections?"

"None I can think of. I noticed Lily is at the hall. Has your father taken her and her child in?"

"Aye, not that it is any of your concern. Now if you will excuse me, I would like to go to my father. I will return later this evening."

Without so much as a backward glance, Wulf spun on his heel and went inside the hall. Something definitely had to be going on around here, Broc thought to himself. Something Wulf did not want him to find out about.

* * * *

The lessons continued and the tension slowly disappeared. Ariel had to admit she could have caused of most of it. As much as she wanted to, she could not forget that night. Every time she looked Broc in the face, she remembered images that would be better off forgotten.

Other factors also brought about the strain. The more time Ariel spent with Broc, the more she found herself liking him and any romantic feelings she carried for him, deepened. To counter act the emotions Broc invoked, Ariel immersed herself in what he had taught her.

Each night she would go to bed exhausted and wake up with every muscle in her body screaming. After a week had gone by the pain eventually went away. Even her shoulder gave her no troubles. Ariel also noticed changes in her body as well. Her shoulders broadened, her arms and legs padded with muscle. She knew she would never be as large as a man, but now with the changes in her body she looked more the part.

Now at the end of November, Ariel felt she had learned all Broc had to teach, but the lessons still continued. The lessons had become a common ground they both tread. In some ways Ariel would miss the time she spent with Broc, but all that would end once he knighted her.

Her days had now become routine. She woke, broke her fast and donned her armor. Her equipment also had changed. In the last month Broc had the blacksmith make her a Norman helmet and a new shield. Instead of the round Saxon variety, Ariel now carried the large triangular shaped shield of a Norman. Her shield carried no emblem or color. The blank white shield would be changed after she became a knight. She already had decided what her emblem would be.

As he had every morning, Broc waited for her at the practice field. But something was different about him today. He had an air of impatience about him. When Ariel finally stood in front of him, she noticed he wore no armor. "No lesson today?"

Broc shook his head. "Nay, something important has come up. The lessons are now over."

Her heart sank. Broc could not be serious, the lessons had to continue. To stop now would be unthinkable. Not when she was so close to realizing her goal. "They can't stop now. You promised to knight me."

Broc smiled. "Aye, I did. I don't break promises I make. Tonight, in fact, you will become a knight."

Flustered, Ariel tried to grasp what he said. "I thought I had to wait until closer to Christ mass."

"There has been a change of plans. While you were at your father's hall a messenger came from William's court. He has requested I come to London earlier than I had previously thought. For some unknown reason, he has ordered I bring you with me."

Ariel did not know if she was happy about this or not "What if I refuse to go?"

"You have no choice in the matter. I was ordered to bring you. If you have forgotten I will remind you, I am your overlord. You must do what I say. Be thankful I'll knight you before we leave. That way you will have some status at court."

Broc started to walk away then stopped. "I suggest you get some rest. For after tonight you will no longer be considered a boy, but a man. It's something to celebrate. It will be a long night I assure you." With that said, he left Ariel standing in the field.

* * * *

Just to spite Broc, Ariel did not go and rest. If tonight was going to be the night all her dreams were to be fulfilled, then she wanted to look her best. Which meant she would need a bath.

Before going to her father's hall, Ariel went to see the blacksmith. He would be the one to paint her emblem on her shield. She had already given him her chosen design so all he had to do was the hard copy.

The smith, Alfward, was a large man with arms and chest heavily muscled from the number of years he spent working the forge. He was Swein's age with hair and beard grizzled with grey. This morning Ariel found Alfward working the bellows, making the forge's fires come to life. At the doorway Ariel cleared her throat to get the smith's attention.

"How are you this morn, Alfward?"

With a smile, the smith looked up and answered her query. "Just fine, lass. Come in and don't look at me like that. The Norman isn't around. I have known you since you were in swaddling bands. You will always be a lass to me no matter what you pretend to be."

Ariel laughed. "I'm sure you know the reason for my ruse. Nothing remains a secret in the village for long."

"Aye. Your boy is the Norman's get. Not hard to figure that out when the boy wears his heritage on his face." Releasing the bellows, Alfward went over to Ariel. "What is it you need?"

"How do you know I need something?"

"Everybody needs something. Come now, what is it to be?"

Ariel placed her shield on the smith's work table. "Will you be able to put my emblem on this before this evening?"

At her words Alfward wrapped his arms around her waist and swung her around. Ariel could not help but laugh with him. The smith put her down on her feet and gave her a slap on the back, hard enough to almost knock her down.

"So he's really going to knight you. I'll be buggered. Have no fear, I will have it finished. It will be the first piece I work on today."

"Thank you, Alfward. Bring it to the main hall when you're finished with it." On impulse, Ariel stood up on tip toes and placed a kiss on the smith's grizzled cheek. She then had the rare opportunity to see Alfward blush. "And if you have nothing else to do, I would like you to come to the festivities. You have always believed in me."

"I would not miss it for anything, lass. You do us all proud." Much to Ariel's surprise, the smith started to bellow with laughter. "I would like to see that Norman's face when he finds out he knighted a woman."

"If I have any say in the matter, that day will never come."

Chapter 17

Ariel thought the day would never end. After her bath, she spent a few hours with Colwyn. But with each passing hour, her nerves started to get the better of her. It became so bad that once Colwyn had gone down for a nap her father demanded she go find something to occupy herself with.

Knowing she would not be able to do anything that would require her full attention, Ariel decided to go for a ride. It seemed to help a bit. The cool fresh air felt invigorating and cleared her head of worrying thoughts. Letting the cold air fill her lungs, Ariel could almost smell snow on it. Galloping her horse through the frozen meadow was a thrill she thoroughly enjoyed.

Without really thinking of where she went, Ariel slowed her mount when she reached the forest and entered the woods. Not until she saw the frozen surface of the pond did she realize where she had come to be. It was a little ironic that she would come to this place, the place where her life first changed, where she had lost her innocence. And after tonight her life would change again.

She hadn't come back to the pond. She had been tempted to go a few days after Broc's leaving, but once she realized she carried his child she hadn't able to come near it. Even now, after all the time that had passed, the memories of their one time together came rushing back. And they were strong. Ariel could almost feel as if it was just yesterday Broc had made love to her.

She had no idea how long she sat there, looking at the pond lost in her thoughts. A feeling of being cold broke the trance-like state that had come over her. Much to her surprise, Ariel felt tears streaming down her face. Roughly, she wiped the wetness from her cheeks with her sleeve. Ariel then turned her horse away from the water's edge. There was no point mourning something that could never be.

Returning to the main hall Ariel went directly to her chamber. She changed into the tunic and trews her father had given her especially for this occasion and sat down on her bed to wait. An hour later, someone knocked on her door. Ariel stood and bid them enter. Her father stepped in and closed the door behind him.

"I was told to fetch you. The meal is almost ready and the Norman wants to knight you before it is served."

Taking a deep breath, Ariel nodded. "I'm ready."

Swein hesitated for a moment. "You don't have to go through with this you know."

"Aye, I do. I know what I'm giving up. I have a son. I don't need to marry."

"It's your decision." Swein pulled Ariel into his arms and hugged her close. "I want you to know I'm proud of you. I only wish your mother could be here. She always believed a woman could do anything a man could. You are proving her theory correct." Releasing her, Swein stepped back and reached for the door handle. "Well, daughter, are you ready to make history?"

Swallowing back tears that had come to her eyes, Ariel nodded her head. Pulling herself together, she stepped through the door and out into the hall.

* * * *

What she noticed first were all the people. The hall was filled to capacity. It seemed every person in the village had come to witness the ceremony. The next was Broc, who stood waiting for her in the middle of the room.

Silence fell as Ariel left her father's side and slowly made her way over to Broc. When she came to stand before him, he motioned for her to kneel. Once she had complied, Broc pulled his sword out of its sheath. He made sure he had every person's attention before he began to speak.

"You come before me as a boy, but no more will you be. From this point on you will be considered a man." Broc placed the tip of his sword on each of Ariel's shoulders. "You may rise."

Ariel stood as Broc sheathed his sword and motioned to her father. Swein moved toward them with her armor and arms. Taking each item, Broc dressed her in chain mail, helmet, sword and then her shield. The look Broc gave it said he hadn't seen it before now. He paused to study it closely obviously confused by it.

Recovering, Broc slid the shield onto Ariel's left arm. He then stepped back. "From this day forward, you will be known as Sir Wulf." A cheer rose up at his words. As if on cue, the serfs started to bring platters of food into the hall.

Now with the ceremony over, Ariel felt the tension leave her body. At the smell of food, her stomach rumbled. The sound reminded Ariel she had not been able to eat all day.

Since the celebration was for her, Broc had her sit in the thane's chair at the head table. The table sat upon a dais, so it permitted her a good view of the revealers below. It seemed Broc had held nothing back for the festivities. From what she could see, the villagers were being served the same food that had been placed at the head table. Mead and ale flowed freely. Ariel picked up the goblet of mead that sat in front of her and took a big gulp. It probably was unwise to drink it on an empty stomach, but she needed it.

Having Broc seated next to her, his scent wafted over her. It had been a mistake to go to the pond. The visit had brought up memories and emotions that had been better left forgotten. Now with Broc so near, Ariel felt them all more intensely.

A trencher filled with food that had been placed before her gave Ariel something to center her attention on. It helped some, but the mead helped more. So as the meal progressed, more mead than food passed Ariel's lips. By the time the meal drew to a close, everything seemed a bit fuzzy and Ariel felt great.

* * * *

The serfs started to clear the tables at Broc's signal. He looked over at Wulf. They had not spoken during the meal, but Broc had seen him quaffing down the mead like water. Swein said nothing to his son about the amount he drank, so Broc figured it was not his place to reprimand Wulf. He had no right to criticize, he was only slightly better off.

During the weeks it had taken to complete Wulf's training, Broc had felt himself becoming attached to Wulf, and it scared the hell out of him. For the feelings he had for Wulf could not be considered normal by any means, especially for him. Whenever Wulf had mastered a stroke or disarmed him, Broc had wanted to pull the boy into his arms. The urge to act on his feelings had become almost too strong to resist at times.

But finding Wulf sitting on his horse, just staring at the pond, had almost been his undoing. Each time he went to the pond Broc felt the loss of the girl. It didn't help that Wulf looked so much like her. That had to be the reason for the strange attraction, it had to be.

Then there was Wulf's emblem. When he had reached for the boy's shield, Broc had been a little shocked to see what had been painted on its surface. Painted white with a red cross separating the surface into four squares, in the top left hand square was his emblem, the gold unicorn, an exact match. In the bottom right hand square was a red heart with a gold sword pierced through it. The emblem itself didn't make any sense to Broc. *Why would Wulf have my emblem on the shield? What did the heart symbolize?* Broc had the feeling Wulf wouldn't tell him even if he asked.

* * * *

As the evening wore on, Swein could not help but see that both Ariel and the Norman were getting a little worse for wear from drinking the mead. But he said nothing to either of them. It was not hard to guess that they were both fighting the same battle—their feelings for each other. The lessons had revealed much.

It had become quite clear to Swein the Norman was attracted to Ariel. The look in his eyes told all, but those same eyes appeared to be blind when it came to Ariel. The fool only saw a young boy. Ariel may have adapted to wearing the clothes of a man, but her body had not. She may bind her chest to make it appear flat, but the rest she could not hide. Her bottom was too rounded for a man's, and her waist too small. The Norman of course saw none of those things. So he thought he had feelings for another male. In a small way Swein felt sorry for him.

When it grew late and the villagers slowly began to make their farewells, both Broc and Ariel were well into their cups. The pair of them had not spoken to each other all night. They would talk to others, but did their hardest not to notice each other's conversations. Seeing the last guest go out the hall door, Swein stood up and turned to his daughter.

"I guess I'll call it a night."

"Are you sure, Father?" Ariel's speech came out slower than usual and somewhat slurred.

"Aye, it grows late. I think you should do the same."

"Once I finish my drink." Ariel waved her goblet, which caused mead to slosh over the edge. Swein shook his head. Ariel was no longer a child. It was not his place to tell her what to do. Knowing she would find her way to bed on her own eventually, he left her sitting at the table beside Broc.

* * * *

He sensed it immediately when they had been left alone in the hall. Broc became more aware of Wulf's presence next to him now, more than anytime during the evening. Instead of dulling his reactions to Wulf, the drink seemed to have heightened them. Taking a deep breath, Broc turned his head and looked over at Wulf. What he saw made his breath catch.

Wulf was asleep. His head was on the table, his arms folded under it forming a make shift pillow. His face affected Broc the most. In sleep, all signs of the stress of daily living were gone. The fan of his lashes lay against his cheeks. Broc had never seen a man with lashes that long before. They were almost too long to be on a man's face. In sleep the boy looked beautiful.

Broc stretched his hand out and gently placed it on Wulf's head before he realized what he did. His hair felt like silk. His fingers splayed, allowing him to run them through the strands. The boy did not awaken. Broc knew he should stop, what with the amount of mead he had consumed he could easily lose control, but the urge couldn't be ignored.

Without removing his hand, Broc slipped off his chair so he knelt beside Wulf. The motion caused his hand to rest on the boy's back. His fingers seemed to have a mind of their own. For they moved down Wulf's arm then back up. Once they reached his shoulder, Broc brushed his knuckles across the soft skin of Wulf's cheek. He felt no roughness that one usually felt when touching a man's face. It almost seemed Wulf was not capable of growing a beard. Something was not right here, but the drink had fuddled his mind, not allowing him to grasp what it was.

A new sensation washed over him. Looking at Wulf's eyes, Broc found them open and watching. No fear or disgust lurked in them. If anything, they told him his touch was more than welcome.

Chapter 18

The sight of Broc's face so close to hers took Ariel's breath away. She had been asleep, but the sensation of someone caressing her cheek brought her instantly to awareness. Even though Ariel knew Broc thought her to be male, she could not bring herself to stop him. It felt too good. It had been so long since he had touched her in this way.

His eyes never left hers as his fingertips softly brushed her cheek once more. Moving lower, he cupped her chin with his hand. With his thumb on her lower lip, he rubbed it slowly back and forth. That was enough to send Ariel bolting upright in her chair.

"Shush. I didn't mean to upset you." In one fluid motion, Broc stood. "You were asleep. Maybe you should retire for the night."

"Aye, I think I will." Ariel pushed back her chair and stood. All the mead she had drunk during the evening rushed to her head. The room began to spin and her legs gave out. If Broc had not caught her around the waist, she would have fallen to the floor.

Broc pulled her closer to his side and started to walk to the chambers at the back of the hall. "I think you may need some help if you are to make it to your bed."

Ariel tried to pull out of his grip, but her legs would not function properly. "I'll manage. Don't worry about me."

"Fine, if that is your wish." Broc released her and Ariel promptly felt herself slip towards the floor once more. A strong arm caught her. "It seems to me that a little help would be in order."

Ariel didn't reply. She could do nothing but accept his assistance. As they staggered to her chamber, Ariel noticed Broc was not very steady on his feet either. They somehow managed to get to the chamber door and walk across the room to her bed. Having made it that far, things decidedly went downhill from there.

Broc released her and her legs promptly gave out on her. On the way down, Ariel grabbed his tunic to stop from falling. As she landed on her back on the bed, she threw Broc off balance and he ended up falling on top of her. They both grew still. Ariel felt the hard length of Broc's body on every inch of her. A small gasp escaped her lips before she could silence it. That little sound was all Broc needed to act.

Broc's head lowered and his lips claimed her own. Ariel's body jerked in surprise, but she made no move to stop Broc. Sensing her acceptance, Broc ran his tongue along the seam of her mouth. At his insistence, Ariel let her lips part, giving him the invitation he needed. The feel of Broc's tongue gently stroking hers, Ariel reached up and wrapped her arms around his neck.

She knew this was bad, very bad. If this went much further there would be no way of hiding what she truly was. But what Broc did to her sent shock waves of desire all through her body. She was not strong enough to stop this. Giving herself up to the sensations that began to pool in the lower half of her body, Ariel groaned.

Broc stiffened and roughly jerked his mouth away from her lips. Ariel watched the passion slowly die in his golden eyes and be replaced with a look of utter disgust. She felt like weeping. He didn't know it was her, he only saw Wulf. Even after what they had just shared. He seemed sickened by what he had done. Broc wiped his mouth with the back of his hand and quickly jumped off the bed.

Ariel reached out a hand to him, to stop him from leaving. She could not do this to him. It would be a cruelty she did not wish upon him, she had to explain. But Broc just stared at the hand held out to him. With a shake of his head, he rejected it and rushed out of the room.

* * * *

He still would not speak to her. It had been days since the episode in her chamber. Ariel had tired to talk to Broc the next day, but somehow he had managed to avoid her. So nothing had been resolved.

They were now half a day away from London. During the day they rode in silence and at night Broc would eat then promptly go to sleep. Ariel decided she would give him some time. But as the days passed, Broc made no attempt to talk to her. He even refused to acknowledge her presence. She had become a spirit in his eyes, an entity he could see through.

When they stopped to make camp for the final night before they reached their destination, Ariel decided it had gone on long enough. This had to end. London was a large city. She had only been there once before and knew no one. No one except for Broc. Ariel could admit to herself she was a little nervous. She could only assume her being a Saxon in a Norman court may not be a pleasant experience for her. She needed Broc for support.

After Ariel had unsaddled her horse and hobbled it, she walked over to Broc. He had a small fire going. The food that made up their evening meal sat spread out on a blanket. Still ignoring her, Broc grabbed his share of the food and began to eat.

Ariel stepped around the food until she stood in front of Broc. She practically stood on him. Still he ignored her. She wondered how long he would hold out before he was forced to look at her. She had no intention of moving until he spoke to her. She could tell she was irritating him.

Broc finally glared up at her. "What do you want?"

"Ah, he spoke. I thought you must have lost your tongue or the ability of speech had left you."

"Well, as you can see, neither has happened. Go eat. We're going to have an early start tomorrow."

Ariel shook her head. "Nay, I think not. At least not until we have a talk."

Every muscle in Broc's body stiffened and he dropped his head, refusing to look at her. "I have nothing to say to you."

Ariel would not let him off that easily. "You may not, but I have something to say to you."

Broc almost growled at her. "Leave me be, Wulf."

"I can't do that. We have to speak of the other night."

Broc surged to his feet. Face red, fists clenched at his sides, he yelled. "Nay! If you want to make it to London in one piece, I suggest you keep your mouth shut!"

Ariel had never seen Broc like this before. He was always so even tempered. With the full force of his anger directed at her, Ariel stepped back. He had hurt her, but no way would she let him know how much. Abruptly she turned away. She picked up her food and went to sit on the opposite side of the fire. She gave up. He could go to hell. Let him drown in his own worries. She would be damned before she put his mind to rest.

* * * *

At dawn the next morning, Broc woke Ariel by giving her a shove in the ribs with his boot. Once her eyes opened, he walked over to his horse and began to saddle it. He spoke not a word to her, which suited Ariel. She had nothing further to say to him.

Ariel rolled her bedding up and went to ready her own horse. When she walked by Broc, he shoved some food into her hands. He most definitely was in a fine mood this morn. She saddled her horse and tied the bedding to the back of the saddle. Once she gained her seat, Ariel hung her shield over the horn of her saddle, keeping it within easy reach should the need arise.

Broc rode them hard all day. He didn't even stop to eat at noon. By the time London came into sight, darkness had fallen and Ariel was extremely hungry. She felt tiredness eating at her. She hoped once they reached the court a bath would be offered to her. After all the days of travel she badly needed one.

Half an hour later, Broc and Ariel rode through one of the city gates. Ariel forgot all about how tired she felt. She had known London was large from her previous visit, but it still cast a spell over her. The sheer number of people living in one place overwhelmed her as it had before. Even at this late hour people moved along the streets.

Ariel felt herself lucky to be with Broc, for she found herself unable to pay attention to where they went. The sights and smells were all still so new to her. She couldn't concentrate on anything else. From her lofty position on top of her horse, Ariel could see a lot more than if she'd been down on street level. At the center of the city a fort had been built. The Normans must have built it once they had arrived. William probably wanted some protection from the citizens of London.

Broc went to the gate and one of the guards stuck his head over the wall. "State your name and business."

"I'm Broc St. Ceneri. King William summoned my companion and me to court."

The guard disappeared from sight. A short time later the gates opened to admit them. Once inside the fort the gates slammed shut behind Ariel and Broc. A feeling of being trapped swept over Ariel. She was now locked inside a fort with her enemy.

A guard took their horses' reins and led the animals to the stable. Ariel stood where she had dismounted not knowing what else to do. There were a number of smaller buildings inside the walls, but one stood larger than the rest, dominating the area. Ariel assumed that had to be William's residence. Almost as if he knew she had been thinking of him, William himself walked out of the building.

Ariel held her ground as the king greeted Broc. Seeing them together, she could tell they were close friends. Neither man paid any attention to her. She didn't let that bother her. William already knew her secret. She just hoped he kept it that way—a secret.

Ariel felt eyes on her and looked up to see William staring at her. He nodded in her direction then waved for her to come closer. Knowing it was an order, Ariel did as she was bid.

With a bit of trepidation, Ariel went to stand before the king. He grabbed her by the shoulder and gave it a squeeze. "Well, Wulf, it seems you have recovered from your wound nicely."

"Aye, sire." Ariel relaxed. For some reason William seemed not inclined to expose her.

"Good. I have informed Broc of the two chambers I had made ready for you both. I will let you get settled in and then I wish to speak to you."

"Just me, sire?" Ariel didn't like the sound of that.

"Aye. There are a few items I need to discuss with you."

After having said that, William left Broc and Ariel. Broc had a strange look on his face. Ariel knew he probably wondered what William needed to talk to her about. That same question kept running through her head as well.

* * * *

With a groan of pleasure, Broc sank down in the warm bath. It was just what he needed. If only it could clean away some of his memories as it cleaned away the dirt from his body.

The days on the road alone with Wulf had been pure hell. Every time he looked at Wulf, memories of how his lips had felt under his flitted through his mind. He felt drawn to him. He had never kissed a man like that ever in his life. What made him feel sick about the whole thing was his reaction to it. He had liked it.

Drawing his knees up, Broc ducked his head under the water. Surfacing, he found William in the room.

"I see you're making use of my tub."

Wiping water off his face, Broc smiled at him. "I figured this had to be yours. There aren't too many tubs that accommodate my size."

"I thought you would enjoy it after your days of travel to get here." William grabbed one of the stools in the chamber and sat down close to the tub. "I see our little Saxon survived."

"Aye, he is a fighter," Broc answered blandly.

"In more ways than one I imagine. I saw the shield slung on his shoulder when you arrived. Does it mean you have knighted the lad?" Broc stiffened at the mention of Wulf.

"Aye, I did. I couldn't let such talent be left to rot. The boy is a natural. He can disarm me without trying very hard."

"Really? Now that is interesting news." To Broc's surprise, William started to bellow with laughter.

"Do you mind telling me what you find so funny about that?"

William chuckled and shook his head. "I think not. Now let me tell you of the activities that have gone on since your departure."

Broc seemed to perk up with the change of subject as he sat up straighter in the tub. "Did you face much resistance?"

"No, actually. Once the dead had been properly buried, including Harold, I went back to Hastings. I didn't stay long though. Food became short in supply. We met no more opposition so I decided to move on."

William stood and went to the table that held a goblet and pitcher of wine. Pouring a goblet full he returned to Broc's side. After he took a sip, he continued.

"Finish your bath before the water cools." Broc complied as William spoke once more. "We went to Dover and burned it to the ground. There, the army took sick. Most of the men suffered from cases of diarrhea and fever, which put most out of commission. Some recuperated, but I ended up having to leave a third of them behind. We next marched to Canterbury, which luckily turned out to be uneventful. The city surrendered without a fight. I have to rule these people, so I was happy for that. It would go much easier for them if they would just accept me."

Pausing, William took another sip of wine. "Then I got the blasted illness. It hit me hard. Laid me up for a month. Not pleasant at all, I might add. But once back on my feet, I headed toward London, and so here I am."

Water sloshed inside the tub as Broc stood. William picked up the toweling and threw it at him. Broc caught it and began to dry himself. "So how did the people of London take to you?"

William shrugged. "Not well, I'm afraid. We arrived at Southwark, which is at the southern edge of the bridge, and met with some resistance there. The citizens of London somehow managed to form a so called army to fight me. They crossed the bridge to meet us and we fought them. Eventually we drove them back and I had Southwark put to the torch. After that greeting I had this fort built. Once completed, I entered London and claimed it as my own."

Broc had known William would not brook any resistance from the people of England. It was just his way of letting others know he didn't relinquish what he called his. "So did they finally accept you as their king?"

William smiled. "You could say that. I'm to be crowned on Christ's birthday in Westminster Abbey. But I doubt it will be the end of any future resistance. I'm sure to spend many years to come exerting my rights."

Pulling on a fresh tunic and trews, Broc filled another goblet of wine for himself. "You know I will always be your man. I have land now and I can supply men for your endeavors."

William stood and returned his goblet to the table. "Does that mean I can have Wulf if I wish?"

"Nay!" That one single word came out with far more force than Broc had intended to use. He took a deep breath to calm himself then continued. "Nay, I need the boy at Elmstead."

William seemed to study Broc intently. "I think you need him more than you would like to admit, dear friend. I will leave you now." William then left Broc to ponder the true meaning of his words.

Chapter 19

Ariel had bathed and changed into fresh clothes. The evening meal would be served shortly, but at the moment she wouldn't be able to eat a bite. She hoped William would send for her soon. Her stomach felt tied up in knots. She couldn't think of any reason why the king wanted to speak to her alone.

After a short knock on the chamber door, William stepped in and closed it tightly behind him. Ariel, who had been sitting on the bed, shot to her feet. "I thought I was to go see you, sire."

William moved closer to her. "Relax, Ariel. I just came to talk, that is all."

Ariel felt some of the tension leave her. "What do you wish to talk about?"

"You and Broc."

Nothing like getting right to the point, Ariel mused. "Well, as you have probably seen, there isn't much to say about us."

William clucked his tongue at her. "Oh, I beg to differ. You have come to my court as a knight, not as a Saxon without rank."

Ariel blushed. "That was Broc's idea. I couldn't pass up what he offered. I now have some rank in your society. A place in what England is coming to be."

"That is most true." William paused and looked at Ariel. "You're very beautiful. I don't understand how Broc can't see you as a woman."

Ariel quickly suppressed the urge to scoff at the king. "Because he's blind. He hasn't figured it out and he probably never will. Even during close contact, that man is too stupid to see what is before him."

From the look of interest on William's face, Areil could see he was intrigued. "What do you mean by close contact, my dear?" Sitting on the bed, he patted the space next to him. Ariel couldn't stop the flush that crept across her face as she seated herself next to William. She hadn't meant for him to know.

"On the night Broc knighted me, we both had a little too much to drink. There is a bond between us, even though Broc fights it with all his being and it grew stronger when he started to train me."

"Are you telling me something happened on that night?"

Ariel looked into William's face and rushed on. "Aye, it did. We kissed and now Broc refuses to talk to me." She put it as simply as she could.

William showed no outward show of emotion to her statement. "Did you tell him you were the girl he seeks during any of this?"

Ariel shook her head. "I tried, honestly I did, but it was already too late. He is so filled with disgust he won't even come near me."

"Now I see the problem here. Poor Broc thinks he kissed a boy. I have always found him to be very perceptive. It's one of the qualities I've always admired in him. I can't understand why he hasn't recognized you."

"He hasn't and I don't intend to tell him either."

The man stiffened at her words. "But what about your son, Broc's son? You cannot keep his son from him."

Ariel scowled at William. Even though he was king, he was crossing the line. "Aye, I can. He gave up that right when he left. I've kept him from Broc and I will make sure he never sees Colwyn."

William shook his head at her show of stubbornness not to listen. "Why? Broc would not do anything to hurt the boy. He has very strong feelings for you. When he returned from England he was not the same man. He kept to himself, more than he had usually done in the past. He seemed to pine for you."

Ariel felt all the blood drain away from her face. Tears shimmered in her eyes. "He may have felt that way at one time, but not any more. He never really did search very hard for me. How he felt before is irrelevant now. It just can never be. He is a Norman and I'm a Saxon, which is a very good reason for us to stay apart."

William shook his head. "For England to live in harmony, Norman and Saxon have to merge together. If you don't do something you will lose him for good. After what happened between you, Broc will try to erase it from his memory by going to another woman. Or he could very well make you leave Elmstead."

"Then that is the chance I will have to take. I can always take my son and leave."

William stood up and looked down at Ariel with a sad look on his face. "I hope you choose not to do that. At the very least, living at Elmstead your son would be sheltered, protected. He won't have to grow up with the word bastard on people's lips whenever he is near." He paused and reached out his hand to brush a lock of hair out of her eyes. "But if you do leave Elmstead, come to me. I'll take care of you and your son. Broc has told me how well you handle a sword. I need all the skilled and trained knights I can get. It would do wonders for your people to see a Saxon knight presiding at my court."

Ariel could only nod her head in agreement then the king was gone.

* * * *

Half an hour later, Ariel went to the hall for the evening meal. Broc already sat next to William. Deep in conversation, the two men did not notice her arrival. Taking advantage of their inattention, Ariel slipped onto one of the benches closest to the doors.

Some of the king's men, who already sat at the table, got up and moved further down away from her. She let the insult wash over her. Instances like this were bound to happen as long as she stayed at court.

Food and a tankard of ale were placed before her. Looking up and expecting to see a serf serving her, Ariel found a young Norman knight standing by the table. Smiling, he sat down on the bench next to her.

"It looked as if you needed some company. You don't mind if I sit with you?"

Ariel turned to look at him. She guessed him to be a few years older than herself. He was tall, but not as tall as Broc. His body was welled muscled. Looking into his face, Ariel found grey eyes crinkled with amusement. No malice could be seen in them. His hair color was the opposite of hers, black, which he wore at shoulder length. "You can sit if you want, but I don't think they would like the idea of you sitting with a Saxon."

The knight looked down the table at the other men and shook his head. "They can think what they like. I don't care if you're Saxon. My name is

Ranulf FitzHugh."

Ariel smiled. "Wulf of Elmstead. I'm glad at least one person here won't shun me."

The knight looked from her to Broc who sat with the king. "But I thought you came here with Broc St. Ceneri. Talk is he knighted you."

"That's correct. Broc knighted me by his own hand. He just isn't talking to me right at the moment." The food sitting before Ariel made her stomach growl. It had been many hours since food had last passed her lips.

Ranulf laughed. "Eat, my friend, then we will talk."

Ariel pulled out her knife and began to eat. The food was simple, but good. Taking a sip of the ale, she found it acceptable as well. Ranulf had brought food for himself as well and steadily devoured it. Ariel risked looking up at the dais.

All the air left her lungs in a rush. Broc looked directly at her. From the look on his face he was not just mad, he was furious. He obviously didn't like Ranulf talking to her. In turn, Ariel felt her own temper rise. Broc had no right to be angry. He wanted nothing to do with her and she would be damned if she sat alone just to please him.

Seeing he had caught her attention, Broc motioned for her to come over to him. Ariel chose to ignore him and quickly looked down at her food. She was no longer his to control. Hell would freeze over before she went to him.

Ranulf cleared his throat. "It seems Broc is not pleased with you. If looks could kill, you would no longer be among the living."

Ariel didn't look up from her food. "Ignore him. It will do him good."

"I will try to take your advice, but I must warn you, he's coming this way."

Just as Ranulf had said, Broc made his way over to their table. When he reached them, he put both of his hands on the table in front of Ariel. Leaning down so only a few scant inches separated them, he yelled right into her face.

"When I motion for you to come to me, you will come! Is that understood?"

The men at the end of the table snickered. Ariel's face grew hot. "You have no right to talk to me this way."

"But I do, I am lord of Elmstead now. You will do as you are told or suffer the consequences."

Ariel's temper exploded as she saw red. She would not let him demean her in this way. "I'm not one of your serfs to be bullied about! You don't own me. So back off and leave me alone."

Before she could react, Broc grabbed Ariel by her upper arms and dragged her across the table. He then dropped her at his feet. Ariel jumped up and tried to leave, but Broc was not through with her. He turned her and the last thing Ariel saw was his fist coming straight toward her. When his fist connected with her jaw, her world went black.

She couldn't have been out for very long because the room sounded to still be in an uproar. Broc growled with rage as William tired to hold him back. He was clearly trying to get at her. Ranulf stood over her, ready to protect her if and when Broc managed to get free from the king's hold.

Ariel took this in with vague interest. Her jaw felt like one massive ache. She opened and closed her mouth a few times to make sure nothing was broken. It didn't seem to be, but it still hurt like hell.

Ariel stood and stepped around Ranulf. She pulled her sword out of its scabbard and calmly placed the tip of it against Broc's throat. He instantly stopped struggling.

"If you ever strike me like that again, I'll leave more than a bruise on your flesh." To make Broc see she meant every word, Ariel applied pressure until a trickle of blood ran down his throat.

Out of the corner of her eye, Ariel saw a flash of steel. Without taking her eyes from Broc, she swung up her sword and blocked the blade coming at her.

Turning her body in the direction of her attacker, Ariel came face to face with one of the Norman knights who had been sitting at her table. His face was red with rage. Pulling his sword free of Ariel's, he once more slashed out at her. She blocked his sword before he could complete the swing. After allowing him to take a couple more swings at her, Ariel finally ended it by disarming the knight. His sword flew out of his hand and landed at the king's feet. Without a backward glance, Ariel stomped out of the hall and slammed the door behind her.

Chapter 20

Bending over, William picked up the sword and walked over to the knight who had lost it. The king's displeasure was easily read on his face. "The next time you ever cross swords with a guest in my hall, other than on a practice field, you will no longer be welcome at court. Now leave me."

The knight gave a quick bow and left the room. William watched him exit the hall. He could not believe what he had just seen. She had disarmed a man twice her size, with a simple flick of her wrist. He found it utterly amazing.

The other occupants of the hall left one by one until only Broc and Ranulf remained with William. Noticing Broc had moved to the hearth with his back to them, William quietly spoke to Ranulf. "Go find Wulf. He ran out of here without a cloak. If he stays out there too long he'll become ill. Tell him I want to speak to him in my chambers."

Ranulf bowed and quickly left the hall to do the king's bidding. William then turned to look at Broc. "I can understand why you knighted the boy. He is a natural."

"Aye." Broc appeared lost in thought as he watched the flames of the fire dance in the hearth. Once he seemed to get his emotions back under control, Broc turned back around. "I'd like to apologize for my actions this evening."

William casually waved Broc's words away with a swipe of his hand. "You should be saying those words to Wulf. You hit him, not I. What I don't understand is why. I thought you liked the boy."

Broc shrugged his shoulders. His expression said he found it hard to explain even to himself. "I do, maybe more than I should."

"Do you want to talk about it?" William could see how affected Broc was by all that had taken place.

"Not particularly. But there is one thing you can do for me."

"And what is that?"

"I have come to the decision that I'm ready to take a wife. I should start begetting heirs now that I have land to pass on. Do I have your permission to marry?"

"Of course. Do you have anyone in mind?" William didn't like the sound of this.

"Not at the moment. I'll tell you when I've made my choice."

Getting the answer he wanted, Broc left William alone. The king shook his head. This did not bode well for the girl. He only prayed Ariel would reveal herself to Broc before it became too late. If she didn't, his friend would not have a very happy life ahead of him.

* * * *

It took a few minutes, but Ranulf finally found Wulf in the stable. He sat inside one of the empty stalls in the clean straw with his legs drawn up to his chest. His head rested on top his knees. At the sound of footsteps he jerked his head up. Tears streamed down his face. With a jolt Ranulf realized Wulf was not what he first appeared to be.

Ranulf wondered why he had not seen it before. "Wulf" was too pretty, even for a boy. Her features too delicate for a man's. And those eyes, shimmering with tears, were a breathtaking blue. All he could do was kneel in the straw before her. The girl automatically tensed.

She looked at him guardedly. "What do you want?"

"The king sent me to fetch you. He wants to speak to you in his chamber." Ranulf could tell she was felt leery around him as she eyed him closely.

"All right."

She stood and scrubbed her face with her sleeve. Ranulf watched her every move. She gave him a questioningly look, then brushed past him and headed back to the hall. Ranulf matched her pace so he could walk beside her. He was still at her side when she reached the king's chamber door. At her knock, William opened the door and stepped aside for her to enter. But before he could close the door Ranulf stepped inside as well. William stared at him before he shut the door.

"I see you've made a new friend. May I ask why you have decided to stay, Sir Ranulf?"

Pulling himself up straighter, Ranulf replied, "Aye, sire. I think Wulf is not what he seems."

The girl gasped in surprise. "At least one of my knights can see what is staring him in the face. It looks as if young Ranulf has seen through your disguise, Ariel."

A shocked look came over Ranulf's face. "You know her, sire?"

The king chuckled. "Aye, I do, Sir Ranulf. I see you have made the girl quite speechless." Stepping closer to Ariel, William put his arm around her shoulders and turned her to face Ranulf. "Sir Ranulf, this is Ariel of Elmstead, or should I say Sir Ariel."

Ranulf opened and closed his mouth a few times before he could bring himself to speak coherently. "You mean she really is a knight?"

"That she is. You saw her performance in the hall. It would be a shame to waste such talent."

"Sir Broc willingly knighted a woman?" Ranulf felt scandalized thinking such could take place.

The king pulled Ariel closer as she stiffened under his arm. "Sir Broc turns out not to be as observant as you. All he sees is a young Saxon boy, not the woman."

"But how?"

William shook his head. "I have no idea. Now let's talk about what happened in the hall. How is your jaw, Ariel?"

Ariel pulled out of the king's grasp and moved so she faced both of them with hands on her hips. The position of her hands made the curves of her body seem more pronounced. There could be no mistaking her for anything else than what she was—a woman.

"My jaw is not broken, but it still hurts."

"Excellent. Now are you going to tell Broc who you are?"

"Nay! You know I will not tell him."

"Your silence will only escalate this situation into an unmanageable problem if you do not speak now."

"I have done some thinking. I would like your permission to go home. You're correct. If I stay everything could easily get out of hand quite quickly. The less I see of Broc the better."

William's brows drew together. He obviously was not satisfied with her answer. "Then what will you do when Broc returns to Elmstead?"

"My father has a separate hall from the one Broc occupies. I will live in my father's hall."

Sighing, William thought over Ariel's request then nodded. "You may leave, but only on the condition you don't go alone."

"That's not necessary, sire. I can find my own way to Elmstead." Ariel seemed to want to protest further, but must have thought better of it.

"I realize you can protect yourself. I would just feel better knowing you didn't travel alone that is all."

Knowing this was a chance to get to know this unusual woman better, Ranulf spoke up. "If it is acceptable with you sire, I would like to accompany Ariel to her home."

A smile formed on the king's lips. "All right, Sir Ranulf. You may go and you may stay at Elmstead for as long as you wish. I've heard of your interest in learning more of the Saxon way of life. What better way to learn than from the Lady Ariel?" William put up his hand before Ariel could protest. "I will hear no more. I suggest you leave with the dawn. Now both of you get some rest. I will tell Broc on the morrow of your departure."

* * * *

The hall was empty except for the king who sat in his chair on the dais. He sipped ale from a tankard. When he saw Broc enter he motioned him to sit with him.

"Well Broc, how do you feel this morn?"

"As well as one can feel after making an utter ass of oneself."

William had to chuckle at his friend's dour expression. "Don't beat yourself up too much about it. I'm afraid the others are applauding you for striking a Saxon, especially a Saxon who had the impertinence to become a knight."

Broc's face became grave. "They really think that way about Wulf?"

"Aye. I have to admit I made a mistake asking you to bring him to court. At least the problem has been rectified in a way that will suit everyone."

"What do you mean?" Broc looked at him questioningly.

"I sent the boy back to Elmstead. After how you treated him last night he asked to go home. To avoid any more problems I gave my consent. And don't worry about him going off alone, I sent Ranulf with him."

Broc didn't seem all that relieved that he would not have to confront Wulf. "Why did Ranulf go with Wulf?"

"It seems the pair has struck up a friendship. Ranulf asked to accompany Wulf and I could think of no reason why he should stay here. I gave him permission to stay at Elmstead as long as he wished." William knew what he was doing to Broc, but the man needed a little prodding in the right direction if he was to be happy.

A full range of emotions flitted across Broc's face—regret, anger then finally acceptance, before he got himself under control to comment. "Since you wish him to stay at Elmstead, I have no objections. Now if you will excuse me, I would like to reacquaint myself with London."

"Go ahead, my friend. We will talk later."

Chapter 21

At the sight of Elmstead, Ariel felt a sense of well being wash over her. She was home and there she planned to stay from now on. She had been away from Colwyn too much in his short life. He was her future and he deserved better from her. Starting now her son would be her first priority. Reaching the outskirts of the village, Ariel pulled her horse to a halt. Ranulf brought his mount up next to hers.

"So this is where you live?" Ranulf asked as he looked around Elmstead.

"Aye, this is Elmstead. I know it probably is smaller than what you are used to, but at least the food is good and the people will welcome you."

"I will be glad for the change. Court life loses its luster after awhile."

Ariel understood exactly what Ranulf meant. "My short experience there has led me to believe it's not all pomp and glitter."

Turning in her saddle, Ariel's gaze drifted over Ranulf. On their travels he had treated her with respect. Not once had he tried anything inappropriate towards her. Now having reached her home, Ariel felt she had gained a new friend. So much so she felt she could trust Ranulf.

"Ranulf, there is something I must tell you before we go to my father's hall." Ariel could see she had his full attention. He had twisted around in his saddle and now looked at her intently.

"What might that be, my lady?"

Taking a deep breath, Ariel started to speak. "There is a reason why I hide my true self and pretend to be a man. That reason is in my father's hall." Ariel looked right into Ranulf's eyes, then plunged ahead. "I have a son and his father is Broc."

Ranulf's eyes widened in shock. "I don't understand. You told me Broc knew you only as a man. How can you have had a son by him?"

"I first met Broc when he came to England when Edward was still king.

He simply doesn't recognize me this way."

Ranulf shook his head in what appeared to be wonderment. "To put it quite bluntly, Broc is a fool. If it had been me, I would be able to see through your disguise. You are too beautiful to be a man, Ariel."

At his words, Ariel flushed. "Well, Broc must not think the same way you do. For after taking what he wanted from me, he left without so much as a backward glance."

"All the more fool is he. I never would have left you."

Ariel grew uncomfortable listening to Ranulf. She had to admit she did find him attractive. Ranulf was a good looking man. If she had met him before Broc, she may have let nature take its course. But after all she had gone through with Broc, Ariel didn't think she could give herself to another man.

Ariel sighed. "Be that as it may, Broc must never know about Colwyn. I trust you to keep my secret."

"Your secret is safe with me. Besides, it's not my place to inform Broc."

That was what Ariel had wanted to hear from Ranulf. Giving him a quick nod, she then started into the village. Ranulf followed her as she greeted the villagers she past. Showing their loyalty to her, they all called her by the name she had given herself.

Ariel knew the village was small, but she hoped Ranulf would notice that the huts were well maintained, which showed her father's goodwill towards his people. She led him past the main hall and took him to the smaller hall that sat a short distance behind the village. As they neared, she could see her father stood out in front of the hall with Colwyn in his arms. Seeing that a stranger accompanied her, he pulled the blanket that was around Colwyn over his head.

She practically jumped off her horse and set off at a run. Ariel threw herself into her father's arms. Ranulf slowly dismounted as she greeted Swein. Taking Colwyn out of Swein's arms, she walked to where Ranulf stood waiting. She then pulled the blanket away from Colwyn's face.

From Ranulf's shocked expression, Ariel knew he could see the resemblance between father and son. Colwyn's small face was so much like Broc's. She hoped he understood why she had kept Broc away from Colwyn, especially now that he had seen Broc's treatment of her while at court.

Ariel's face beamed with maternal pride. "Ranulf, this is my son, Colwyn."

"My God, Ariel, he is the very image of Broc. I don't see how you'll be able to keep him a secret for very long. You cannot keep him locked away for the rest of his life you know."

"I know. I'll decide what has to be done when the time comes. For now, a blanket will suffice."

* * * *

With the Norman away, Swein could almost believe their lives had gone back to what they once had been. A smile absently formed on his lips as he watched his daughter playing with her son. He did have to give the Norman credit though. He had given Ariel a beautiful child.

Now another Norman had come to Elmstead. Sir Ranulf was younger than Broc and truly seemed to be forthright and honest. He didn't share most Normans' attitudes that Saxons were of a lower class. Not that Broc had ever treated them that way, but he had come and taken Elmstead as his own. This other man seemed interested in the Saxon way of life. If his old eyes saw clearly, the young man also seemed extremely interested in Ariel.

Ranulf sat on the floor beside Ariel, sharing in a game with Colwyn. Swein had to admit to himself, he could find nothing to really dislike about this Norman. In some ways this young man would be better for Ariel than Broc, but his daughter was not responding to him in that way. It was a shame because Ranulf seemed to treat her better than Broc had so far.

He had seen the bruise on Ariel's jaw, even though she had tried to hide it from him. It was not hard to guess who had left the mark on her. Broc's continued absence told all. Why else would he still be at court and Ariel return home before the expected time? Even though he had pushed his daughter to tell him what had happened, it had been Ranulf who told him what had taken place. Ariel would never have told him.

The sound of Colwyn's laughter filled the hall. It was a sweet sound to his ears, one that Swein had missed through the years. His wife had only been able to give him Ariel. Swein sighed. His wife would have loved her grandson very much.

Swein watched as Ariel brought playtime to an end and picked Colwyn up. "It's time for this young man to get ready for bed. Can you entertain Ranulf, father? I have to bathe Colwyn before he goes to sleep."

Swein nodded. "Aye, daughter. I'm sure we will find something to keep ourselves amused."

Ariel disappeared into her chamber leaving the two men alone. Signaling Ranulf over, Swein poured two goblets of mead and handed one to him. Already sitting at a trestle table, Ranulf sat down next to him.

"So how do you find Elmstead? I'm sure it does not compare to London."

Ranulf smiled. "What I have seen of it so far, I find appealing. It's nice to get away from the court once in a while."

"Ariel told me you have come here to learn about the Saxons."

"Aye, we must now live together. We should have a better understanding of how each of us lives." Swein could see Ranulf meant what he said.

"Not too many of your countrymen would agree with that. They only have one interest in us—taking over what lands we have and making them their own."

"That's why I wish to know more of your way of life. Maybe with the knowledge I learn here I can make the changes easier on your people."

Swein laughed. "I'm afraid that will never happen. We are a proud people. We have been on this island for generations. I can tell you, William will never have a peaceful moment now that he has made himself king. We never wanted him in the first place. Now he takes away our lands to give to others as he sees fit. We will fight him."

Ranulf's eyes narrowed. "Are you saying you would fight against him?"

Swein chuckled. "Nay, I'm too old for such goings on. Besides, I must think of Ariel and Colwyn. I would never jeopardize them in that way. Broc so far has treated us well, I have no complaints. I would not like another to take his place."

Ranulf relaxed at Swein's words. "William respects him. He even calls Broc a friend."

Swein refilled their goblets. "I didn't know Broc was so close to the king."

"He is. The friendship started shortly after Broc came to court. He is a younger son, so he will inherit no lands from his father. What else could he do but go to court? I don't know much about Broc, he mostly keeps to himself. I would not say we're friends, more like acquaintances. What little I do know about him, I know he will not be too pleased having me stay here. Even with the king's permission."

Swein had a feeling Ranulf would not be too far off the mark with that. Especially if Broc saw how well Ariel got along with Ranulf. "Just how long do you plan to be at Elmstead?"

"However long it takes to learn what I need to know."

"It should prove interesting when Broc returns."

Ariel returned to the hall. Sitting down on the bench next to Swein, Ariel accepted a goblet of mead he passed to her. "How did the bath go?"

"Very well. He had fun soaking everything in the chamber as well as himself. Now he's asleep."

"Ranulf told me he will be staying at Elmstead for a while. Since he will be here for the Christ mass, we will be able to show him how we Saxons celebrate the season."

"It would only be the proper thing to do. With Broc still at the king's court, we should be able to celebrate without having to pretend what we are not."

Wisely, both men remained silent.

Chapter 22

The Christ mass revels had come and gone and William was now truly the King of England. The coronation had taken place on the day of Christ's birth. It had been a moving sight for Broc, to finally see all of William's dreams realized. All had culminated in the placing of the crown on his head. This was what they had all fought for, to see this day come to be.

To get the Saxons to more readily accept him as their king, William had used the ancient English rites. He had only made a few changes to it, thinking of his Norman nobles. All went smoothly and no one could deny William his throne.

Now with some misgivings, Broc was now on the road heading back to Elmstead. It would be interesting to see the boy's reaction at the sight of him arriving with the others who traveled with him. Looking over his shoulder Broc saw the four other people who followed him a few paces behind. His betrothed was among them. She was Lady Alwen, a Saxon lady, whose father had been the Earl of Essex. Her father, Lord Theodoric, rode beside her with two of his men acting as guards.

Broc had met the lady and her father while at court. The earl had found accommodations in London shortly after losing his lands to another. Once settled, he promptly started to worm his way into William's good graces.

The man himself disgusted him. In his middle years, Theodoric looked his age. His brown hair had thinned and was cut quite close to his head. He may have been well built during his youth, but now he had let his body go to fat. It was not too hard for Broc to guess Theodoric had taken full advantage of his high status. The man's eyes always looked red and puffy from too much drink.

The Lady Alwen was nothing like her father. In fact, she was the most beautiful woman he had ever seen. Even prettier than the Saxon girl and that was the only reason why Broc had chosen her for his wife. She would give him beautiful children and not much else could be said about her.

The lady's yellow blond hair fell in waves down her back. Her eyes were blue, but not as blue as the other Saxon girl's. She had skin so white Broc figured she never allowed the sun's rays to touch it.

Alwen gave him a shy smile. Broc quickly looked away. He had no love for the lady and probably never would. She would only serve one purpose. All he expected of her was to bear him children and take care of his home. He wanted nothing more from her. They were going to be married at Elmstead after they arrived. Broc wanted to get it over with as soon as he could.

William had given his consent to the marriage, but Broc had sensed his friend had not been too pleased with his choice of bride. He had gone as far as to say Broc would be miserable if he went through with it. He also warned Broc life at Elmstead would be turbulent with Lady Alwen in residence. Broc still had no idea what William had meant.

Up ahead, Elmstead came into view. Kicking his horse into a canter, Broc stepped up the pace. Without looking back to see, he knew the others would keep up.

* * * *

Ariel stepped out of the main hall as Broc charged through the village with four strangers following him. When all the horses came to a halt in the yard, only then did she realize a woman was among the strangers.

Watching Broc, Ariel saw him go to the woman and help her dismount. She was very beautiful. From the way she smiled at Broc, her appearance heralded changes at Elmstead. Broc took the girl by the hand and led her over to Ariel. She wanted to run, but it wouldn't change the inevitable.

"I'm glad you're here, Wulf. It will save me the time in sending for you. I would like to introduce you to the Lady Alwen, my betrothed."

At those two words, my betrothed, Ariel felt as if Broc had slammed his fist into her stomach. "Nice to meet you. When is the wedding to take place?"

Broc smiled at Alwen. "Just before the evening meal, tonight."

He was slowly killing her and Broc had no idea what his words were doing to her. "Well, then I will leave you. You have much to do before the ceremony."

The sound of Broc's voice stopped Ariel from making a quick retreat. "There is one more thing, Wulf. I have chosen you to act as my witness to the marriage. I will expect you back at the hall." Ariel tried to refuse, but Broc wouldn't allow it. "You have no say in the matter. I'm your lord and you will do as I wish."

Ariel gave way this time and nodded her head in acceptance. She then roughly brushed past him and stomped off to her father's hall.

* * * *

Swein found her there a little while later. Ariel paced the floor, cursing Broc one moment and wailing in anguish the next. "You can stop the marriage, Ariel."

Ariel stopped her pacing and looked at her father. Her eyes showed how much Broc had hurt her. "I will not do it."

"Then you will watch the man you love marry another."

Swein watched his daughter silently start to cry. He wanted to go to her and hold her, but right now she had to get her emotions back under control. He could see she tried to pull herself together when she took a deep breath and lifted her head up to face him.

"I made a vow never to tell Broc. No matter how much he means to me, I will not stop the marriage."

Swein acknowledged what Ariel said with a nod of his head. "It would be a blessing if you did tell him. His betrothed will only make problems for Elmstead."

"Why? She looks harmless enough."

"Aye, she is. You left before you saw who her father is. It's Theodoric, Earl of Essex. Well, at least he used to be."

Ariel gasped. Swein knew Ariel had seen Theodoric's cruelty to others first hand during the summer. She had found him revolting to say the least. His presence at Elmstead boded ill for both of them.

* * * *

At the time specified by Broc, Ariel returned to the main hall. Broc watched her every move shortly after she arrived. Letting him know she would not be intimidated by him, Ariel stared back.

"You can stare at him all you want, but Broc will still marry the girl."

Ariel tore her eyes away from Broc and turned to look at Ranulf. "I know. He was the one watching *me*. I do believe Broc thought I would go against his wishes."

Ranulf peered down at Ariel with a sad look on his face. "Can you go through with it?"

Ariel lightly shrugged Ranulf's question aside. "Of course, I'm not a coward. Besides, I have no choice in the matter."

A look of pity washed over Ranulf's face, but it quickly became replaced with rage. "How could he do this to you? Has he no feelings? He must be able to see what you actually are."

Deep down inside Ariel asked herself those very things, but what good would it do. "That is exactly the problem when it comes to Broc, he does not see. He probably never will. It just shows how much our short time together had meant to him."

Ranulf took a step closer to Ariel. He moved so he was a mere inch away then lowered his voice so only she could hear what he said. "If it had been me, I would never have forgotten. Ariel, you need not be alone. I would be proud to have you as my wife."

Ariel at first didn't know what to say. To be truthful, she couldn't find much wrong with Ranulf. He was virile and handsome. The fault lay with her. She was just not ready to accept another man in her life.

"I can't accept your offer, at least not yet. I can tell you one thing that will never change. I will never go back to what I once was. I'm as much a knight as you are. I will not give that up for any man."

Ranulf bent his head so he could whisper into her ear. "I would have you any way you choose. I've seen you fight. You may be better than I. It's in your blood. I would be a fool to make you give it up. It would only drive you away."

Before she could answer him, a hand grabbed Ranulf by the neck and roughly pushed him away from Ariel. She knew who it was without even looking. Broc stood where Ranulf had been a moment before. His eyes practically shot sparks. If Broc had the ability to kill with a look, Ranulf would have been a dead man. Once more Ariel felt her temper rise at the man standing before her. Lately, the most prominent emotion Broc elicited from her was rage.

"Leave Ranulf alone. You have no rights over him."

That only made Broc's eyes flash sparks in her direction. "So it would seem, but the same cannot be said for you. It's time. Come with me now."

Tamping down her fury, Ariel silently followed Broc to the dais where a priest, Lady Alwen, and her father waited for them. Reaching the others, Broc took Alwen's hand and the priest started to say the words that would bind them together.

With each word the priest spoke, Ariel's rage turned to despair. When the couple kissed to seal their vows, Ariel felt the sensation of drowning in a deep dark lake wash over her. It killed any hopes she had of one day sharing her life with Broc. Now it was too late.

After signing her male name to the marriage document, Ariel sat down on the bench next to Ranulf. She felt completely numb.

After the newly married couple sat down, the serfs started to serve a lavish meal. None of it passed Ariel's lips. Afterwards, she wouldn't even remember what had been served. A full goblet was all that mattered. She never once looked at the raised dais where Broc sat with his bride.

If she had been watching, she would have seen Broc was not exactly acting like a bridegroom should. He ignored his food and his bride. A goblet never stayed for very long out of his hand. When Ariel's eyes weren't on him, Broc's gaze never left her face.

The time for the bedding approached and the Lady Alwen left the hall with some of the village women. They took her to Broc's chamber where she would be prepared to receive her husband. Broc didn't even look up when she stood to leave. The two guards, who had come with Broc's now father-in-law, came to stand on either side of the bridegroom's chair. They had to gain Broc's attention by giving his shoulder a tap. Broc jerked and turned to look up at one of the men.

"Come, my lord. It's time for you to join your new bride in your chamber."

At the man's words, Broc drank a whole goblet of mead in one gulp. He then tried to stand and failed in the attempt. In the end, the two men had to each take one of Broc's arms and half carry him to his chamber. More than one person present wondered aloud if Broc would be able to perform his marital duty this night.

* * * *

With a flick of her wrist, Alwen dismissed the village women. They had disrobed her and helped her into her husband's bed. She had no further use of them. She had only allowed them this close to her because there were no other women of her class available. Now she waited for her husband.

It had been unbelievably easy to hook Broc St. Ceneri. Almost too easy if the truth was told. For some unknown reason he seemed to need her. Theirs would not be a love match by any means, but she found her husband attractive and counted herself lucky to even have that.

The chamber door crashed open. Alwen watched her father's men drag Broc into the room and roughly dump him on the bed beside her. Without a backward glance, they left her alone with her new husband.

A person would have had to be blind not to see Broc had managed to drink himself into a stupor during the meal. Only Alwen hadn't realized how much he had consumed. It had to have been a great quantity for him to be in such a state. Looking over at her husband, she found him asleep and dead to the world around him.

Chapter 23

A week had gone by since Broc had brought his bride to Elmstead and life was a far cry from being normal. The presence of the former overlord and his men made everyone jumpy. The biggest problem was worrying over Theodoric. He wasn't making any preparations to leave Elmstead.

The days after the marriage Ariel found to be exceedingly hard. Having to watch Broc take his vows had made her come to grips with her true feelings. She had started to fall for him during her training. Her feelings for him had not changed no matter how many times she told herself he meant nothing to her. Now it was too late to tell him. Every night in the privacy of her own chamber, Ariel mourned over her lost chance.

If Ranulf had not been such a steadying force in her life, Ariel probably would have run from Elmstead. The sight of Broc and Alwen together tore her apart. At times it became almost too much for her to bear. During those instances, Ranulf would make her put on her armor and take her out to the practice field. There, he let her vent her frustrations out on him. After a few hours of steady sword play, Ariel felt ready to once more face Broc.

Today was no exception. Sensing her mood, Ranulf donned his armor and told Ariel to meet him on the field when she was ready. Instead of going directly to Ranulf, Ariel slung her armor over her shoulder and went to the meadow. The day felt cold, but the sun shone down brightly, giving a slight reprieve from the winter dullness. A light dusting of snow covered the ground.

Not until she reached the meadow did Ariel realize she was not alone. The earl's guards were a short distance behind her. Ignoring them, she hoped they would go away and leave her in peace, but they were not to be put off so easily. When Ariel refused to acknowledge their presence they forced her to. Ariel steeled herself as they slowly approached her.

"Well, the little knight is alone. Where is your Norman friend? Did he finally get tired of looking after you?"

When Ariel did not respond, the man grew angry. "It looks as if this boy thinks he's better than us. Isn't that right, Godwin?"

"It would seem so." The one named Godwin stepped in front of Ariel and pulled her amour out of her hands. It clanged when it landed on the ground near her feet. Seeing temper flash in her eyes, he laughed. The one who had spoken first moved to stand beside his companion.

"What do you think, Godwin? Should we teach this young one to respect his elders?"

"Aye, Hugh. I think he needs to be taught a lesson."

Before Ariel could move away both men lunged at her. They were larger than she, but Ariel fought them with all of her might. In the ensuing scuffle, the front of Ariel's tunic ripped open. Feeling the cold wind hitting her bare skin, she automatically tired to clutch the material together with her fist. That was her downfall. Ariel's attackers took the advantage as she tried to close her tunic. They both grabbed her and threw her to the ground. The air left her lungs in a whoosh as she landed in the snow. Gasping for breath, Ariel realized the two men had seen what was under her tunic.

The one called Hugh, straddled Ariel's middle and grabbed her by the throat. "I think this is our lucky day, Godwin. I think we have stumbled onto something here."

When his friend didn't seem to understand, Hugh took his dagger out of its sheath. Hooking it into Ariel's tunic, he cut it and the bindings around her chest. At the sight of her bared breasts, Godwin sucked in his breath.

Ariel panicked as Hugh started to work on her belt buckle. Arching her hips, she tried to throw him off, but it was no good. All it accomplished was Hugh putting more pressure on her throat. Still she struggled until lack of air made the world blacken.

One minute Ariel struggled to take her next breath and then the next, she sucked in large amounts of air. She remained oblivious to what went on around her. All that mattered was getting her breath back. The silence that suddenly fell was ominous.

Breathing normally again, Ariel looked around her. Her attackers had gone, but she was far from being alone. Broc stood above her with his eyes glued to her chest. While fighting to get her breath back she had made no attempt to cover her chest.

Jerking the material together, Ariel shot to her feet and started to back away from Broc. His eyes bore into her with each step she took. She had to get away. He now knew who she was. Turning, she started to run and brushed past Ranulf who had just reached the meadow.

Seeing her disheveled condition, he shouted to her as she ran by him. "Ariel, wait! What did those two do to you?!"

Ariel didn't stop or even let on that she had heard him. She had to get away from Broc. Behind her, she heard Broc bellow for her to stop.

* * * *

She didn't stop running until she reached her father's hall. She had nowhere else to go. Knowing Broc, he would search for her. He would want answers and Ariel had no choice but to tell him. At least here his wife wouldn't overhear what they would say to each other.

Throwing open the door, Ariel saw Lily was the only one there. "Where's Colwyn?"

Lily gasped at the state of Ariel's clothes. "He's asleep in your chamber. What happened to you?"

Ariel had to make sure Lily was not there when Broc showed up. "I'll explain later. Right now, I need you to leave."

Lily hesitated as if she were unsure whether or not she should leave Ariel alone. "Are you sure you're all right?"

"Aye, just go. I'll be fine."

Giving her a reassuring hug, Lily silently walked out of the hall. A minute later Broc burst through the door. As he came to stand just inside, he looked her up and down taking her measure. "Why? Why would you pretend to be a boy?"

When he tried to move closer to her, Ariel held up a hand to stop him. "Don't come any closer. I won't be able to say what needs to be said if you come any nearer."

Seeing Broc had heeded her words, Ariel attempted to answer him. "It was the only way I could go and fight with the fryd. My father needed to stay at Elmstead, so I took his place."

Broc roughly ran his hands through his hair in apparent agitation. "But why not tell me who you are? You had to have known me."

Ariel made a sad little chuckle. "Aye, I did, but you didn't know me. No matter how close you came, you were blind to what was in front of you."

That statement caused a groan to slip past Broc's lips. "Oh, god. The women and what I did to you in London. You could have told me."

Ariel pulled herself up straighter. "Nay, I wanted you to see me as I am. I knew you the instant I saw your face on that battlefield. I've never forgotten you."

At Ariel's words, Broc seemed unable to stay away from her any longer. Crossing the room he tried to wrap his arms around her, but Ariel wouldn't allow it. She backed away out of his reach.

"Aye, I was blind, but that doesn't mean I had forgotten you. You have been in my dreams since I left. That was the reason why I asked for Elmstead, I wanted to look for you. You have become a part of me."

Ariel cringed at his words. "Really? Yet you can take another as your wife?" Knowing she had hit a sore spot, she continued. "Well, now you will have to forget about me. You belong to another. You were never really mine in the first place."

All the blood drain out of Broc's face as his pallor turned white. "I could have been. If you had only told me who you were, I would never have married Alwen."

Ariel found this harder to do than she had first thought, but she pushed on. "As I said before, it's too late. Alwen is your wife, not I." Seeing Broc open his mouth to speak, she quickly cut him off. "And I refuse to be your mistress. I have other people in my life to think about, and someone in particular who could be hurt if I did."

She could see her words hurt him, but Broc had brought much of this on himself through his inability to see clearly. He looked at her now, his expression showing her he realized how stupid he had been not to see through her disguise. Now with the truth out in the open, Ariel knew Broc would never see her as a boy again. It was through his stupidity alone that he had ended up with a woman he apparently did not want.

Neither one of them seemed to know what to do next. Ariel didn't want him to comfort her. If he touched her, she wouldn't be able to let him go. It hurt that he couldn't be hers. He had to realize he had to let her go. It was the only way.

Broc opened his mouth to say something when the sound of a child crying came from one of the chambers. Ariel's eyes widened in panic. Then without saying a word she went to the chamber where the cries came from.

When Ariel didn't return, Broc crossed the room and stepped through the open chamber door. The sight that met his eyes made him pause.

Ariel sat on the bed with a child in her arms. Her head was bent over the child's face, obscuring it. Feeling his presence, Ariel lifted her head. The child forgotten for the moment, Broc watched a single tear slip down her cheek.

"I never meant for you to find out this way. After your marriage, I planned never to tell you."

* * * *

It wasn't until Ariel turned the child to face him that Broc saw what she had truly meant. The child's face spoke volumes. It was an exact miniature of his.

Unable to stop himself, Broc sat beside Ariel on the bed. His eyes never left the child's face. "He's mine?"

Ariel swallowed. "Aye. His name is Colwyn."

Without asking, Ariel lifted Colwyn and placed him on his lap for the first time. At first Broc held his son feeling a bit uncomfortable, but when Colwyn turned and looked up at him giving him a winning smile, he felt himself relax.

He had a son. That thought alone almost overwhelmed him. He had never been this close to a small child, until now that is. Broc never realized a baby could smell so good. They actually had a scent all their own.

Looking at his beautiful little son, Broc felt the loss of not seeing him grow to what he was today. It saddened him and it made him angry as well. So angry in fact, he stood up and walked out of the chamber with Colwyn still in his arms. He made it as far as the hall before Ariel let out a shout of surprise.

"Stop Broc! You can't take Colwyn."

Turning on his heel, Broc gave Ariel the blast of his anger. "Why ever not? He's my son as well. A son you have kept from me. I had a right to know!"

Ariel walked slowly toward Broc as she spoke. "Maybe I should have told you, but it was my decision to make. Most of Colwyn's life you haven't been a part of."

Broc became more agitated. He started to pace the floor. "Through no fault of my own, I might add. So in my absence, you arbitrarily took away my rights to my son."

Now Ariel became irritated as well. "You gave up those so called rights when you left. Do you know how I felt when you just turned and left? It became quite clear to me you had had your fun and nothing else seemed to matter to you."

What she said washed over Broc, calming him as if someone had thrown a cold bucket of water over him. "That's not true."

Oblivious, Ariel continued to speak in a raised voice. "Aye, it is. You mistakenly took me for a peasant; therefore fair game. You never even asked me my name. You assumed I didn't speak French. You could have taken the time to find out those things."

Broc was about to tell Ariel he had made more than a few mistakes with her, when the hall door opened and Swein walked inside. He walked up to Broc and took Colwyn out of him arms.

"I will take the child. He should not be listening to the two of you go at each other like this. The sound of your yelling can be heard outside." Swein gave Broc and Ariel a pointed stare. "Settle this in a quieter manner. We don't want what is going on here to reach the ears of those who have no business knowing."

They remained in silence after the hall door shut behind Swein. They just stood looking at each other. Broc broke the silence between them.

"At our first meeting, I may have gone about it the wrong way. Do you honestly believe I make a practice of using peasant women for my own pleasure? Well, I can tell you I do not." Reaching out, Broc snaked his hand through Ariel's hair and pulled her up close so her body was flush against his own.

"I wanted you, I still do. You have always been with me, even after I left. I have wished to go back to that day, to do things differently, but I cannot. Please, don't push me away."

He had to kiss her. Desire pounded through his body now that he held her close. He slowly lowered his head, letting his mouth hover a hair breath above hers. Ariel stiffened, but when his lips closed over hers, her body relaxed against him.

Releasing Ariel's hair, Broc wrapped an arm around her waist and pulled her even closer. He swept his tongue along her bottom lip. Ariel opened her mouth allowing him entrance, which caused his body to crave her even more. A moan escaped her. Broc shifted so Ariel felt the full hard length of his cock pressed against her belly. He wanted her. She had to be able to feel the proof of it.

Broc reached inside the rip in her tunic and placed his hand on her bare breast. Her skin was soft and warm beneath his hand. His touch had Ariel stiffening once again. She wrenched Broc's hand away from her breast and gave him a hard shove. Not expecting her to reject him so violently, Broc lost contact with her lips. With his body still burning with unfulfilled desire, a questioning look flashed across his face.

"We have to stop this, Broc. We cannot do this. It can go no further than this."

Desire still pulsed through his body. His heart beat wildly inside his chest. No other woman made him feel this way. Broc had felt strong desire before, but not to the extreme that existed between Ariel and himself. He wanted not to just possess her body, but her soul as well. Emptiness washed over him now that he no longer held Ariel in his arms. He needed her. It was as simple as that. Nothing could ever change that.

"What would you have me do? I need you and Colwyn to be a part of my life."

Tears came to Ariel's eyes once more. "I will not keep Colwyn from you any longer. You can be a part of his life now. There will have to be some conditions made. If you break them, I'll make sure you never see him again."

Broc would do anything to see his son, and as much as she would allow, still be a part of Ariel's life as well. "I understand."

"You must never tell your wife about Colwyn or me. I will still be Wulf if those guards have not already spoken to the earl."

A spark of anger flashed in Broc's eyes at the mention of Ariel's attackers. "I agree with the conditions. Don't worry about those two. Let me assure you they will be taken care of."

The door opened before Broc could finish all he wanted to say to her. Much to his disgust, Ranulf stood in the doorway. Seeing the man's eyes look so intently at Ariel made Broc tremble with anger. What hurt the most was seeing Ariel look at Ranulf with such familiarity. He knew if he didn't leave now he would in all likelihood do something to upset Ariel. Broc gently caressed her cheek and left the hall.

Chapter 24

Her new life as wife to Broc had not turned out to be as pleasant as she had hoped it would be. Alwen had known there would not be much of a relationship between them from the start. It was only to be expected given the circumstances, but she had thought Broc would not have any problems performing his marital duty.

Since the disaster that had been their wedding night, Broc had not shared a bed with her. He wouldn't even so much as come close enough for a fleeting touch. Something had to be definitely wrong with her husband.

Before the Normans' arrival on English shores, Alwen had been considered one of the most beautiful women on the island. Men had fought each other just to gain her attention, but her Norman husband wanted nothing to do with her. Before their marriage he had shown signs of willingness to bed her, but all that had changed.

Looking at Broc where he sat beside her in the hall, Alwen felt nothing but anger toward him. Something had happened two days before, something that had turned Broc completely away from her. Her husband now didn't even acknowledge her as being alive.

Other slight changes had happened as well. Her father's guards had all of a sudden disappeared, and they had left in a very great hurry. If the rumors going around Elmstead were accurate, Broc had run them off, threatening them with their very lives. It had all centered on Wulf, who was another thorn in her side. The boy was just too beautiful for the male gender. Broc had started spending a great deal of time with Wulf at the old thane's hall. Alwen had not been asked to join in any of those visits.

Broc ate beside her, trying hard not to have any kind of speech with her. Alwen didn't have to look very hard to find out why he was so silent. He watched Wulf and Ranulf. Now that the boy had started having the evening meals in the main hall, he always sat with the other knight. Broc's eyes never left them during the entire meal.

Something had to be done. When the first opportunity presented itself, she would confront Broc and demand to be treated as his wife should be.

* * * *

God she's beautiful in full armor, Broc mused to himself.

A week had gone by since that fateful day. Broc just couldn't get enough of Ariel. Every day he found little excuses to be around her, even making it a point to go to the practice field to watch her train with Ranulf, something that took place right at this very moment.

He knew he caused himself undo pain watching them together, but he was afraid of what would happen if he left them alone, especially now with Ranulf always at her side.

The sun flashed brightly off their chain mail. The sound of their swords clashing together echoed around the field. Broc focused on Ariel's moves and knew the moment she would send Ranulf's sword flying. He still had a hard time believing this extraordinary woman had actually given him a son.

Thinking of Colwyn brought a smile to his lips. He had come to mean a great deal to Broc, which surprised him a little. Small children had not been a prominent feature in his life. To be quite honest, he hadn't been very interested in any he had seen. Even William's children had not interested him. Now that he had Colwyn, Broc had begun to understand how William could be so attached to his children.

The sound of laughter brought Broc out of his musing. Ariel's laugh was music to his ears. He hadn't heard much of it since he returned from London. It irked him to know he was not the one to make her laugh.

After the training session ended Broc walked over to the pair. Both Ariel and Ranulf fell silent as he approached. "Well, Ranulf, I see you're keeping Ariel in fighting form."

Ranulf refused to look at Broc and kept his eyes on Ariel. "It would seem so. Truth be told, Ariel is the one who comes to me to train with her."

Ariel let out a small laugh at Ranulf's words. It seemed they had a joke only they knew about. Reaching the end of his patience, Broc barked an order at Ranulf. "You may leave us. I need to talk to Ariel alone."

Ariel opened her mouth to protest, but Ranulf stopped her with a shake of his head before she could utter a word. He then left the field.

Broc watched until Ranulf was out of sight. He turned to look at Ariel and found the flat of her sword swinging toward him. Caught completely off guard she managed to land a blow on his shoulder.

Broc yelped in pain. He then watched Ariel leave the field. "Wait, you have to hear what I want to say."

Ariel angrily marched back to Broc. "Whatever you have to say to me, I do not want to hear."

Broc grabbed her and stopped her from leaving. "Aye, you will listen. It has to do with you and Ranulf."

"What about us? I know what this is all about. You don't like Ranulf spending so much time with me. In fact, you damn well hate it. Correct?"

"Maybe it does bother me."

Ariel shook her head. "That would explain a lot, you watching us whenever we're together. You can't take your eyes off us. How dare you? If you're going to tell me to stay away from Ranulf, you can just keep it to yourself. I enjoy being around him and I will continue to do so, no matter what you say."

Broc gritted his teeth. "That is exactly what I was going to say. Stay away from him."

"Nay." Ariel glared at him with anger showing in her eyes.

"You will. Remember, you are the mother of my son. You have to think of him first before yourself. It's bad enough you walk around wearing men's clothing, wielding a sword as a man, but you will not flaunt your lover around Colwyn."

Ariel went completely still, her face showed no emotion. When she spoke, she talked in a quiet, level voice. "Is that what you truly think of me? As for Ranulf being my lover, he's not. Not that it is any of your business anyway. I may be the mother of your son, but I'm not your wife. For your information, Ranulf is not ashamed of what I was forced to become. If anything, he likes that I'm a knight. He has asked me to be his wife on a number of occasions. I have given it a lot of thought lately. So I'll let you be the first to know, I will accept his offer."

Leaving Broc to stew over her words, Ariel walked away.

* * * *

Feeling as if everything right in his life had now gone completely wrong, Broc walked into the main hall. It was deserted except for his father-in-law. Theodoric sat before the hearth, drinking as usual. The man had done nothing except drink the days away since he arrived at Elmstead. Broc disliked the man immensely.

At the sound of Broc's footsteps, Theodoric looked up. "Ah, there you are. My lovely daughter was looking for you."

Exactly what he needed now—a confrontation with his wife. "Was she? I was at the practice field." Needing a drink himself, Broc headed to the table where a jug of mead and goblets sat.

Theodoric didn't seem to notice Broc's foul mood and kept on talking. "Watching Swein's son again? He is good with a sword. I remember seeing him cross swords with the other warriors of the fryd. Never seen one so young handle a sword with such ease. I can understand why you trained him to be a knight."

Broc responded blandly, trying to show his lack of interest in the subject. "Aye, Wulf is talented."

"That he is. Oh, by the way, Alwen is waiting for you in your chamber."

Broc downed the mead in one gulp and headed to the chambers at the back of the hall. Just what he needed. He wondered what the hell Alwen wanted now.

At first Broc thought the chamber empty. Then he happened to glance at the bed. Alwen was stretched out in the middle of it with the covers tucked around her chest. Her arms lay on top of the covers, bare. Glancing at one of the chairs in the room, Broc noticed her gown had been neatly draped across it.

Broc had not touched Alwen since the night they wed. He didn't remember that night since he had drunk too much mead. In the morning the bloody sheets were evidence enough to show Broc had done his duty. But now that he knew about Ariel, he had no urge to take his wife again. Even her beautiful face couldn't make his body stir to life.

Alwen smiled an invitation at him. Broc stared back. The woman in the bed was his wife, by rights he could take her anytime he wanted. After his conversation with Ariel, Broc decided to use what was his.

Moving toward the bed, Broc slipped off his cloak and unbuckled his sword belt. Alwen flung her arms wide, catching him close when Broc stretched his full length atop her. Before his lips met hers, he closed his eyes. He knew if he had to look at Alwen's face he would not be able to go through with this.

Her lips were warm and soft. At first Alwen followed Broc's lead, letting him possess her mouth, but soon she responded with passion. Pulling the sheet away from her chest, Broc fondled one of her breasts. Alwen arched her back and pushed herself closer as he rolled her nipple between his thumb and finger. Releasing her breast, Broc skimmed his hand down her body until he reached the spot between her thighs.

A moan escaped Alwen as he moved his thumb, rubbing against her clit. He then slipped a finger inside her. What he found caused him to rip his mouth away from her lips and jump off the bed.

Alwen reached for him, trying to bring him back down onto the bed. "What's wrong?"

He rubbed the back of his hand across his mouth. "How can this be? How can you still be a virgin?"

Alwen sighed. "Is that what is bothering you? Well, that can be easily rectified. Come back to bed."

Broc stepped away from the bed. "Wait a moment. The morning after we wed, the sheets were stained with blood and I lay beside you naked."

Alwen cleared her throat. "Very well. You were so far gone in drink you passed out soon after you came to me. I wasn't going to let everyone see you had not made me your wife. I took your clothes off and cut my arm to stain the sheets."

A small cut could be seen on the inside of Alwen's forearm, a mark that proved what she said was true. Broc felt angry over her duplicity. Then all she had said hit him hard. It felt as if a great weight had been lifted from him.

He picked up Alwen's gown and flung it at her. "Get dressed. I've decided you don't interest me as you did before." Grabbing up his cloak and sword, Broc left a confused Alwen lying on the bed.

Chapter 25

Ranulf watched Ariel fling off her armor with more force than was necessary to relieve her of it. Obviously she was not in the best of moods. Whatever had happened between Broc and herself must not have been to her liking.

Seeing the tankard of ale in his hand, Ariel took it from him and drank it down. Ranulf accepted the empty tankard back and laughed. "You just had to ask and I would have happily poured you a drink."

Ariel chuckled. "Sorry. Broc is a pompous ass. He actually had the gall to tell me who I could associate with."

"Ah, let me guess, he doesn't want me around you. Right?"

"Aye, but I put him in his place."

"Just exactly how did you manage that feat?"

Ariel took Ranulf's hand and pulled on it so he stood before her. "I told him you had asked me to be your wife."

Ranulf sucked in his breath. "And?"

"I told him I probably would accept your offer."

Ranulf pulled her close and bent his head down so he could rest his forehead against hers. "Why the sudden change of heart, Ariel? You said you were not ready to have another man in your life."

She sighed deeply. "I know. Maybe I hoped in the back of my mind Broc would still be mine one day. But that has all changed, he has a wife, he has no need of me. Besides, he is not happy with what I have become. He would prefer me to don gowns and do nothing more strenuous than lift a needle."

Kissing her forehead, Ranulf pulled her head down so it lay against his chest. "The bastard. He told you this? How could he, especially when it was he who brought about all the changes in your life?"

Ariel gave Ranulf a little squeeze. "Don't let him upset you so. I'll let him be a part of Colwyn's life, but that's all he will have. I want to start a new life, with you."

"You know how happy that makes me. I just think you still need some more time. You're not ready yet, but I won't let you get away that easily. Tomorrow, you and I will sit down with your father and sign betrothal contracts. Then, when you are truly ready, we will wed."

* * * *

He walked for what had seemed like hours. Finally pulling himself together, Broc found himself standing behind the hall where Ariel and her father lived. It was inevitable. Ariel had been the one and only constant thought on his mind. Seeing Ariel's chamber still held light, Broc moved around to the front of the hall. It was time to make a decision before it was too late.

The main part of the hall was cloaked in darkness. The only light came from the banked fire in the hearth. It was just enough for Broc to quietly make his way across the room. At the closed chamber door he paused, not sure what he was about to do was the right choice.

Without knocking, Broc plunged into the room before his courage left him. What he saw made his heart skip a beat. Ariel was stretched out on top of her bed in a deep sleep. The tunic and trews that she usually wore had been taken off for the night. In their place a chemise clung to Ariel's curves. The light, white material only came to the tops of her knees, exposing a great deal of her legs. With her chest unbound, Broc had a view of the tops of her breasts. The sight of Ariel lying there, free to be herself, almost undid him.

As quietly as he could, Broc stepped over to the bed. He stood over her, unable to stop staring at her. She was a vision, a vision of what could have been his.

Taking the opportunity given to him, Broc sat down on the edge of the bed next to Ariel's sleeping form. He had to touch her, hold her. It was an urge too strong to put aside. With hands that shook, Broc reached out and gently stroked her face. Ariel slept on without waking. Growing bolder, he cupped her cheek, only to have her snuggle her face deeper into his hand. Broc knew he couldn't turn away. He crawled into the bed beside her.

* * * *

She was having a dream and a very erotic dream. Since Broc's return Ariel had been having them on a regular basis, but this one felt so real. almost as if Broc actually touched her body, doing delicious things to it. Not wanting it to stop, Ariel let the sensations that engulfed her body have free reign.

An ache started between her legs along with heat and wetness that pooled in her core. Broc's dream hands played her body so knowingly. Ariel needed the sweet release only he could give her.

A moan that came somewhere deep inside her body, escaped Ariel's lips bringing her fully awake. Shocked, Ariel realized she was not having a dream after all. Broc lay stretched out on the bed beside her. His fingers were still devastating her body with infinite finesse.

Seeing Ariel was fully aware of him, Broc moved so he was partially lying atop her. He was fully aroused. She could feel the long, hard length of him pressed against her side. This was not right. No matter how much she had dreamed of this, wanted this, it had to stop.

Fighting the sensations that took over her, Ariel tried to speak. She found she couldn't even manage the smallest of sounds. Broc bent his head and took one of her nipples into his mouth. All the fight drained out of her. Through her chemise, he used his tongue to lave and suckle her, until she ached for him.

Broc's fingers moved to the ribbon at the neckline of her chemise. Giving it a tug, he untied it then pulled down, causing her chemise to slip down to her waist. He once more bent his head, only to stop before he reached her breast.

Following his line of sight, Ariel knew he saw the ring. The ring he had given her. She still wore it on a gold chain around her neck. She hadn't been able to bring herself to take it off.

Broc smiled. He growled with pleasure, swooped down and took her exposed nipple deep inside his mouth. Unable to control herself any longer, Ariel laced her fingers into his hair, holding him to her. She arched her back offering more of herself.

Releasing her breast, Broc claimed her mouth. His kissed her demandingly. At the feel of his tongue sweeping her bottom lip, Ariel opened her mouth to allow him access. Their tongues mated, tasting one another. There would be no going back for both of them. Ariel needed him just this one time more than anything.

His lips left hers. Ariel opened her eyes to see Broc staring at her, intently. His gold eyes darkened with passion. Without taking his eyes from her, he reached down and pulled her chemise up her body then threw it to the floor.

Ariel fought the urge to cover her breasts with her hands. This was the first time she had ever been naked before a man. Sensing Ariel's hesitation, Broc moved off the bed. With her attention focused on his movements, he stripped off his clothes until he stood gloriously naked before her.

Ariel gasped. He was beautiful. There was no other way she could describe him. The thick slab of muscle that made up his chest was covered in curly dark blond hair that arrowed down past his navel. His arms were heavily muscled as were his legs, and covered with the same curly hair that could be found on his chest. What caught Ariel's attention though was what he had between his legs.

His cock was fully aroused. All Ariel could think was how large he appeared. She couldn't believe her body had easily accommodated him the first time their bodies had joined together. She couldn't seem to take her eyes from that part of him.

Broc seemed to sense her reservations. He climbed back on the bed and pulled her into his arms. He once more swept her away on a wave of passion. He moved to stretch his full length on top of her. His legs came to rest between hers. The feel of his weight on her was glorious. Clutching at Broc's back, she tried to pull him closer.

Keeping his lips on hers, Broc devoured her with his mouth. Trailing his fingers across her ribs he shifted so he lay on his side next to her. His hand moved lower until he reached her hot slick channel. He groaned. Ariel knew she was wet. His cock jumped in response. Rubbing a finger against her clit, he pushed her arousal higher. Ariel moaned his name. He slipped one finger, then two, inside her wet opening, sliding them in and out of her. His tongue mirrored the movement of his hand.

He was driving her wild. Ariel needed more of him. Even though his skilled fingers were devastating her, they were no longer enough. She needed his body inside her. Whimpering with need, Ariel pulled at Broc's back urging him to take her.

Broc spread Ariel's legs with his thigh then entered her slowly. Inch by inch he pushed his hard cock into her body until he was buried to the hilt. He kissed her tenderly, making Ariel feel completely loved.

Broc moved inside her, pulling out until he was almost at the point of leaving her body then slowly entered her again. Ariel arched her hips matching his strokes.

Pleasure built to greater heights with each thrust of Broc's body. Keeping his movements steady, Broc's hand drifted down between their bodies until he reached her clit, the center of her pleasure. He rubbed the little nubbin of skin back and forth. It was enough to send Ariel plunging into an intense climax. As her body clamped around Broc's shaft, she moaned her pleasure into his mouth. Broc thrust powerfully a few more times. His body stiffened then he filled her womb with his seed. He collapsed on top of her.

Ariel let her eyes drift shut as little spasms of pleasure still gripped her. She held Broc tightly in her arms. She felt loved and cherished.

Chapter 26

Rolling onto his side, Broc pulled Ariel up against his body. Her eyes were closed, but he knew she didn't sleep. He quietly studied her face. She was lovely. After what they had done, he loved her even more, if that was possible. He knew he would never be able to give her up now. She had become a necessity, like the air he breathed. Ariel stirred, her sky blue eyes fluttered open and she gazed up at him.

He smiled warmly at her. "Hello."

Broc watched the blood drain from Ariel's face until it appeared quite white. "My god, what have I done?" She tried to sit up, but he pulled her closer and wrapped his arm around her waist holding her to him.

"Shh. You have done nothing wrong."

Ariel fought his hold and managed to slip out of his arms to sit up on the bed. "Nothing wrong?! I've done it again. I don't know what it is, but whenever I'm around you I lose my senses. I vowed I would never give myself to you again."

Broc couldn't keep the smug smile off his face. "Well, you did. I for one do not regret it."

Ariel had to stop herself from trying to smack the satisfied look off his face. "Of course you wouldn't. But what if we made another child?"

"If we made another child, I will be happy for it."

"You would be glad to have another child born illegitimate?"

Broc shook his head. "Nay, I never said that."

Ariel looked at him with a confused expression on her face. "It will be. If you have forgotten, you are married to Alwen."

"Not after I go to London and meet with William."

"You are making less sense with each word you say. How exactly is that going to be of any help?"

Reaching for her, Broc stroked Ariel's cheek. "I learned something about Alwen today. It seems she's still a virgin."

"How can that be? Everyone knows the bedsheet had blood on it the next day."

He had shocked her, he could tell by the blank look on her face. "On our wedding night I drank myself into a stupor. To put it bluntly, I could not perform my husbandly duty. I passed out."

"Then explain how the sheets had blood on them,"

Broc chuckled. "Alwen decided to hide the fact she remained untouched. While I slept she cut her arm and divested me of my clothes. In the morning I assumed I had truly made her my wife. I had no memory of that night."

"You just found this out today?" Broc knewAriel had started to piece together the information.

"Aye, I know what you're thinking. I couldn't bring myself to touch her. She wasn't you."

Ariel brought Broc's head down and thoroughly kissed him. Ariel was the frist to break the contact. "All the nights I lay in my lonely bed picturing you making love to Alwen, and she was a virgin. What will you do in London?"

Already feeling the absence of her lips, Broc pulled himself back under control. He could understand Ariel's need to have all her questions answered. "I'm going to ask William to give his support in having my marriage to Alwen annulled. I don't love her, I never did. I want to be free of her."

"So where does that leave us? I need to know."

Broc smiled and kissed the tip of Ariel's nose. "That depends entirely on you, my lady. When we last spoke you said you were going to wed Ranulf. If I obtain an annulment, will you wed me instead?"

Ariel nodded her head. "Aye, my lord, I will become your wife. I'll talk to Ranulf. I hope he underdstands my decision."

With a whoop, Broc hugged her close to him. "I will leave for London in the morning."

Ariel managed to pull back far enough to look intently at Broc. "I will be your wife, but I'll not change what I am. I'm a knight. Just because you take me to wife, it does not mean I will go back to wearing gowns and sit sewing the whole day through. If you can't accept that, then I suggest you don't go to London."

The smile on Broc's lips disappeared as he turned serious. "I would never ask you to change." Ariel opened her mouth to speak. Broc pressed a finger across her lips to silence her. "I know what I said this afternoon. I only said it to hurt you. Every time I see you with Ranulf I go a little crazy. I love you just the way you are. I would be proud to have a wife who is a knight. One who fought with the fryd and was one of Harold's house carls. We could protect Elmstead together."

Ariel smiled. "Well, then I will be your wife. God speed on your trip to London, my lord."

* * * *

The moon was full with not a cloud to cover its bright face. The thousands of stars that hung in the heavens glittered like diamonds. Alwen noticed none of these things.

A heavy, hooded cloak covered her form. She stood in the shadows a few yards from the old thane's hall, waiting. Even though the hour was late and no one else stirred, she patiently waited. Alwen knew he was in there. It was only a matter of time before he came out. Broc would not be able to get rid of her so easily. She was still his wife, and he could not treat her so.

At the sound of voices, Alwen stepped deeper into the shadows. Broc walked out into the night. He turned to talk to the person who stood in the doorway. The light shining in the hall cast enough brightness for Alwen to see who it was. It was Wulf, but a very different looking Wulf. The face was his, but the body was that of a woman. Wulf wore nothing but a lawn chemise. Everything suddenly became quite clear. Wulf was actually a woman. Obviously Wulf was not her real name. Alwen wondered why the girl posed as a man.

The voices stopped and to her horror, Awlen watched her husband pull the girl into his arms and kiss her passionately. He never kissed her that way. Now all made sense. Broc rejected his wife only to make a woman who acted as a man his mistress.

Silently, so as not to make her presence known, Alwen moved back in the direction of the main hall. One thing ran through her mind—revenge. Broc would pay for the grave insult he had given her. He would pay if it was the last thing she did.

* * * *

Broc knocked on Alwen's chamber door. It was dawn. The time had come to tell her of his intentions. At her call, he entered the room and shut the door behind him. She stood at the window with her back toward him. Even though she didn't turn, Broc knew Alwen was aware of his presence.

"I'm leaving Elmstead for a few days. I go to London."

Still not turning to face him, Alwen spoke. "I bid you God speed, my lord. I hope nothing distressing has come about."

"Nay, nothing like that." Broc hesitated for an instant then forged on. "It has to do with our marriage."

Alwen spun around. Her face twisted in a scowl of rage. "What do you intend to do, my lord?"

Broc took a deep calming breath. This was not going to go very well. "Since our marriage has never been consummated I wish to petition for an annulment, with William's permission."

"How dare you?" Alwen shrieked the words at Broc. In an unexpected move, she threw herself across the room and slapped his face.

She hit him with enough violence to snap his head to the side. When it looked as if she would strike him again, Broc caught her wrist in a vise like hold. "Do not do that again, my lady. We are ill suited. We would only make each other miserable if our marriage continued."

All the fight drained out of Alwen. With eyes that shimmered with tears, she spoke in a quiet voice. "Am I not beautiful enough for you?"

"I find you quite pleasing to look at, that's not the problem. There is another."

That turned out to be a mistake. Broc's words set Alwen off once more. "Is it that whore in the other hall? The one who pretends she is a man?"

Broc stiffened at the insulting way Alwen spoke of Ariel. "How did you know?"

Alwen's laugh was anything but pleasant sounding. "That bitch is your mistress. I saw you together last night. She was practically unclothed and you had your hands all over her for the entire world to see. How could you do that to me? I'm still your wife."

Broc released Alwen's arm and took a step away from her. "You followed me? You have overstepped yourself. Whoever I decide to associate with is my business. You have no say in the matter. As to you being my wife, when I return from London you no longer will be. Now, I bid you adieu."

"What will become of my father and me? Where will we live?"

Broc shrugged his shoulders. "I guess you had better sober up your father long enough to make plans for your future. You may stay at Elmstead until my return then I want the both of you gone."

* * * *

Ariel nervously paced the floor. With each step she took the scent of the flowers mixed with the rushes beneath her feet wafted around her. She had watched Broc ride out of Elmstead on his way to London. Now she had to face Ranulf. She didn't want to hurt his feelings, but there was no other way around it.

She continued to pace, the sword that hung at her side slapped her thigh with each step she took. Deep in thought, she didn't become aware of Ranulf's presence until he came up behind her and pulled her up against his chest.

"I hope it's thoughts of me that have you so distracted."

Ariel turned in his arms and tried to smile at Ranulf, knowing she failed miserably. Ranulf's smile slowly left his face. "What has happened?"

With a sigh, Ariel stepped out of his arms. "We have to talk, Ranulf."

Ranulf folded his arms across his chest. "I have a feeling I'm not going to like what you are about to say."

"I don't wish to hurt you."

"But you probably will. Is it about our betrothal?"

"Aye, there is something you should know." Taking Ranulf's arm, Ariel led him to a bench. Once he was seated she sat down next to him and took his hand in hers. "Last night something happened between Broc and me. It made me rethink a few things."

Ranulf grew stiff and in an emotionless voice he said, "So, he came to you. Have you decided you would rather be his mistress than my wife?"

"Nay! It isn't like that. He has gone to London to seek an annulment."

It seemed to take him a minute for all of Ariel's words to sink in. "Are you telling me Broc has never slept with Alwen?"

Ariel nodded her head. "Precisely. He only found out about it. It seems Alwen hid the fact Broc had passed out on their wedding night, even from him."

"So he came to claim you. I should be angry, but I'm not. I know you don't love me. You have feelings for me, but nothing compared to how you feel about Broc."

Ariel bent forward and kissed Ranulf softly on the mouth. "You are a true friend. I would hate to lose you over this."

Ranulf sighed. "I wouldn't turn from you now. Broc probably told Alwen what he intended to do. With Broc away from Elmstead life may not stay so peaceful."

* * * *

William watched Broc pull his mount to a halt and dismount in the yard. One of the guards had come to tell him Broc St. Ceneri was at the gates. He was not completely surprised by his friend's arrival. It had been only a matter of time.

Broc nodded at William and relinquished his horse's reins to a guard who led the animal away to the stables. Slinging his pack over his shoulder, Broc went over to William. "I see you were told of my arrival."

"Aye, come to the hall. You can quench your thirst with some wine."

Broc nodded. "I could do with some. When it permits, I have to discuss something of great import with you."

"When you have rested we will talk. Come."

William knew Broc probably did not need to rest. That he was able to discuss his problem with his king right at this very moment, but for some reason he felt like playing with Broc.

William motioned to one of the serfs who worked in the hall to bring them wine. Once it was poured he watched Broc take a sip from his goblet. He seemed to savor the taste. William threw back his head and laughed. "What's the matter? Have you not been able to get any good French wine at Elmstead?"

Broc chuckled. "Nay, I'm glad you find it so amusing. Try having to drink mead and ale all the time."

William cringed dramatically. "While you're here I will arrange to have a shipment of wine sent to Elmstead. God forbid if you have to drink English ale every day."

Broc grew silent while they sipped their wine. Serfs busily cleared out the old rushes so fresh ones could be laid out. No one else was about.

Broc broke the silence with a question. "How have the Saxon people adjusted to being under your rule? The last time I was here you expected some problems."

The king shrugged. "There were a few incidences of unrest. I had them put down easily enough, but I don't think it will be the last. I must say these Saxons are a proud people. I cannot help but wonder if by taking the throne, my reign will not be a peaceful one."

"I know what you mean about these people, but you will do what must be done."

"Aye, even if I must fight them with my last breath. They will have to accept me as their king." Seeing Broc had finished his wine, William stood. "If you're rested enough, let's go to my chambers so we can talk privately."

Broc picked up his pack and followed the king to the back of the hall. Once inside, William sat behind his desk and motioned Broc to take the chair across from him.

"So, my friend, you finally have opened your eyes and saw Wulf was your Saxon girl."

Broc gave William a surprised look. "You knew all along as well?"

"Of course."

"But how? You never told me. Was I the only person so utterly stupid not to see through her?"

"It was by accident that I found out Ariel's secret. Remember when I helped you tend her wound? When you went to see the healer I found the bindings around her chest. After further investigation, I found out the boy was not what he pretended to be. I promised Ariel not to tell you."

Broc rose out of his chair and began to pace the floor. "How could you, William? I thought you would never keep something so important from me. You could have saved both Ariel and I a lot of heartbreak."

"Sit down. You're giving me a headache with all that pacing." Once Broc was again seated across from him, William leaned over the desk to look at him closely. "I don't know exactly why I didn't tell you. Maybe because there was a child involved. I figured you both had to work this out on your own."

Broc spoke with irritation in his voice. "To the point you would allow me to wed another?"

"If it came to that. I had no idea how you would react when you found out you had a bastard child. I was lucky. My father loved my mother and made me his heir. The way it stood, Colwyn had a strong protector in the form of his mother."

"How could you say that? I would never do anything to harm Colwyn. He is my son and he will be my heir."

William nodded his head in approval. "I'm glad to hear it. Now tell me what brings you to London." The king leaned back in his chair and waited for Broc to collect his thoughts.

"I want an annulment from Alwen. I wish to wed Ariel."

It was William's turn to be surprised. He sat up straight once more. "Are you saying you didn't make your Saxon bride your wife?"

"That's correct. On the night we wed I drank heavily and didn't perform my husbandly duty. I've not been able to bring myself to touch her since."

William steepled his fingers in thought. "How did you find out who Ariel was?"

Broc scowled. "The guards my father-in-law brought to Elmstead decided to have some fun with her. I witnessed the attack and ran them off. Ariel's tunic and bindings had been cut open."

So the chit had not told him, William thought to himself. He had to give Ariel credit for not backing down on her decision. "I see she held firm to her word not to tell you. Seeing how the Lady Alwen is still untouched, I can see no foreseeable problem in obtaining what you wish. I will have my brother, Odo, get the process started. As to your marriage to the Lady Ariel, you have my permission on one condition."

"Whatever it is, I'll do it."

William chuckled at how fast his friend agreed. "It is nice to see a man do anything for his future wife. It's something easy. I wish to return to Elmstead with you. I would not dream of missing your nuptials."

Broc smiled and let out a hearty bellow. "You honor us both."

Chapter 27

Life at Elmstead moved at its regular pace with only a couple of changes that took place. With Broc in London, the villagers once more came to Swein with problems that needed handling. He was the thane and always would be regardless of who actually owned Elmstead. The other dramatic change was Alwen and her father's disappearance. A few days after Broc's departure they were found missing.

Ranulf had retired for the night and in the morn, they were gone. All they had brought to Elmstead they had taken with them. Ariel was just glad to see the back of Alwen and her father. Ranulf on the other hand, predicted their late night departure would not bode well somewhere down the road. Ariel told him his fears were unfounded.

A week passed. Ariel spent her days in arms practice with Ranulf and caring for Colwyn. During the evenings, she spent relaxing with her father, Lily and Ranulf. This evening had been no different from any other. The others had already retired, but Ariel was not quite ready to close her eyes for the night. Thoughts of Broc whirled madly inside her head.

She missed him. There was no doubt about that. She missed his touch and her body ached for him. The night before he had left for London he had reawakened her body to desire. It now demanded what Broc could only give it.

Looking out at the night sky, at the millions of twinkling stars, Ariel wondered if Broc looked at them at the same time. Even though leagues separated them, they would be sharing the wonder of the night together. Ariel shook her head at her silly musing. Love made her a romantic fool.

Turning her back on the night, Ariel walked to her chamber. She stripped out of her tunic and trews and replaced them with a chemise, the only feminine piece of clothing that graced her body these days. Moving to the other side of the chamber, she checked on Colwyn. He slept on a small bed low to the floor. Smiling at her sleeping son, all soft and warm looking, Ariel gently placed a kiss on his chubby cheek. He didn't stir.

Gaining her bed, she climbed into it and buried herself beneath the covers. In moments sleep claimed her. She would never know what had actually brought her out of her deep sleep. One moment she was oblivious to the world and the next Ariel came fully awake.

Something was wrong. Ariel sat up in bed trying to get her bearings. The smell of something burning tipped her off that all was not right. Glancing at her chamber door, Ariel saw a cloud of smoke drift under the bottom of it.

Ariel bounded out of bed and picked up Colwyn, wrapping the covers around him. Before she left the room she gathered up her armor and threw it out the only window. She looped her sword belt over her arm. She wouldn't leave her armor to be burnt.

Throwing open the door, Ariel saw the hall was engulfed in flames. Panic tried to take over her senses. If the flames reached the thatching of the roof it would start falling in on them. Trying to focus through the thick haze of smoke, Ariel made her way to her father's chamber.

Pushing open the door, she spied her father's sleeping form. "Father! Wake up! The hall is on fire!"

At Ariel's shout, Swein jerked awake. It didn't take him long to pull on some clothes. Once dressed, he reached for Colwyn. "Give him to me, Ariel. I'll carry Cowlyn."

Colwyn was now awake and had begun to cry. Ariel gently passed him to his grandfather. Before she left the room, she strapped her belt around her waist so her sword hung at her side.

The smoke so thick it was hard to see through it. Their eyes watered and with heat so intense each breath seared their lungs. With the hall burning all around them, they gradually made their way to the hall entrance. The few minutes it took to cross the hall felt more like hours to Ariel. By the time they reached the outside they were coughing from all the smoke they had inhaled.

The alarm had been raised in the village. A couple of village men came to help them. Once they moved safely out of range of the fire, the wife of one of the men placed a blanket around Ariel's shoulders. In her haste, Ariel had forgotten she only wore a thin chemise.

Swein wrapped his free arm around his daughter's shoulders. "Are you all right?"

Ariel coughed, trying to dispel the smoke from her lungs. "Aye, father."

Now that they were out of danger, Ariel turned to look at the hall. Some of the villagers were trying to fight the fire, but it was a losing battle. The building was totally engulfed by greedy licking flames. There would be nothing left once the fire ran its course. They would lose everything. It was then Ariel remembered her armor.

"Father, are you able to stay with Colwyn?"

Swein nodded. "Aye, where are you going?"

"I threw my armor out my chamber window before I left. I want to retrieve it."

"Fine. Just be careful you don't get too close to the flames. The rate this is burning, I would not be surprised if the whole building collapses."

"I'll be careful." Ariel had already started to walk away.

Wrapping the blanket more closely around her, Ariel made her way to the back of the burning hall. It wasn't hard to find her armor. The flames reflected off the chain mail making it flash in the darkness. Ariel had thrown it far enough away, so she didn't have to come into close contact with the fire. But even at this distance the heat of the flames could be felt.

Ariel let go of the blanket and bent down to pick up her armor. As she bent over she had the feeling she was no longer alone, that someone watched her. Straightening up, Ariel slowly turned around.

One of Theodoric's guards stepped into view, the man called Hugh. "Did you think you could get away from me so easily? Your Normans will not be able to come to your rescue this time. Especially with one in London and the other knocked senseless."

When Hugh lunged for her, Ariel threw her armor at him, hitting him square in the chest. The weight of the metal slowed him down giving Ariel enough time to draw her sword. With a bellow of outrage the guard drew his sword and advanced on her.

His skill did not match hers, but he made up for its lack in brute strength. With each block, Ariel's arms felt as if they were being ripped out of their sockets. There was only one way to defeat this opponent, she would have to out maneuver him.

Blocking a few more hits, Ariel found Hugh's weak point and lunged, effectively disarming him. She placed the tip of her sword at the base of his throat. Instead of yielding, he laughed at her. Opening her mouth to cry out for help, Ariel felt a blinding pain at the back of her head. Before the blackness engulfed her, she saw the other guard, Godwin, step into view. She had underestimated her enemy. Her sword dropped from her hand as Ariel silently fell to the ground.

* * * *

The sound of voices brought Ariel out of the darkness she had fallen into. That and the sickening jolt her stomach made with each bump in the road the cart hit. Cracking her eyes open produced the same sensation. Ariel quickly shut them again.

She tried to move and found it beyond her capabilities. After the events of the night before, she was not surprised to find both her wrists and ankles bound by thick ropes. Ariel could only wonder what Theodoric's men had in store for her.

A heavy blanket wrapped her body from head to toe, rendering her blind to her surroundings. Ariel shifted her head trying to find the opening of the cover. A stabbing pain shot through the back of her head at that small movement.

The cart rumbled on and the blanket became stifling. Ariel had no idea how long they had been traveling, but judging by the sounds her stomach made it had to have been quite some time. She hoped they would reach their destination soon. The pressing need to relieve herself was becoming great as well.

A short while later the cart came to a stop. Straining to hear, Ariel heard a new voice, but through the thick blanket the conversation was too muffled to hear what was being said. The voices fell silent. When the blanket was pulled away from her head, she closed her eyes against the bright glare of the sun. After the darkness beneath the cover the bright light blinded her. It took a few minutes for her eyes to adjust to the sudden change. When she could see again, Ariel was not pleased with the situation she found herself in.

Theodoric leaned over the side of the cart and smiled at her, it held no warmth. It was obvious to her who had been behind her abduction. He reached out his hand and grabbed a handful of her hair. His grip grew painful as he moved her head from side to side, studying her face intently.

"Well, well. I see my daughter was correct. I almost did not believe her when she told me you were actually a woman. You fooled a lot of people, my lady."

"What do you want with me?" Ariel's voice came out in a croak. It had been many hours since she last had anything to drink.

"It's quite simple really. You are going to be an instrument of revenge. The Norman has to pay for his treatment of my daughter. The slight he gave her cannot be easily overlooked." Theodoric seemed to be pleased with his plans for Broc. He even rubbed his hands together in pleasure at the thought of it.

"I refuse to do anything that will hurt Broc."

"Such loyalty. Too bad you will not have a choice in the matter. My plan is simple. What better way to wound him then to sell his woman into slavery. That way he will never be able to find you."

Ariel felt a wave of real fear wash over her. "What makes you think Broc will even care I'm gone. He may not even search for me."

Theodoric's laugh was sinister. "Come now, of course he will search for you. How could he not try to get back the mother of his son?"

At his words, Ariel felt her stomach roll over. "How...how did you know?"

Theodoric shook his head as if to say Ariel should know better than to ask such a silly question. "My men watched you for a few days before they set out to capture you. What a surprise they had when they saw the face of the child. It was not hard to guess his heritage when he wears it on his face for all to see."

The urge to protect her child made Ariel momentarily forget her situation. "If you harm my son in any way, I will kill you."

Her captor chuckled at her. "In your present position, I think that is an impossibility. Do not worry. I have no interest in harming your son. He will better serve as a reminder of you every time the Norman looks at him and he will feel your loss. He will represent everything that could have been."

A chill ran down Ariel's spine. She was indeed powerless. Right now she would not be able to fight the plans Theodoric had for her. She only hoped an opportunity presented itself so she would have the chance to free herself.

Chapter 28

Broc returned to Elmstead triumphant. The annulment had been granted with the help of the king and he now carried the papers safely among his belongings. He did not return alone. As planned back in London, William rode at his side.

It was still the early part of the day when they dismounted in the yard. So early in fact, none of the villagers or anyone else for that matter moved about. Taking the reins of both horses, Broc led them to the stable. It didn't take him long to wake the stable boy and leave the animals in his care.

William stood in the middle of the yard giving Elmstead a thorough inspection. Seeing Broc had returned, he nodded. "I can see why you asked for Elmstead, other than the obvious reason of Ariel coming along with it. Speaking of which, let's go see your Lady Knight."

Broc motioned for William to follow him. On the way he thought of what the king had called Ariel. Lady Knight. The title was appropriate in more ways than one.

The sight of the smaller hall burned to the ground knocked the air out of Broc's lungs in a rush. *My god, who could have done this?* Broc wanted to shout that question until someone answered his cries. Then he thought of another question, an exceedingly important one. What of Ariel and Colwyn?

Taking off at a run, Broc headed back to the main hall. He didn't even take the time to see if William followed behind him. Broc called Ariel's name in the empty hall. The sound reverberated off the walls. When Ariel didn't appear, he called for her again. It was Swein who finally stepped out of a chamber. He carried Colwyn in his arms. His son quietly whimpered. Broc met him halfway across the room.

"Where is Ariel? Why did she not come when I called?"

Swein whispered to Colwyn, trying to soothe the baby. "Calm down, you're frightening your son. There are a few things you need to know."

"Give Colwyn to me." Swein passed the child to Broc and Colwyn settled at the sight of his father.

Broc kissed the top of Colwyn's head. "How did your hall come to be burned to nothing?"

Swein sighed. Broc saw lines of tiredness etched into the older man's face. "We don't know exactly how the fire started, but we think it was deliberate to draw our attention away."

"Away from what?"

"From Ariel, she's missing. She disappeared during the night of the fire. I have a good idea who is behind it though."

"And who would that be?" Both Swein and Broc looked at William, shocked to realize they were not alone in the room. Swein was the first to recover.

"Who, may I ask, are you?"

"William, your king."

Swein's mouth dropped open as if he did not know what to say at first. "I'm sorry, sire. I did not realize who you were."

William waved away his apology. "Never mind that, tell us what you know about Ariel's disappearance."

The older man pulled himself together and nodded. "Well, to start with, Alwen and Theodoric left Elmstead shortly after you, Broc. They left in the dead of night, with no word to any of us about their intentions."

Broc had to admit all thoughts of his former wife had fled his mind at the sight of the burnt hall. Now taking the time to look more closely around him, he noticed another person was also missing. "Where is Ranulf?"

"Gone in search of Ariel. He left after she was discovered missing. He has been gone for four days now."

A thought flitted across Broc's mind. One he was not proud of, but that did not stop him from voicing it. "What makes you so sure Ariel was taken? Who is to say she and Ranulf had not planned this all along so they could be together?"

Swein's face turned red with indignation. "How dare you accuse my daughter of ever doing something as dishonorable as that? She would not ever leave here willingly. She would never have left Colwyn behind or you for that matter. Ariel loves you. She waited for your return."

A wave of pleasure swept over Broc. "I apologize. I did not mean what I said, please continue."

Giving Broc a stern look, Swein spoke once more. "You are forgiven. Ranulf couldn't have planned this. He was bound and knocked unconscious. We found him trussed up and he never saw his attacker either."

Hearing one of his knights had been assaulted, William took over the questioning. "What else led you to your conclusions that Ariel was taken forcibly?"

Swein switched his attention to the king. "During the fire Ariel had tossed her armor out her chamber window. She didn't want to lose it to the flames."

"How any knight would feel. Continue."

"After we escaped the hall safely, Ariel went to retrieve her armor. When fifteen minutes turned into an hour, I started to become concerned for her. I found her armor lying in a pile behind the hall and her sword a short distance away. She had been wearing it when she left Colwyn with me."

"Not a good sign. Who do you think is behind this? I'm sure you have your suspicions."

"Aye, I do. I think Theodoric, along with his daughter, set this into motion."

William scratched his chin and nodded his head in affirmation. "That does seem to be the most logical choice, but from what I remember of him, he spent most of the time in his cups."

Swein shook his head. "Pardon, sire, but you do not know the man as well as me. Before your coming he was Elmstead's overlord. I have had to deal with Theodoric for some years now. He is not what he seems to be. I warned Ariel to be cautious around him when she went to join the fryd. The former earl can be ruthless when the notion takes him."

William's eyes turned hard and forbidding. "Then let's hope Ranulf returns with something to aid us. If not, we have to find Theodoric ourselves. He will have much to answer for."

* * * *

Late that afternoon Ranulf returned. Seeing Broc and William he felt a surge of hope. But taking one look at their faces he knew Ariel had not returned. Wearily shaking his head, he let them know he had found nothing promising in his search.

Taking a few staggering steps, Ranulf slumped down onto one of the benches in the hall. William came and sat down beside him, placing a tankard of ale on the table next to him.

"So I take it you found nothing concrete in regards to Ariel's whereabouts."

Ranulf scrubbed his face with his hand. "Nay, I've been on the road since I left here. I could find no sign of her, but I did find out one thing. Theodoric must be behind Ariel's abduction. One of the villages I passed through gave me that piece of information. A villager noted a pair of rough looking Saxons driving a cart pass through. The men he described matched Theodoric's guards exactly. They had something in the back of the cart. The villager didn't see what they carried. That was the day after the fire."

William nodded. "Did the villager tell you which direction they were headed in?"

"Aye, they were driving the cart north."

Giving Ranulf's shoulder a squeeze, William stood up. "You did well. Eat then get some rest. You look like you need it."

Ranulf had to agree with the king. "Aye, I do. In the last four days I have hardly taken the time to eat or sleep. I stopped only long enough to rest my horse. Give me a few hours to sleep then I will be ready to continue the search."

"Get your rest. We will not leave without you. Three are better than two."

"Make that four." Swein had kept silent while Ranulf spoke, but he spoke up now. "Ariel is my daughter. I will not be left behind."

"Are you sure you want to leave Elmstead unprotected?"

"The villagers can look out for themselves. I doubt there would be any trouble during our absence in any case."

William turned to Broc. "What about you? Are you willing to leave your son behind?"

Broc, who up until now had only listened to the exchange between the king and Ranulf, spoke. "Aye, Lily will continue to provide the care Colwyn needs. I need to be there to confront Theodoric. If he is indeed behind Ariel's disappearance, I will smite him a blow he will soon not forget."

"I give you leave to deal with him as you see fit. Then if we are all agreed, we continue the search for Ariel with the dawn."

The others nodded their heads in acceptance. Out of concern for the woman who meant so much to them all, they hoped the dawn would not be long in coming.

* * * *

If there truly was a hell then Ariel was in it. Her life had become a misery, fraught with pain and suffering.

Theodoric had not kept her long. He had wanted her gone before her presence would arouse suspicion. But he kept her long enough to make a few changes to her person. After their brief meeting, Theodoric had ordered her taken to a small storage shed. The ever obedient Hugh quickly jumped out of the cart and roughly picked Ariel up. From what she could see in her position over Hugh's shoulder, she saw a building that appeared to be a small hunting lodge. Where exactly they were, she had no idea. The most distinguishing feature was all the trees. The lodge was surrounded by them.

The shed sat a short distance away from the lodge. Hugh unceremoniously dumped her to the floor once he opened the door of her temporary prison. Before he took his leave of her, he cut the bonds that had secured her ankles. At least she was to be allowed to move around on her own two feet. He slammed the door shut and locked it from the outside.

Sunlight filtered through the chinks in the walls, allowing enough light for Ariel to see her surroundings. They were not pleasant to behold. The same spaces that provided the light also permitted the cold winter air entrance. Her only cover was the thick blanket that had hidden her from view. Grabbing the edges of the blanket she pulled it tightly around her.

A pile of straw lay in one corner affording her some protection from the hard dirt floor. An empty pail occupied another corner reminding Ariel of the pressure building in her bladder. Not relishing the idea, she quickly used the pail as best she could with her hands bound together. After taking care of that particular piece of business, there was nothing else to do but wait and see what Theodoric would do next.

The day wore on and Ariel remained undisturbed. With the coming of night the door was unlocked to allow Hugh into the shed. He carried a bowl of steaming food and a jug. He silently placed each item on the floor beside her. Giving her a sly smile, he left her once more, locking the door behind him.

Shifting on the straw, Ariel moved to see what she had been given. The jug contained water. Seeing no cup included with what she was given, she picked up the jug and drank thirstily from it. Her thirst was as great as her hunger. As time crept by, Ariel had figured she was not going to be fed or given anything to drink. She was most thankful that was not to be the case.

With her thirst now quenched, she turned to look at the bowl of food. It contained a thin looking stew of meat and onions. It was not much, but it would fill the space in her belly. Dipping her fingers into the hot stew she ate greedily.

Ariel had just finished her meager meal when the door to the shed opened once again. This time Theodoric crossed its threshold. He silently watched her as he cut the ropes at her wrists. Letting him know she would not be cowed, Ariel stared back. Theodoric chuckled at her show of bravery.

"It's good to see you are not easily scared. When you are sold it will go that much harder on you. A few stripes placed on your back will put you in your place."

Ariel remained silent. She would not give him the pleasure of hearing her defend herself. There was no point anyway.

At her continued silence, Theodoric threw a bundle of clothes at her. "Take off your chemise and put on these clothes."

Ariel picked up the bundle and found it to be peasant garb. The material was rough home spun and the hem of the skirt was frayed, and from the look of it, far from clean. Her mind rebelled against the notion of donning such.

Noting her hesitation, Theodoric took a threatening step closer. "Either you put it on or I will rip that chemise off you and dress you myself."

The thought of him touching her body was incentive enough to make her do what he asked. With her eyes downcast, Ariel hurriedly stripped off her chemise and dressed in the peasant clothes. When she finished Theodoric shouted for Hugh.

Before Ariel could move to resist, Theodoric grabbed one of her arms and painfully wrenched it up behind her back. With her subdued, Hugh easily slipped the collar around her neck locking it in place with a bolt and lock. Having completed those tasks they then left her alone.

The metal sat cold against her bare skin. The weight of it was more than enough to make its presence felt. Already the rough edges dug into the tender flesh of her neck. Having to wear the collar was humiliating enough, but it also made the chances of Ariel's escape that much harder. As long as the metal collar graced her neck, she would forever be marked as a serf. No matter what she told others she would not be believed.

Chapter 29

Ariel spent a fitful night tossing and turning on her straw pallet. She was too anxious thinking what the dawn would bring. Her life would be hanging in the balance. As the first rays of the new day chased away the darkness, Ariel's makeshift prison door opened. Her time of reckoning had come.

This time it was Godwin who entered. He shoved a hunk of cheese and bread at her. "You have one minute, then you have to come with me." He turned around and closed the door. Ariel could hear him moving around on the other side.

Glad to at least be allowed to relieve herself without Godwin watching, she moved to the pail. With that chore taken care of, Ariel picked up the jug and drank the rest of the water. Who knew when she would be given something to drink next?

Wolfing down the bread and cheese, Ariel stood in the middle of the floor and waited for the door to be opened. Godwin did not keep her waiting long. He opened the door, and taking her by the arm he pulled her out of the shed. Once more she was put in the back of the cart. This time however she was not kept out of sight. Obviously Theodoric felt confident enough to have her traveling out in the open. After giving her the once over, Theodoric mounted his horse and signaled for the cart to follow. Hugh snapped the reins and the cart jerked into motion.

Ariel watched the scenery pass trying to guess what part of England they traversed, but it was no use. She had not spent enough time out of Elmstead to even begin to guess. The only thing she knew for sure was the direction they traveled. From the direction of the sun, it was easy to see they were steadily moving northward.

The road was full of holes and ruts and at times Ariel had to hold onto the side of the cart to prevent from being tossed about. When the sun was at its highest point in the sky, Ariel caught sight of buildings in the distance.

Theodoric kicked his horse into a canter leaving the cart to follow at a slower pace. Apparently they had reached their destination.

The buildings turned into recognizable shapes the closer they came. There appeared to be a few peasant huts with a hall that dominated the area. But they didn't hold Ariel's attention for very long. A short distance away from the cluster of wooden buildings a structure of stone was being erected. Ariel could only guess that upon its completion it would replace the hall made of wood. Only a Norman would build such a fortress.

As part of her training as a knight, she spent some time learning of Norman fortifications. From hearing Broc's descriptions, the castle would be unlike anything her people had ever attempted. There would be a moat and the earth taken from the moat would then in turn be used to make the parapet walls, making them sit higher. Next would be a strong palisade wall made out of tree trunks. Inside the palisade walls you would find barns, outbuildings and barracks. Last would be the donjon, or the castle proper.

The donjon would not be much to behold. Its primary function would be defense. It didn't have to be pleasing to the eye. The huge square tower would defy attack by mere solidity. The only entrance would be a single small door on the second story. If under attack and the palisade walls were ever forced, the gangway to the door could easily be knocked down providing a safe haven in the tower. Taking a closer look at the construction, Ariel could make out the completed moat and partially completed parapet walls. It already overshadowed the original Saxon hall.

Hugh pulled the cart to a halt in front of the hall. Theodoric waited for them with another man standing at his side. At his master's signal, Godwin pulled Ariel out of the cart and brought her to stand before the two men.

"This is the serf I told you about, my lord."

The man Theodoric addressed took a step closer so he could take a better look at her. Ariel took the opportunity to study him as well.

He was Norman. Up close he appeared to be a lot younger than Ariel had first thought him. She guessed he was probably only a few years her senior. The eyes that looked at her so intently were a dark brown. They were so dark it was hard to see the pupil in the center. He too shunned the Norman style of hair and wore his midnight black hair to his shoulders. He was tall, but his height was no match for Broc's. Like all warriors, his body was heavily muscled from his years of training with a sword.

Taking in all the details of his face, she noted a straight nose, finely arched brows, a square chin and full lips, which at the present time was shaped into a smile. From the look in his eyes, Ariel guessed he knew what she had been doing, taking his measure.

Without taking his eyes from her, he spoke to Theodoric. "She's a hard worker?"

"Aye, my lord. She's stronger than she looks."

"Why is it you wish to sell her?"

Theodoric must have thought of all possible answers, because he answered the Norman easily. "I originally purchased her for my daughter, but alas Alwen found her abilities lacking. She wished to be rid of her."

The Norman nodded and swept her body up and down with his eyes. "I will find a use for her. In the spring my wife will be coming to England. Until she arrives I'll have the girl work in the hall."

"I'm pleased, my lord, but there is one thing you should know about this serf."

"And that is?"

Theodoric cleared his throat, gaining the Norman's full attention. "She thinks she is more than what she actually is. At times she can be very believable. I pray you not to listen to her, they are all lies."

"I will take that into account. Here is your payment, you may leave now." Tossing a bag of coins at Theodoric, the Norman dismissed him. Signaling to his men, the older man left Ariel without a backward glance.

"What's your name, girl?" Geoffrey asked her.

Pulling herself up straighter, she answered. "Ariel."

"I'm Geoffrey de la Roche, your new master. Come with me."

Ariel followed Geoffrey into the hall. There were men sitting at the trestle tables eating their midday meal. They all looked up when she stepped into the room. The further she moved into the hall, the harder it became for her to ignore the remarks being made about her. She was now considered a serf, a female serf, which gave every man in the hall the right to use her in any way they wished. Ariel prayed she would be strong enough to survive what she would have to endure. She hoped Broc would come for her, but she did not put much stock in that happening any time soon.

Stepping into one of the chambers, Geoffrey closed the door behind them. Geoffrey stood in front of Ariel studying her face. He reached out and touched her hair. "Undress. I want to see what Theodoric brought me."

Knowing that if she refused he had the right to rip the clothes off her back, Ariel slowly began to undress. When she at last stood naked before him, she locked her eyes on a point just over his left shoulder.

She stood stiffly before him, trying not to flinch as he circled her. He stared at her body, and from the smile on his face she knew he liked what he saw. He gaze drifted to her breasts and down to her hips. He circled her again. Ariel knew the moment he saw the scar she had on her shoulder. He was a warrior, he had to have seen scars such as that and recognize it for what it was. He had to carry some of the same type of scars on his body.

He nudged the crude metal collar that hung around her neck, She gritted her teeth as the metal brushed against the fresh chafe marks. If she had been a collared slave for as long as Theodoric undoubtedly told Geoffrey, those marks would not be on her skin.

Standing once more facing Ariel, Geoffrey took hold of her chin and forced her to look at him. "You may get dressed. I think Theodoric was not honest with me."

Ariel nodded her head in agreement and reached for the rags Theodoric had forced her to wear. Maybe Geoffrey would return her to Elmstead. He looked like a sensible man.

Geoffrey stopped her before she could get dressed. "Wait. Don't put on that foul thing. I'll give you something better. That is only fit for burning." Crossing the room he knelt down in front of a chest and rummaged through it.

Finding what he sought, Geoffrey shut the lid of the chest and walked back to Ariel. He held out a man's tunic and trews. Without hesitation, she quickly donned the items she had been given.

"I'm sorry it isn't your typical female attire, but at least they are better than those rags."

"They're fine. I prefer man's clothing."

Geoffrey watched her adjust the clothes so they fit her smaller frame. He sat down in one of the chairs in the room and motioned for her to sit in the other. He quietly looked at her. "You are not a serf, are you?"

Shocked at Geoffrey's question, Ariel shook her head. "Nay, I'm not."

"Then what exactly are you?"

"My father was thane to Elmstead before William's coming."

Geoffrey ran his fingers through his hair in agitation. "So that would make you a lady. Then why do you have a warrior's body and a disdain for women's clothing?"

She hesitated before answering. There had to be somewhere Geoffrey was going with all these questions. "If I tell you, will you release me?"

"I can honestly say I'm not willing to do that right now."

That was definitely not promising in Ariel's way of thinking. "Then I do not have to answer your question."

Geoffrey didn't push her. "All right, but I want you to answer this next question. Do you have a husband?"

"Nay."

"Are you betrothed?"

Ariel paused for a second. Broc was going to marry her, but he hadn't returned in time for betrothal contracts to be drawn up so technically she was not. "Nay, I'm not."

With that answer he seemed to come to a decision. "Well in that case, you stay. I'm sure Theodoric was smart enough to cover his tracks, so it'll be hard for anyone looking to find you here."

"Why will you not let me go?" Ariel could not understand his reasoning. He all but admitted he knew Theodoric had lied to him about her, but still he would not release her. What kind of man had she been sold to?

"I'll be honest with you. You are the most intriguing woman I have ever come across. I want you to be mine, pure and simple. If by keeping you a serf it will bind you to me, I will keep you a serf. It is my right."

"What exactly do you expect from me?"

"During the day you can look after the hall, but at night you will warm my bed."

Chapter 30

"Why can we not find her, damn it!" Broc slammed his first on the table in agitation.

"Don't work yourself up so, we will find Ariel." Swein said in a reassuring voice.

"It has been a fortnight since she was taken and we still haven't found anything. Not even Theodoric and Alwen can be found. It's almost as if they have disappeared off the face of the earth."

"I should have anticipated his moving against us. Ariel foiled his plans. With Alwen wed to you he was that much closer to the king. You after all are a close friend to William. I should have realized he would want revenge."

Broc ran his hands roughly through his hair. "Don't blame yourself. I am responsible for bringing him to Elmstead. If I ever see Theodoric again he will be lucky to walk away with his life."

Feeling spent, Broc threw himself into a chair near the hearth. A small fire burned within it. The days had gradually become warmer, but there was still a need for a fire to keep the hall comfortable. Spring was not too far off and Colwyn would be turning a year old in a week. His mother would not be with him to share this special day.

Almost as if she had heard his thoughts, Lily walked into the hall carrying Colwyn on her hip. When his son caught sight of him he started to wriggle in Lily's arms, trying to get down. Winning the struggle, Colwyn toddled over to his father.

Broc still found his son's ability to walk an amazing sight to behold. How he managed to propel himself forward on his chubby little legs, he did not know. The only sad thing about it was Ariel had missed Colwyn taking his first steps.

When Colwyn reached him, Broc picked him up and tossed him into the air. Catching him, he pulled his son up against his chest, Colwyn snuggled close.

Looking at Swein, Broc kissed the top of his son's head. "We have to find her soon. Colwyn should not have to grow up without his mother."

"Then let's hope William can find out where Theodoric is hidden. London holds many people, and there is Ranulf. I'm sure he will continue to search."

Broc nodded his head in agreement. William had left Elmstead two days before. When their initial search had uncovered nothing, William had decided it best to return to London. He had said he would try and use other means to find Ariel. And it was imperative that he not stay away from London for any length of time. If his absence became noted, it could give others ideas of taking the throne from him. Ranulf had decided to leave with the king. With Ariel missing it was for the best.

Time was running out. Broc knew if no clue as to Ariel's whereabouts was found she could very well be lost to them forever.

* * * *

Straightening, Ariel wiped the sheen of sweat from her brow. She then surveyed her handy work. Her days were spent toiling in the hall. Shortly after her arrival it had become apparent there were no other women at Kilsmere. The hall had been full of filth, which no woman would have tolerated.

It had taken Ariel almost a whole day just to clear out the rushes from the hall floor. They had become full of remnants of past meals. Along with the bones and scraps of food, the rushes had begun to molder. She was surprised anyone could even eat a meal there. The stench would have had her retching. Clearing them out had been bad enough.

Cooking the meals had also been an experience. Back at Elmstead, Ariel had only made small meals for her family. Preparing food for all the people at Kilsmere was a monumental task. But there had been no complaints so far, giving Ariel the notion that whoever had been in charge of the cooking before her had not been very good.

By the end of the day, Ariel had been totally exhausted. She had eaten her meal by the hearth trying not to be noticed. Some of the men had given

her sly looks but no one bothered her, not even Geoffrey. After she had
finished her bowl of food, she had stretched out before the fire and fell
asleep in the fresh rushes. She didn't stir again until the dawn broke over the
horizon.

Every day after that, her hours were spent cleaning the hall and
preparing meals. And every night she slept before the hall fire. For some
reason Geoffrey still had not insisted she come to his bed, which had taken
some of the pressure off her. As the days went by, Ariel had come to an
even more startling conclusion. She was once more with child.

Only one night spent with Broc and she was pregnant once more. That
made her situation all the more unbearable. If she didn't gain her freedom
before the child came, it would be born a serf.

Ariel rubbed her aching back trying to alleviate some of the tightness
she had there. The hall was now put to rights. The trestle tables had been
scrubbed clean along with all the walls. Her days would be easier now that
all the back breaking work was completed, but she had not minded doing it.
The work had kept her mind off what her life had become.

Looking out a window, Ariel realized how late in the day it was. She
would have to start preparing the evening meal. At least she found that part
of her duties a little easier.

Placing another piece of wood on the fire, Ariel saw that more would
have to be brought in from outside, which meant she would have to seek out
Geoffrey. He had forbidden her to leave the hall. If she needed wood or
anything removed from the hall he had one of his men do it. Ariel had the
feeling he even kept her presence a secret from the villagers.

A pair of strong arms wrapped around her waist and pulled her back
against an equally strong male body. Her first reaction was to free herself
until she looked down at the arms that circled her. She recognized the
material of the sleeves. It was Geoffrey who held her.

He nudged her hair aside and kissed the back of her neck, Ariel stiffened
causing Geoffrey to chuckle. "Come now. You knew I would seek you out."

"I had thought you had changed your mind."

"Nay, I have been watching you. You have worked hard to get the hall
set to rights. I let you rest without making any further demands on you. Now
the hall is completed and I want you in my bed."

Even though she knew there would be no getting around it, Ariel still had to try to hold Geoffrey off. "What if I refuse you?"

Geoffrey released her only enough for her to turn in his arms and face him. "You have no choice in the matter. You are a serf now. I own you and can use you as I see fit."

Ariel's spirit rebelled at the notion of being another person's property, and to such extent they could decide whether she lived or died. She had been independent for far too long. As for sharing a bed with Geoffrey, it would make her situation seem more permanent. If Broc were to find out he would more than likely shun her. Not knowing what else to do, Ariel used the only piece of information she could think of to stop Geoffrey from carrying out the plans he had for her.

"You cannot bed me, I'm with child."

Geoffrey blinked in surprise. He then looked down at her still flat stomach. "How far along are you?"

"Almost two months."

His reaction was not what Ariel had hoped it would be. Geoffrey just smiled. "Then I will just have to be extra careful with you."

"Does it not bother you that I carry another man's child?"

"Not in the least. Whoever he was, he's no longer a part of your life. I will provide for the child's up keep, just as I do yours."

She had lost. She would have no choice but to submit to him. "You may own my body, but you will never own my soul or my heart. They have been given to another." She stepped away and went back to the chore of preparing the evening meal.

* * * *

The sight of Ariel sitting before the hearth almost made Geoffrey hesitate. He had given her all the time he could, allowing her to adjust to her new station in life. He could no longer wait for her. Tonight he would make her his.

Placing a hand on the top of Ariel's head, Geoffrey made his presence known to her. She continued to stare into the fire. "Ariel, it's time to retire for the night."

"Aye, I know."

"Please don't make me do this. I just can't do what you ask of me. If you were an honorable man you would leave me alone."

"I am an honorable man. I just can't do what you ask. Come, I won't hurt you." Geoffrey held out his hand. Ariel took it and he helped her to stand.

"Let it be known, Geoffrey de la Roche, you may use my body, but do not expect me to do anything to increase your pleasure."

"We will see. For now, I will accept whatever you can give me."

Ariel allowed him to lead her to his chamber. Once the chamber door closed behind him, Geoffrey moved about the room snuffing out all of the candles only keeping a single one lit next to the bed. The room was plunged into semi-darkness. Ariel stood near the bed, waiting.

True to her word, Ariel showed no sign of taking an active part in their love making. Divesting her of her clothes, Geoffrey found it very much like undressing a doll. Her limbs moved where he placed them as if they had no will of their own.

When she was gloriously naked before him, Geoffrey sucked in his breath. The mere sight of her caused his blood to pool in his loins, causing his cock to harden. Her lips were hard and unresponsive. Wrapping his arms about her, Geoffrey pulled Ariel close. Her woman's scent engulfed his senses.

He kissed her eyes, her cheeks, her neck. Geoffrey felt a tremor rack her body. She would fight him, but he would teach her to accept. Lifting Ariel off of her feet, Geoffrey gently placed her on the bed. He stretched out beside her.

Hoping to arouse her, Geoffrey cupped her breast in his hands. He flicked his tongue around each of her nipples. Ariel held herself ridged. Letting his hands roam her body, he caressed her, working his way to her sex. Slipping a finger between her folds he pushed against the opening to her body. He found her dry. Peering down at Ariel, he saw she had her eyes closed. As he watched, a single tear slid down her cheek. Groaning he rolled off her so he lay on his back beside her.

Ariel turned her to look at him with questioning eyes still bright with tears. Turning his head away Geoffrey took hold of his throbbing cock and slid his hand up and down it. He continued the motion until he ejaculated.

"Why didn't you take me?"

Turning over onto his side, Geoffrey stared at Ariel. He knew he would kick himself for doing it, but it was the right thing to do. "I don't rape women, and that is what it would've been if I took you. I admit I was being thoroughly selfish in wanting to bed you. I wasn't thinking how it would affect you. I apologize. I won't force you to endure my touch."

Ariel leaned forward and gently brushed her lips across Geoffrey's. "Thank you. If you no longer wish to bed me I'll return to the hall."

Geoffrey grabbed her arm before Ariel could get out of bed. "Wait. I still want you in my bed." At her confused look he shook his head. "I told you I wouldn't bed you. I want you to sleep in the bed beside me. Just sleep. It will protect you from my men. They don't have to know we aren't having sex."

Understanding Geoffrey was only looking out for her, Ariel laid back down on the bed and allowed him to pull the covers over them both.

Chapter 31

The market place was crowded with all manner of people. Alwen didn't care whether she brushed elbows with Saxon serfs or Norman nobles. Spring had finally come bringing new life to the land, just as she had a new life now.

She was back in London living in modest accommodations far enough away from court, so as not to draw attention to herself. So far no one had realized she was back in the city.

Her father had yet to return from his excursion, but he had not left her alone during his absence. He had hired a maid to look after all her needs. Today she had left the girl at home, wanting to go to the market alone.

Moving from one stall to another, Alwen purchased fresh vegetables and meat. Coming to a stall that held bolts of material and other trinkets, she paused to look over the goods offered up for sale. The vendor stood behind the table ready to be of service if anything caught Alwen's eye. She smiled at the man as she browsed through his wares.

The material was of good workmanship, but Alwen didn't feel like making herself a gown. What caught her eye were the gloves. They were made of kid skin and were soft to the touch. Spotting a pair of dark green ones, Alwen picked them up and tired out the fit. A child's high pitched shrieking drew her attention.

The gloves forgotten, Alwen watched Broc coming toward her. He hadn't seen her yet. He was too absorbed in the child he carried in his arms. The boy child was probably no older than a year and his face was a match for his father's. Broc had never mentioned he had a son.

Hurriedly stripping the glove from her hand, Alwen moved to leave before Broc became aware of her. Before she could replace the glove she felt Broc's eyes on her. Too late, she found she would not be able to avoid him now. Sure enough a large hand clamped down on her shoulder before she managed to step away from the stall. Spinning around, Alwen looked up to find Broc towering over her. He held the child in his other arm.

"Where is she?" Broc roared the question at her causing others to stop and stare at them.

Flustered, Alwen lowered her eyes. "I don't know what you mean."

"Aye, you do. We are going to talk and you will tell me what I need to know." Tightening his hold on her, Broc led Alwen through the market until they came to an open stretch of lawn.

"I will ask you again. Where is Ariel?"

"Why should I tell you anything?" Alwen snapped.

"Because if you don't, it will go badly for you."

"Are you threatening me?"

Broc shook his head. "Nay, I'm only stating a fact. If you do not tell me I will take you to the king. He is very fond of Ariel. He's not too pleased with you or your father at present. It would be best if you spoke to me instead."

That was all the convincing Alwen needed. All her aggressiveness drained out of her. "Then what will happen to me?"

"Nothing, you will be free to carry on with your life. I only want your father."

Knowing it would be better for her to deal with Broc rather than the king, Alwen gave in. "Very well, I will tell you, only because it will do you no good."

"I will be the judge of that."

With a shrug, Alwen told Broc what he wanted to know. "My father was going to sell her. To whom, I do not know."

Broc sucked his breath in sharply. "By what right does your father have to do that?"

Some of Alwen's antagonism resurfaced. She laughed. "It's simple enough. He made her a serf. Whoever he sells her to will believe her to be a serf. She is lost to you, Broc."

Broc scowled at her. "No one would believe Ariel to be a serf. Her bearing is not that of a slave's."

"My father thought of that so he collared her. You know as well as I it's a mark of a serf. As long as the collar is on her person she will not be believed."

Broc swore. The hand holding her shoulder tightened, with punishing force, causing her to shout out in protest. The child must have sensed his father's mood because he now started to cry. The sound of his son's sobbing seemed to bring Broc's anger down to a simmering point. He released her and cuddled the child close as he reassured him by stroking his back.

"Does your precious Ariel know you have a child?"

"Of course. That is just another reason why I want your father. You see, he stole Colwyn's mother away from me."

Alwen's face flushed red. "She gave you a son? Then why the charade? You acted as if she was a man. You even knighted her."

"So I did. That is all the explanation you deserve. Are you sure you have no idea where Theodoric took Ariel?"

"I told you, nay. He never spoke of where he was going. But I will tell you this, I'm glad my father's plan worked."

Broc's lips curled into a sneer. "You know Alwen, your looks could rival those of an angel's, but inside, you really are a heartless bitch."

Alwen gasped at the insult. Without a by your leave she stomped away. Broc let her go.

* * * *

William lifted his face into the sun. He had been spending far too much time indoors. There was always someone demanding his attention, more so now with the work having begun on the stone tower that would replace the wooden fort.

It was rejuvenating to be outside, breathing in the fresh spring air. Taking advantage of the time free from the demands of others, William leaned against the side of the hall enjoying the sights. It relaxed him just to see his people going on with their daily lives.

Spotting Broc as he walked through the gates with his son in his arms, William straightened and walked out into the yard. Since Ariel had disappeared Broc was never far from his little son. Colwyn even slept in the same bed with his father.

"How was your outing to the market place? See anything special?"

"You could say that. Alwen was there."

The smile on William's face vanished. "She's back in London? She has more nerve than I had thought. What of Theodoric?"

Broc shook his head. "Not with her, but Alwen did have some information that may help find Ariel. She says Theodoric has made Ariel a serf and has sold her."

"That bastard. Did Alwen know where he took her?"

Broc's shoulders slumped. "Nay. Theodoric made sure she was ignorant of his whereabouts. He probably wanted to make sure if we found her Alwen would not be able to lead us to Ariel."

"He is very apt at covering his trail." At the look of hopelessness on Broc's face, William gave his shoulder a reassuring squeeze. "Fear not, friend. We're now one step closer than we were before. It's time to send out some of my men. If they pose as peddlers they will be able to gain entrance to any hall. We will find her. It's only a matter of time."

Chapter 32

Life moved on. Two months had passed since her abduction by Theodoric. Ariel had finally eased into her new life enough for her to sleep at night.

After her first night spent with Geoffrey she had withdrawn into herself. Even though she hadn't made love to Geoffrey, in a small way she felt as if she betrayed Broc by accepting her fate. It didn't sit very well with her. Ariel's continued silence had worried Geoffrey. Being a patient man, he gave her the space she needed to adjust to her new life.

But now Ariel didn't find the nights quite so hard to bear. If anything, they gave her a degree of comfort from the harsh reality of what her life had become. To have a warm body to lie beside at night and not have to worry about being mistreated eased her mind, making it easier to accept what couldn't be changed. During the day she was treated as any other serf would be. The only difference was Geoffrey forbad his men to abuse Ariel in any way.

Today was more strenuous than the normal course of a day. The donjon of the castle had been completed and Geoffrey wanted everything moved out of the hall and to be placed in his new residence. The packing, therefore, fell onto Ariel's shoulders.

Watching the last few items being carried out the door by a couple of burly guards, Ariel stretched the kinks out of her back. Being only three months into her pregnancy it still wasn't noticeable. Placing her hand on her stomach, she felt the slight rounding of her middle. The new life inside her thrived. It was the only link she had with her former life.

Shaking off her musing, Ariel took a final look at the hall to make sure nothing had been left behind. Finding it empty, she stepped out the door and into the yard. The day was still warm even though the sun was on its decent. Summer was just around the corner.

Taking the now well worn path to the castle, she headed to what was to be her new home. Geoffrey was at the gates waiting for her. She waved to him.

"Is that the last of it?"

"Aye, the hall is empty." Ariel allowed Geoffrey to pull her close and softly kiss her forehead.

"Good, I can't tell you how glad I am to finally have stone walls around me again. I don't know how you Saxons can feel protected in a flimsy wooden structure as your home."

Ariel shrugged her shoulders. "It's all in what you are used to."

"I suppose." Slipping his arm around Ariel's shoulders, Geoffrey led her to the donjon.

The square tower dominated the yard. Ariel wondered how anyone could feel comfortable living in such a cold looking dwelling. She would take her Saxon wooden walls any day over stone. Following Geoffrey up the stairs, she looked around the yard. Some of the outbuildings were completed, but construction still continued. The barracks, that were closest to the donjon, was one of the finished buildings. Ariel could see a couple of guards talking in front of it.

Stepping through the tower door was like walking from the bright sunshine and into the dim light of darkness. The warmth of the day didn't penetrate the thick walls and there were no windows to let in light. Taking the stairs inside the donjon to the second level, Ariel noticed the slits in the walls. Places for archers to fire their arrows down on intruders.

The hall was not as large as the one in the Saxon building since there was no need for a room that size. The guards would have their meals in the barracks. Only family and selected others would reside in the tower.

This was the first time Ariel had been to the castle. She was impressed with its defenses, but coming to think of it as a home, she couldn't see it as a place a family could live in comfortably. But as she had told Geoffrey before, it was all in what you were used to.

Looking at Geoffrey, she found him standing waiting patiently beside her, watching her reaction to her first sight of the donjon. "Well? What do you think?"

"I can see what you meant by being better protected here."

"I know it is harsh looking, but I'm sure you can make it into something livable."

Ariel smiled weakly, she highly doubted that would happen. She was not a miracle worker. "I will try."

Geoffrey beamed at her. "Good, do you think you can be finished in a month's time?"

"Possibly. What is the rush?"

"That is when my wife will be coming. I want everything ready when she arrives." Kissing her once more, Geoffrey headed back down the stairs leaving Ariel standing alone in the hall.

His wife was coming. Ariel couldn't see any good coming out of it. How would this unknown woman take to her? Especially when she found out her husband was sharing his bed with a serf.

* * * *

Later that evening Ariel lay in bed waiting for Geoffrey. He was down at the barracks talking to the captain of his guards. Now that the castle was occupied, guards needed to be posted on the walls. At the sound of his footsteps on the stairs, Ariel rolled onto her side feigning sleep. Closing her eyes, she hoped he would just let her sleep.

Geoffrey stripped out of his clothes and slipped into the bed beside her. Rolling onto his side he cuddled up close to her. "What's wrong, Ariel? I know you aren't asleep."

Ariel took a deep breath and opened her eyes, but didn't turn to look at Geoffrey. "I'm thinking about your wife."

"What about her?"

"I'm worried about what she will think of me."

Geoffrey pulled her closer and kissed the back of her neck. "Have no fear. She won't be sharing my bed."

What kind of relationship did Geoffrey have with his wife? Ariel wondered. "What about your wife? She hasn't seen you for months. Maybe she would like to have you near her again."

Geoffrey grunted. "I doubt that, we have never met."

Confused, Ariel turned to her other side and stared at Geoffrey. "What do you mean you have never met? You did have a wedding ceremony?"

"Aye, but I was not there. We were married by proxy."

Ariel had heard of marriages being performed with another standing in for an absent participant, but she had never seen it actually done. "When did the marriage take place?"

"After William was crowned king. My parents thought it best for Lisette to be my wife instead of my betrothed when she made the crossing to England."

It was obvious this did not bother Geoffrey in the slightest by the matter of fact way he answered her questions. "So yours is not a love match?"

"Hardly."

Ariel knew Geoffrey wanted to drop the subject when he closed his eyes, but she wasn't ready to let it go just yet. "If she is unknown to you, she may not be what you expect. You could very well end up liking her you know. She may be the woman of your dreams."

Geoffrey threw his head back and laughed. "That's not possible. I don't believe there is a woman out there who could be my perfect match. It rarely happens where someone finds a love so great." Seeing Ariel's look of concern, he tried to lay her mind to rest. "If it will make you happy, I will try to look objectively at my marriage. I just hope my wife will be pleasant enough looking. That way I won't find it hard to bring myself to consummate the marriage. Now that's all I intend to say pertaining to my new wife. You have had a hard day, go to sleep."

Letting Geoffrey snuggle her against his chest, Ariel closed her eyes. She knew it was possible to find a person you could give your heart to. Broc already had hers in his possession. Ariel hoped Lisette would be to Geoffrey what Broc was to her.

* * * *

The sound of cart wheels rumbling into the yard took Ariel away from her work. She stood looking out one of the slits in the wall. Through the small space, she watched Geoffrey help a woman dismount her horse. Keeping his hands on her waist he smiled down at her. She had to be Lisette. His wife had finally come to England.

The month had gone quickly for Ariel. There had been much work to be done at the donjon. A chamber had been readied for the new mistress of Kilsmere, along with a larger room for Lisette and her women to use.

Everything had been completed at the expected date, but Lisette hadn't come. Now, after another month had gone by, she had come to Kilsmere to be with her husband.

Backing away from the opening, Ariel waited for the couple to come into the hall. The baby moved within her, which caused Ariel to smile. She was now five months along and her pregnancy was quite noticeable. She finally had to give up her tunic and trews. She needed the room only a gown could provide.

They were laughing. Ariel could hear them coming up the stairs together. She took that as a good sign. Her biggest wish had been for Geoffrey to like his wife. Just maybe, if he grew fond of her, Ariel would be able to convince him to release her.

Lisette stepped into the room first. She was tiny, only coming to Ariel's shoulder in height. But what she lacked in stature Lisette more than made up for it with a large personality. This was no soft spoken lady. Even now she was talking excitedly to Geoffrey, making him laugh all the more.

One of Lisette's women, who had come up the stairs after her lady, noticed Ariel first. The woman stopped in her tracks and gasped, drawing Lisette's attention.

Taking control of the situation, Geoffrey took Lisette by the elbow and led her over to Ariel. "Lisette, this is Ariel. She does all the work inside the hall. I'm sure she will see to any of your needs."

Ariel watched Lisette's deep green eyes look at her from head to toe. Ariel found Geoffrey's wife to be beautiful. She had thick chestnut colored hair that fell in waves down her back. Flipping her hair over her shoulder, Lisette addressed Ariel.

"You are a serf?"

"Aye."

Lisette's eyes roamed down to Ariel's protruding stomach then back up to her face again. "I see you are with child. I will tell you right now that will be the last child my husband will sire off of you. Henceforth, you will stay out of his bed." Geoffrey just about choked when he heard Lisette's words. Ariel smiled.

"The babe isn't Geoffrey's."

Lisette blinked. "Are you telling me you have never slept in my husband's bed?"

"Nay, I'm not, but it isn't what you are thinking. I will gladly step aside, I would not presume to take your rightful place."

Lisette smiled, taking no offense at Ariel's straight forward manner. "I'm happy with your decision, but there is one thing. If the babe is not Geoffrey's, then who is the father?"

"That is something I keep to myself. I was already pregnant when Geoffrey bought me."

This last remark caused Lisette to blink then she smiled. "Whoever the father is, have no fear for your child. It will be well provided for."

Obvioulsy not liking how the conversation progressed, Geoffrey interrupted. "Don't worry, Lisette. I already told Ariel that exact same thing. Now come, I'll show you to your solar."

Watching Lisette and Geoffrey, followed by the other women, leave the hall, Ariel smiled. Geoffrey would have his hands full with his new wife. She would not stand to be ignored. Ariel knew Lisette and she would get on famously.

Chapter 33

As she had predicted, Geoffrey came barging into the small chamber Lisette had given Ariel for her use. It had originally been intended for Lisette, but Geoffrey's wife had moved into his chamber instead. She had told Ariel, Geoffrey would just have to get used to her being in his bed, because she had no intention of leaving it.

Now, after darkness had fallen, Geoffrey stood in her chamber. He was not happy. "I thought I told you before, you will still share my bed."

"Aye, you did. Lisette decided otherwise."

"I don't care what she wants."

Ariel shook her head. "It can't be helped. What's the matter, Geoffrey? Don't you find Lisette appealing?"

Geoffrey appeared to think about his answer before he spoke. "She does appeal to me. I just would prefer you next to me."

"Why? Your wife is beautiful and could make you a happy man if you would only let her. You two seemed able to get along. I think your problem is you're afraid."

"I'm not afraid of Lisette."

Ariel smiled. "Oh, but you are. She's not exactly what you expected."

Geoffrey's brows drew together to form a scowl. "True. My father led me to believe she was a weak willed and easily controlled female."

Ariel burst out laughing. Lisette was nothing of the kind. She wondered how Lisette managed to fool Geoffrey's father into believing she was weak willed.

"Obviously your father only saw what Lisette wanted him to see. Be that as it may, she is your wife. You should at least spend tonight with her. Once you have consummated the marriage then you can decide who you would prefer in your bed."

Moving closer to Ariel, Geoffrey gathered her into his arms. "Maybe

you're right. I should share my bed with Lisette at least for tonight."
Pausing, he looked closely at her. "Is it true what you told Lisette, that you
would never try to take her place in my bed? I thought you were
comfortable with me now.

Looking Geoffrey in the eye, Ariel told him the truth. "Aye. But just
sleeping next to, being held in your arms, I feel as if I'm betraying the father
of my babe. I love him very much. I would never want to jeopardize what I
have with him."

"You never said anything about this before."

"I'm a serf, my feelings mean nothing. I'm a possession, not a person.
As long as you keep me a serf I will never be treated with any respect."

Sighing, Geoffrey kissed her forehead. "I don't know what to say. When
I bought you, I thought you could make up for what could be lacking in my
new wife. Now that Lisette is here I may have to rethink the situation."

Ariel brightened at his words. "Are you saying you'll release me?"

"I need time to get to know Lisette. At least give me until the babe is
born."

Ariel adamantly shook her head in denial. "Nay, I don't want my child
to be born a serf."

"I understand. I'll try to make my decision before your time comes."

"I know you'll make the right choice. Now go to your wife, she is
probably waiting for you."

Releasing her, Geoffrey brushed his lips across her mouth. "I will go
and leave you to your rest."

After he was gone, Ariel felt optimistic about her predicament for the
first time since arriving at Kilsmere. If she could bring Lisette over to her
side maybe Geoffrey would set her free.

* * * *

The cooking area was on the lower level of the tower along with the
storage rooms. Ariel was down in their gloomy depths preparing the
morning repast the day after Lisette's arrival. The young couple had not yet
left their bedchamber. Ariel took that as a positive sign.

Footsteps descending the stairs drew her attention away from the
cooking fire. One of Lisette's women walked into the room. Ariel groaned

to herself. It was the one who had been shocked at her presence in the hall the day before.

Lisette had brought only two women with her from her home. Their responsibilities were to care for Lisette and her belongings. The one who stood before Ariel now was the eldest of the two. The woman was quite plump and carried herself with pride. She was at that moment looking down her nose at Ariel. The woman did nothing to hide the disgust she felt for her. Choosing to ignore the older woman, Ariel turned her back on her. The woman huffed in indignation and moved across the room.

"How dare you, a lowly serf, turn your back on me? I will not tolerate any disrespect from the likes of you."

"Then I suggest you leave." Ariel didn't even bother to turn her head to look at the woman.

"Well, I never. You may have graced the lord's bed, but that does not make you any better than what you are."

"Why are you here and who are you?" Ariel sighed in exasperation.

The woman drew herself up to stand to her full height. She was still a few inches shorter than Ariel. The gown she wore was a drab brown and a white wimple completely covered her hair. She was not a great beauty and her personality did nothing to make one forget her plain face.

"I will have you know I am Lady Lisette's personal maid. I am Dame Marguerite and you should treat me with the respect I'm due. I'm here to see to my lady's meal."

"If you were to leave me alone then the meal would be finished quicker."

Dame Marguerite raised her hand to strike Ariel, but the sound of Lisette's voice stopped her before she could follow through. At the sight of her lady stepping down the last remaining steps, she lowered her arm and smiled.

"What are you doing down here, my lady?"

"I was about to ask that of you," said Lisette.

"I came to make sure this serf prepared your meal to your liking."

With a wave of her hand, Lisette dismissed the older woman. "You may leave and if I ever see you try to strike Ariel again you will be sorry. Is that understood?"

"Aye, my lady." With her face flaming, Dame Marguerite disappeared up the stairs.

Lisette moved to stand next to Ariel and smiled at her. "I apologize. I had no idea she would come down here to pester you. She sometimes takes her duties too seriously."

"I'm a serf. She can treat me any way she deems fit."

"But you aren't a serf, are you?"

Ariel moved away from the fire and went over to the work table that stood in the center of the room. Rolling her sleeves up past her elbows, she began kneading the huge mound of dough on the table's surface, Lisette followed her.

"It's all right, Geoffrey told me about you. He thinks you're a warrior."

Ariel stiffened. "And what if I am?"

"I have never met a woman warrior before. Truth be told, I at times wished I could wield a sword instead of a needle."

Ariel pulled the dough into sections and busily formed it into loaves. "I too felt that way, especially after my mother's death. Father was so depressed at her passing. I had to take on his duties. I took up the sword to help protect my home."

"Could you teach me?"

Ariel looked at Lisette. She could see the girl was serious by the total lack of humor on her face. "What would your husband say?"

With a smile, Lisette moved closer to her. "He doesn't have to know. I could find a place not too far from the castle walls where we could go. No one would have to see us."

Shaking her head, Ariel continued to shape the bread. "That's not possible."

"Of course it is, as long as we don't draw attention to ourselves."

Ariel shook her head once more. "You don't understand. I have work to do in the hall. My duties take most of the day to complete. Besides, Geoffrey does not allow me to leave the hall."

Shock registered on Lisette's face. "Why would Geoffrey keep you locked indoors?"

"I think he's afraid I will try to run or someone from the outside world would recognize me."

Lisette frowned in concentration. "I will have to speak to Geoffrey about allowing you more freedom. For now I will have, Elaine, my other woman, take over the cooking. I brought her with me to fulfill that task anyway. I figured Geoffrey would not possess a decent cook. Finish baking the bread and then come to my solar. I will give you some other duties."

Ariel found herself speechless as she stared at Lisette's retreating back. Geoffrey's wife was nothing like she had expected. Ariel wondered how Lisette would get Geoffrey to allow her outside the castle walls.

Chapter 34

The solar was awash in bright sunlight causing Ariel to blink at the glare. When her eyes grew accustomed she stepped into the room. Lisette sat near the windows working intently at an embroidery frame. Her needle flashed expertly through the material. Ariel watched Lisette perform her woman's work. She was totally useless when it came to stitching. Her mother had tried to teach her how to wield a needle, but Ariel was never very interested in learning how to do it properly. Eventually her mother had given up and let her follow her father about Elmstead. She had turned out to be a quick learner when it came to running the land.

Sensing Ariel's presence, Lisette's hands stilled and she beckoned her closer. "Did Elaine come to relieve you?"

"Aye. She seemed most eager to begin her work."

Lisette laughed. "She enjoys cooking for a large amount of people. She is very talented. My father was not too happy to give her up, but I finally won her from him. Elaine wanted to come to England, which helped to win my father over to my side."

Ariel chuckled. "Well, she will be greatly appreciated here. I may know how to cook, but my talents in that area are very limited."

"I'm glad all has worked out then. Now, we must find something else for you to do. I didn't want you working over a hot fire all day in your condition. How are your stitches?"

Ariel flushed and shook her head. "I'm afraid I have no great skill when it comes to a needle and thread."

"All right, let me think a moment." Lisette paused. Ariel watched a frown crease her forehead in concentration. A few minutes later, Lisette's face brightened.

"Do you know anything of healing?"

"Very little." All Ariel had learned was from Osbern. He had taught her how to take care of minor wounds. He had told her if she could learn to inflict the wounds, she could learn how to heal them. Even now, with all the time that had gone by, Ariel still mourned the loss of Osbern. Just thinking of him caused her pain.

Ariel managed to pull herself out of her past as Lisette grabbed her hands and squeezed them in hers. "This is perfect. I should have thought of this before."

Confused, Ariel looked at Lisette in askance. "What will be perfect?"

"My mother is a healer. She taught me all she knows. I will teach you. That will be our excuse to leave the castle walls. We will have to go out into the forest and gather the plants we will need."

Ariel doubted it would be that easy. "You still have to talk to Geoffrey. Even if he does allow me to leave the hall he may send one of his men to watch over me."

Lisette smiled knowingly. "I know how to handle Geoffrey. As for the guard, I will simply tell him a woman in your condition could not run very far on foot."

Lisette did have a point. Even if Geoffrey granted Ariel her freedom there was no way she could make it back to Elmstead alone. She would never endanger her unborn child by taking such a risk, but there was still something Lisette had not thought of.

"Your plan is logical enough, it could work, but there is one problem."

"What is that?"

"Just what do you expect us to practice with? There is no way we could obtain two swords without them being missed."

Frowning once more Lisette looked at Ariel. She then laughed. "I'm afraid I tend to get carried away with myself once in awhile. My mother is always telling me I rush into something without thinking out every detail. You are quite right. I will obtain the swords, it may take a couple of days, but I will get them."

Knowing Lisette to be a resourceful woman, Ariel did not doubt she would follow through with her promise. "However you get them, be careful. Men don't like women sticking their noses into their work. I know from first hand experience."

"Have no fear, I have my ways. I always get what I want, even with Geoffrey."

Ariel could not help but laugh, something she had not been able to do much of before Lisette arrived. She seemed to be the type of woman who knew how to look out for herself. Ariel was positive she would present her with two swords on the morrow.

* * * *

The following morning Geoffrey came to her chamber. Ariel had just finished dressing when the door opened to admit him. He said nothing at first. He stared at her with his hands clasped behind his back. After a few moments of being under Geoffrey's scrutiny, Ariel couldn't take anymore.

"Is there something you want?"

"Nay, not really."

"Then why are you looking at me like that?"

Geoffrey paced the room a couple of times then stopped directly in front of her. "Lisette has decided to take you under her wing and teach you the skills of a healer. She even went so far as to ask me to free you. I refused to remove the collar, but I agreed to her teaching you. There is one problem though. It seems she would need to take you out to the surrounding countryside to collect certain plants. She assured me you would not run, and that one of my men breathing down your neck would not help the learning process. Before I grant my permission, I need to feel I can trust you not to try to flee."

Ariel could not help but smile. During the night she had doubted Lisette's ability to sway Geoffrey to her way of thinking. It looked as if she had succeeded. It was too bad she could not convince him to take the damned collar off.

Looking Geoffrey straight in his dark eyes, Ariel did what she needed to. "All I have to give is my word. I promise not to flee. The risk would be too great for my babe." To add emphasis to her statement, Ariel laid a protective hand on her rounded belly.

Geoffrey nodded. "Then I will inform Lisette of my decision." He turned to leave only to pause at the door and look over his shoulder at Ariel.

"Just so you know, you were right. Lisette is nothing at all what I had expected. You don't need to worry about me taking you to my bed again. I've found my wife gives me all I need." With that said he walked out of the room and quietly closed the door behind him.

Feeling her spirits soar, Ariel spun around the room. Her life was definitely going for the better. With Lisette's coming she had been given more freedom than she had before, and she need no longer worry about how Geoffrey felt about her when she only thought of him as a friend. And that was what Geoffrey had become. He still owned her, but he had always treated her with respect. She could not hate him for that. All her hate was directed at one man—Theodoric. If he crossed her path again he would pay for his underhanded dealings with her.

* * * *

A very excited Lisette awaited Ariel in her solar. It was apparent Geoffrey had spoken to her and had given his permission. Lisette already had a basket in her hand. She rushed up to Ariel and grabbed her hand. Before she could speak, Lisette pulled her into a small storage room just off of the solar.

"Come here, Ariel. I need help getting these out of the castle."

Going over to a chest that sat up against the wall, she pulled out two swords. They were unlike any Ariel had seen before. The blades had intricate scrollwork running up and down their length. The pommels were gold with rubies and diamonds set into them. The grips were wrapped in white leather. Ariel could only stare at the beauty of them.

"Well, what do you think? Will they serve our purposes?"

Ariel gulped. "Aye. Wherever did you get these?"

"I brought these with me from home. I planned to give them as a gift to Geoffrey, but I think I will keep them for myself instead."

"Why two swords?"

Lisette giggled. "The blacksmith had made these as a matching set. I just could not bear to separate them. They are quite breathtaking, are they not?"

That was an understatement in Ariel's opinion. "Aye, but they are too fine for what we would use them for."

"But these are all I have. Take one," Lisette urged. "We can strap them to our backs under our cloaks. There are matching scabbards as well."

Hesitantly, Ariel took a sword from Lisette. It felt good to have the solid weight of a sword resting in the palm of her hand again. Too much time had passed since she held a sword. She had missed that part of her old life. Backing away from Lisette, Ariel tested out the balance of the sword by slicing the air before her. Looking up she found Lisette watching her.

"I can see you do know what you are about with that."

Unthinkingly, Ariel said, "I should. I'm a knight." She didn't realize what she had revealed until she heard Lisette's sharp intake of breath.

"Are you serious?"

Knowing she wouldn't be able to talk her way out of what she had said, Ariel nodded. "Aye."

"How can this be? You're a woman. No man would train a female let alone knight her."

"I passed myself off as a boy. I already knew how to wield a sword, so it was easy to make everyone believe I was male."

"From what I heard Saxons do not have knights."

"That's true, we don't. I was knighted by a Norman."

Taking a scabbard out of Lisette's hand, Ariel slid her sword into it and slung is over her back. She already said too much. She hadn't even told Geoffrey that much about her past life. Ariel felt so comfortable around Lisette she had let her guard down.

Knowing Ariel wouldn't talk about that subject any further Lisette passed her a cloak and placed a basket over her arm. With both swords adequately concealed she led Ariel out of the solar.

Dame Marguerite was in the hall and sneered at Ariel as she walked by. Obviously she still held her in contempt. Ariel chose to ignore the other woman and followed Lisette down the stairs.

Crossing the yard to the castle gates proved uneventful. When the gates loomed before them, Ariel held her breath. After months of being forced to remain inside, doubt assailed her. It was hard to believe Geoffrey would allow even this small amount of freedom, but their passage through the gate didn't meet with any hindrance. Ariel's breath left her lungs in a whoosh once the gates were safely behind them.

Lisette looked back at the castle then set out at a steady pace toward the forest. Ariel's step lightened the farther away from the castle she got. Taking a deep breath of fresh air, she plunged into the woods behind Lisette. They didn't have to travel very far before they came to a small clearing. It was a perfect spot, not too far from the castle, but the trees offered sufficient cover to hide their activities.

Taking off the cloak from around her shoulders, Ariel drew her sword. Lisette followed suit. Swinging the sword, Ariel stretched out her muscles. She would more than likely feel today's exercise in the form of aching muscles on the morrow. Looking at Lisette who valiantly tried to duplicate her moves, Ariel watched her struggle to lift the sword before her. Ariel took a small measure of comfort in knowing Lisette would be in worse shape than she. Moving to the center of the clearing, Ariel signaled Lisette to follow.

"We won't do too much today. For the little we do now will leave your muscles shrieking in protest tomorrow."

Lisette nodded. "I agree. Besides, I think we should spend half the time teaching you to be a healer. If Geoffrey should question you on your progress, you should be able to tell him about some of the plants and their uses."

Ariel agreed with her. "You're right. It wouldn't do to have Geoffrey become suspicious. Our outings would be stopped."

Taking up a stance, Ariel held her sword before her. "Today I will show you some moves that will help strengthen your arms and shoulders."

Nodding her head, Lisette moved to stand near Ariel and took up the same position. And so began Lisette's education in sword play and Ariel's in herb lore.

Chapter 35

Days passed and Ariel found Lisette to be a true friend. She made her life more bearable. Having the excuse of teaching Lisette how to handle a sword, a familiar routine had been established once more. Even though six months gone, what little Ariel could do gave her a sense of normalcy.

Lisette turned out to be an apt pupil. She would not be able to progress as far as Ariel, but she would be able to defend herself. As for Ariel becoming a healer, she had already learned enough to be considered passable.

Each day started the same. Ariel would wake up, dress and go to Lisette's solar. There, she would help Lisette dress and then they would both go to the hall to break their fast. When Geoffrey finished his meal and left the donjon, Lisette and Ariel would return to the solar and collect the swords. Shortly after that they would go to the clearing to practice. Today was no exception to that routine.

The day was warm and bright. With each stroke of their swords the sun flashed reflectively off the blades. The jewels in the pommels sparkled, colored lights mixing with the myriad collection of flowers that were scattered throughout the clearing. The sounds of their clashing swords mingled with the songs the birds in the surrounding trees made.

When the sun moved to shine directly above them, Ariel held up a hand bringing a halt to their exercise. Lisette lowered her sword so the tip of the blade rested on the ground. She stood puffing while giving Ariel a stare.

"How is it that at the end of our lessons you are hardly winded? Where as I huff and puff like a bellows. You are six months pregnant and you still could out last me."

Ariel smiled reassuringly at Lisette. "It takes time. You have only been at this for a month. Six months from now you'll be able to keep up with me."

"Something to look forward to. At least my muscles don't ache at the end of each day as they did in the beginning. I thought the pain alone would kill me."

Smiling, Ariel shook her head. "Hardly. You have grown stronger. I am surprised Geoffrey hasn't noticed the difference. Your body has become stronger."

Lisette giggled. "Geoffrey is more interested in another part of my body, one that I don't use for sword practice."

The girls' laughter filled the air, echoing among the trees. Before the sound of their mirth fell away to nothingness, four men stepped out of the trees and into the clearing. Slowly they moved to surround Ariel and Lisette.

Letting her eyes quickly fall on each man, Ariel realized they were Saxon. They had to be some of the men who had taken to living in the woods after the Normans had come to England. Their long hair hung in scraggly, greasy sections. Their clothes were rough homespun, dirty and torn. From the looks on their faces, Ariel guessed the men would not be too friendly. Each man carried either a battle axe or a sword. The latter probably coming from the Norman victims they had robbed.

Edging closer to Lisette, Ariel looked at her briefly. She hoped Lisette wouldn't try anything that could get her hurt. She had raised her sword, making Ariel afraid that Lisette intended to use it against their attackers. She was not ready to confront an enemy with killing on his mind.

The men moved in closer, drawing the circle tighter around the two women. The one closest to Ariel smiled wickedly at her. His teeth were black and the stench of his breath wafted over her.

"What do we have here?"

"Looks like a couple of lovelies. They would make good sport, even that one with the child in her belly."

The man who stood closest to Lisette was the one who had spoken last. Both he and his companion had spoken in English. Ariel was glad Lisette only spoke French. It was better she remained oblivious to what was being said.

When the man who spoke last poked at Lisette with the tip of his sword, Ariel knocked the blade away with her own. The one with the foul breath chuckled. "It looks as if this one will give us a fight. She holds a sword well enough, but will she be able to wield it with any kind of skill is the question."

That made the three other men laugh. They obviously were over confident, taking their success for granted. Ariel knew they really didn't expect any kind of resistance from two lone women. They would be in for a big surprise. Nothing would turn out the way they thought it would.

When the sword poked at Lisette once more, Ariel's reaction was automatic. Pushing Lisette out of the way, she moved to match her sword against the man. She put her full strength behind the blow and her opponent's sword flew out of his hands. A look of utter surprise crossed his features before he turned to retrieve his weapon. The others' mood of light banter changed to aggression after that.

With a growl of rage, the first man who had spoken lunged at Ariel. Making sure Lisette stayed behind her, she let her training take over.

The man with the bad teeth raised his battle axe above his head. Ariel blocked the blow and made one of her own, catching the man across the ribs. Her slice cut through his clothes, causing blood to well. He bellowed in pain. After that everything became a blur.

When Ariel finally lowered her sword, there were three bodies on the ground before her and one man was running back into the woods. Breathing heavily from her exertion, she realized Lisette was no longer standing behind her. Quickly turning around, Ariel looked for Lisette only to come face to face with Geoffrey. Lisette stood a few feet away.

The utter silence that had fallen in the clearing became ominous. At least to Ariel it did. Here she stood with a bloody sword in her hand facing the man who owned her. She had no idea what Geoffrey would do to her. Before he could act against her, she let the sword fall out of her grasp so it landed on the ground at her feet. She could do nothing about the blood splattered on her hands and clothes. Pulling herself up to her full height, Ariel watched Geoffrey bend down and pick up the discarded sword.

"Who are you, Ariel?"

Before she could answer, Lisette spoke to her husband. "She's a knight."

Geoffrey roughly ran his fingers through his hair making it stick out in places. "How can you be a knight?"

Ariel held up her hand to silence Lisette before she could answer for her. Her friend closed her mouth and nodded her head in agreement. "Easy,

I passed myself off as a boy and a Norman finished my training. In the end, he knighted me."

"Your training could not have lasted very long. We have only been here since this past October."

Ariel shrugged her shoulders noncommittally. "I know that, I fought at Hastings. I was part of King Harold's house carls."

In shock, Geoffrey sucked a breath in through his clenched teeth. "That scar on your shoulder, did you get it at Hastings?"

"Aye."

"And the knight, the one who knighted you, who was he?"

Ariel was not ready to divulge that information just yet. "His name is of no importance to you. Now, if you do not mind, I'm going back to the castle to clean up."

Brushing past Geoffrey, Ariel started to walk out of the clearing. She had only taken a few steps before Geoffrey thought to stop her. "Is he the father of your child?"

Without slowing her steps, Ariel answered. "Aye, he is."

* * * *

Slipping through the castle gates without drawing attention to herself proved easy enough. Nobody ever noticed a serf. Ariel gained the donjon entrance and quickly climbed the stairs. She literally ran into the peddler who had been waiting in the hall.

Keeping her head down while making excuses for herself, Ariel tried to step around the man. He didn't allow it. He kept his hands around her upper arms.

"Are you all right? You have blood all over you."

Still not looking at the man, Ariel shook her head in denial. "Aye. It's somebody else's, not mine."

Geoffrey bounded up the stairs. The peddler quickly released her, allowing Ariel to continue on her way. Geoffrey halted her once more. "Ariel, please stop."

Knowing Geoffrey would follow her, Ariel made no move to walk away from the peddler. Steeling herself for a confrontation, she took a deep breath and turned to face Geoffrey.

"I need to change."

"Give me a moment. I want you to keep this." He carried a sword, the one she had used during Lisette's training. Stepping forward, he held it out to her with the pommel pointed in her direction. Ariel couldn't bring herself to take it.

"I'm a serf. Weapons are forbidden to me."

Geoffrey shook his head and offered her the sword again. "Take it. You kept Lisette from coming to any harm when those men attacked. You handle a sword better than I. Ariel, you're a knight, a knight needs a sword."

With a shaking hand, Ariel accepted the sword. Clasping the cold metal to her chest, she made a hasty retreat to her chamber. She didn't want Geoffrey to see the tears that could no longer be held back.

Chapter 36

The peddler stayed at Kilsmere only long enough for the Lady Lisette to make a purchase. He managed to get one more look at Geoffrey de la Roche's serf and then slipped out the castle gates. He could not tarry. London was his destination and he had many days of travel before he reached that great city.

He rode well into the night, only stopping long enough to rest his horse and eat. He continued the grueling pace until London could be seen in the distance. Pulling over to the side of the road, he paused only long enough to change his travel stained tunic and pull on his chain mail. His sword followed. Once it hung at his hip, he hopped into his saddle and rode the final distance to London.

* * * *

London was a hot and foul smelling place during the high summer months. Broc felt like he had been in the city for an eternity, but he couldn't bring himself to go back to Elmstead. Too many memories were there, memories of Ariel. They were too much to bear.

William's tower neared completion and like every other day, the king was there watching over the construction. Broc headed in the direction of the tower hoping William could provide some distraction, anything to keep his mind off Ariel. All these months and nothing could be found of her. The not knowing constantly ate at him.

William was there. He stood among the workmen, pointing out any faults he could find. Moving closer, Broc held back a chuckle. William's presence had all the workers on their toes. When the king finished speaking to the foreman, Broc went and stood beside him.

"Have you finished harassing the workers?"

William laughed and turned to look at Broc. "What is this? No child attached to you? I rarely see you without your son in your arms."

"He's sleeping and Lily is watching over him." Even though William had exaggerated a bit, he was right. Colwyn had become a big part of his life now. With Ariel gone, his son filled some of the gap his mother's disappearance had made.

Knowing what was going through Broc's mind, William squeezed his friend's shoulder. "I know. Something will happen soon."

"It has been too long."

"Do not give up hope. She will be found."

The sound of a horse's hooves pounding into the yard drew their attention. Seeing the king, the knight dismounted and made his way to William. Bowing to the king, the man waited for William to acknowledge his presence.

"Sir Thomas, you have returned. Do you have anything to tell us?"

Quickly glancing at Broc, Thomas nodded. "Aye I do, sire. I think I may have found the girl."

"Where?" Broc all but shouted that one word, drawing the attention of the workers nearest to them.

William squeezed Broc's shoulder. "Calm down, Broc. Let the poor man tell us what he has found. Continue, Sir Thomas."

The knight gave a nod of his head and then continued. "Far to the north there is a new castle called Kilsmere. It's owned by a Geoffrey de la Roche."

"I know of him. He's a second son of one of my barons."

"He has a serf who matches the girl's description. When I arrived she came into the hall with blood on her clothes and hands. Geoffrey de la Roche followed her. He gave her a sword and called her a knight. Apparently she saved his wife from some Saxons who had attacked her and the serf. He made her take the sword."

Broc became very still. "Did you hear what name the serf was called by?"

"Aye, I did. He called her Ariel."

Broc closed his eyes, sending up a silent prayer of thanks. They had found her. He would go to Kilsmere and take back what was his. God help Geoffrey de la Roche if he had harmed Ariel in any way.

* * * *

The lessons continued, only now Geoffrey took an active part in them. They still used the clearing as their practice field, having no fear that their attackers would return. Ariel had dispatched most of them and the one remaining man would be a fool to return. A week had gone by and no trace of the man could be found.

Word spread quickly throughout Kilsmere of Ariel's victory over the Saxon men. Since coming to live with Geoffrey, she had been treated with little to no respect, now that had changed. The guards went out of their way to talk to her. They no longer leered at her, making her feel like a piece of meat they wished to devour. Even Dame Marguerite had grudgingly accepted Ariel's part in Lisette's life.

The practice that took place this day was a bit of a surprise to Ariel. Before she and Lisette could begin Geoffrey went to stand between them. "It's time I tested my skill against Ariel's abilities. I have to know if she is really better at handling a sword."

Ariel chuckled. "If I should be the better?"

"I will remove the collar from around your neck."

Ariel could tell Geoffrey meant every word he said. She couldn't stop herself from making sure she had heard him right. "Truly? If I disarm you, I will no longer be a serf."

"Aye, you should never have been one in the first place. But be prepared, I will not make it easy on you. I really don't wish to see you leave Kilsmere."

"Just because I would leave Kilsmere does not mean I would never return. I have come to think of you both as friends."

Ariel's words sobered Geoffrey from his bantering mood. "Even after the way I treated you?"

Looking at Lisette, Ariel tried to see whether she was bothered by what Geoffrey had asked. Lisette smiled reassuringly at her. "I consider myself lucky Theodoric sold me to you. Another owner could have treated me much worse. Sharing your bed for a short time was far from being a hardship. I expect Theodoric thought you would use me terribly."

"I'm glad you can think of me on such friendly terms."

Smiling, Ariel raised her sword. "Enough talking. Let's get down to business here. You also be prepared, I will not make it easy for you either."

With Lisette watching on the side lines, Geoffrey and Ariel crossed swords. The clearing filled with the ringing as their blades met. For the first time in months, Ariel allowed herself to be what she truly was, a knight who happened to be a lady.

Laughing, Ariel pushed Geoffrey across the clearing with blows of her sword. True to her word, she gave it her all. Once she figured she had proven herself, she made her move to disarm Geoffrey, but at the last moment he dropped his sword. He appeared to be staring at something just over her shoulder. Before she could turn around to see what had caught Geoffrey's attention, Ariel heard a deep voice call to her. One she had thought at one time to never hear again.

"Ariel, is it really you?"

Turning in the direction the voice came from, Ariel found Broc standing a foot away from her and he wasn't alone. William was there, along with the peddler. But from the appearance of the "peddler", Ariel realized he really was a knight.

Seeing how Broc's eyes stared at her protruding stomach, Ariel placed her hand on it. Her simple movement caused fury to kindle in the golden eyes that stared at her. Ariel opened her mouth to speak, but Broc's eyes had moved to Geoffrey.

"Are you Geoffrey de la Roche?"

"Aye."

Broc's fist came up and slammed into Geoffrey's jaw. Not expecting it, Geoffrey lost his balance and fell to the ground. Broc stepped closer, ready to hit the downed man again. Ariel moved to stand over Geoffrey.

"Stop it, Broc! There's no reason for you to hit Geoffrey."

Broc's eyes seemed to burn right through her. "Really? I have every reason. Look at you. The collar is bad enough, but to see you carrying his child makes it even worse."

Ariel was shocked that Broc would think the baby wasn't his. "You think the child is Geoffrey's?"

"Are you telling me he never took you to his bed?"

Ariel hesitated in answering him. If she lied to Broc it could cause further problems down the road. It was best to get it all out and in the open.

"Aye, he did."

"Did he force you?" Broc growled.

"Nay."

Broc's face lost all traces of emotion. He turned and started to walk away from Ariel. This was not working out the way she had thought. He had to understand.

"Broc, wait. I can explain."

Without stopping, Broc said, "You do not need to explain. It's very clear to me, you allowed another man to take you."

Realizing Broc had no intention of listening to her Ariel stuck out her sword and tripped Broc. When he fell Ariel moved so she could sit on his chest.

"You will listen to what I have to say. Aye, I did sleep with another man, but not in the way you think. Besides, a serf has no rights. He wanted me there. I had to do what he wanted. As for giving myself to him, I was already pregnant with your child when Geoffrey bought me. This babe was all I had left of you. I wouldn't have done anything to harm it."

Broc's expression never changed. "Are you through? I would like to get off the ground now."

A wave of pain washed over Ariel. He wouldn't listen to her. "Did you not hear what I just said to you?"

"Aye, it changes nothing. Now get off."

Devoid of all feeling, Ariel slipped off of Broc. As she climbed to her feet, Broc stood up and retrieved his horse from William. Mounting, he left the clearing.

When Ariel could no longer see Broc, she allowed herself to look at the king. He had left his horse with the knight and came to her side. Geoffrey and Lisette had also moved closer to her. Ariel just barely managed to pull herself together.

William looked Ariel up and down then glared at Geoffrey. "You have not done well by this, Geoffrey de la Roche. Give me the key to this collar. I can no longer stand seeing it around her neck."

Reaching into the pouch that hung at his belt, Geoffrey pulled out the key and handed it to William. "I wish to seek your forgiveness, sire. I knew nothing of Ariel's past and Theodoric didn't inform me. I only wished to keep her at Kilsmere."

Removing the collar, William disgustedly threw it to the ground. His eyes narrowed at the mark the collar had left around Ariel's neck. "The woman next to you must be your wife. Was she not good enough for you?"

"I bought Ariel before Lisette came to England. I have kept only to her. Concern for Ariel made me hesitate in removing the collar. I was afraid if I did she would try to make it to her home alone. With her this far gone I planned to release her. She's smart enough not to endanger her child."

William nodded. "So, Colwyn is to have a brother or a sister I see."

"How is my son?" Both Geoffrey and Lisette turned shocked looks in Ariel's direction.

Smiling, William answered. "He is fine, my lady. Broc has kept his son at his side since your disappearance. The boy even sleeps in the same bed as he."

Ariel closed her eyes on the tears that welled to the surface. "I have missed him so. He probably won't remember me. I've been gone too long."

Seeing the tears in her eyes, William pulled Ariel close to him and held her in his arms. "He will quickly learn you are his mother. In time this will only be a memory. Broc will come around."

"And if he doesn't?"

"Do not fret, I will handle Broc. Everything will be put to rights. I will personally see it comes about."

Chapter 37

Broc sat in the donjon in the hall drinking a tankard of ale. Ariel didn't seek him out. She needed the solitude of her chamber to think out what she would do about him.

The brightness of the day turned into the shadows of evening and Ariel stayed in her chamber. When the evening meal came and Ariel still didn't come out, Lisette went to her. At her knock, Ariel bid her enter.

"Ariel, you can't stay in this chamber indefinitely. You will have to face Broc at some point."

Ariel sighed. "I know. I just don't have the energy to fight with him today."

Lisette slipped onto the bed beside her. She put her arm around Ariel's shoulders. "You have to eat. Think of your baby."

Smiling weakly, Ariel agreed. "I know. Could I have some food brought here?"

"Nay. If you hide in here, Broc will think he's right. That you did something you are ashamed of. You're stronger than that and you will not be alone. Geoffrey and I will be there, along with the king. He has been scowling at Broc. He believes you."

Knowing Lisette had made a valid point, Ariel stood up and brushed at her gown. "I guess I do need to show him he has not brought me low. Lead on."

Linking her arm through Ariel's, Lisette led her out of the chamber and into the hall. She did not stop until they reached the head table. All conversation ceased. There were two empty seats. Lisette took the one beside Geoffrey, leaving the chair between William and Broc for Ariel. Squaring her shoulders, Ariel went and sat down. Ignoring Broc, she smiled at William as he filled a trencher of food for her.

"Here you go my, my lady. I'm pleased you decided to join us."

"Lisette has a way of changing one's mind."

William glanced over at Geoffrey's wife. "You like the Lady Lisette?"

"Aye. I've come to think of both Geoffrey and Lisette as friends."

"I bet you do," Broc said condescendingly.

Choosing to ignore him, Ariel began to eat her meal, but Broc did not let her get away that easily.

"Come on, Ariel. He means more to you than a friend. He had you, for Christ sake."

Ariel spoke each word carefully. "You can believe what you will. I'm not in the mood to argue with you."

"What if I am in the mood? Maybe I'm in the mood to take you to bed. You seem not to mind whose bed it is you jump into."

Ariel stared at her food while she tried to hold her temper in check. She would not give Broc the satisfaction of seeing her succumb to anger.

"What, nothing to say? If I treat you like a serf, would you accept my offer?"

William slammed his fist on the table. "Enough, Broc. Ariel deserves better from you. I thought you loved her. This is no way to treat your future wife."

Broc snorted rudely. "Who says I will take her to wife now. What I felt for Ariel before, she killed when she went to another man's bed." Pushing back his chair, Broc nodded to William and then stomped out of the hall.

* * * *

The remainder of the night Ariel spent tossing and turning on her bed. William had tried to reassure her Broc would eventually come around. He said once back in London everything would be taken care of. They would be leaving early the next day. Ariel doubted Broc would be in a more agreeable mood anytime soon, no matter where he happened to be.

Still tired from lack of sleep, Ariel gathered up her pitifully few belongings and went to the hall. William was there with Geoffrey and Lisette, but Broc was nowhere to be seen, which pleased her. If he had been present she more than likely would have tried to take his head off, metaphorically speaking.

Seeing the sword slung over Ariel's shoulder, William smiled. "I see my

Lady Knight has her sword."

Giving a noncommittal shrug, Ariel joined them. "I don't look much like a knight with my stomach sticking out before me." The others laughed at her quip.

Broc stepped into the hall at that moment. "How nice. I'm sorry to break up this little tête-à-tête, but the horses are ready and I would like to leave."

With an apologetic look, Ariel bid Geoffrey and Lisette farewell. Kissing Lisette's cheek, she told them to come to Elmstead and visit her when they had the opportunity to do so. Broc cleared his throat in an effort to hurry her along. Lisette glared at him.

"We would love to come. When your time of lying-in is near I will make sure to be at Elmstead."

"I would like that."

Ariel moved to Geoffrey next. Placing her hands on his shoulders, she reached up and kissed him on his cheek. "You may come to Elmstead as well."

Before Geoffrey could answer, Broc grabbed Ariel by the arm and herded her down the stairs. He didn't stop until he had her mounted atop a horse and her belongings strapped behind her.

William entered the yard a minute later. Seeing Broc and Ariel already mounted, he jumped onto his horse's back. He could only shake his head at Broc's behavior.

* * * *

By the end of their first day of travel, Ariel was so tired she barely could get off her horse. Thanks to William who helped her to dismount, her legs didn't collapse under her. Tsking, he led her to a fallen log and gently helped her to sit down. He then moved to set up a fire while Broc took care of the horses. Ariel curled her lip at his back. He obviously didn't care she tired faster than he and William. With each league traveled, Ariel began to feel something akin to hatred for Broc. She had also come to a decision. If he wouldn't treat her civilly, why should she act any different around him?

All three ate in relative silence, only speaking when they wanted something passed to them. When the meal finished, they lay down around the fire and fell asleep. The coming dawn they set out once more.

The days flew by with Broc never once slowing their pace. He didn't seem to notice Ariel barely made it through her meals without nodding off to sleep, but William did. By the end of their journey, he was sending just as many scathing looks in Broc's direction as Ariel did.

Reaching the city gates, William left Ariel's side and rode past Broc. He soon disappeared leaving her and her unwanted companion to make their own way through the city. Looking neither to the right nor left, Ariel blindly followed Broc through the busy city streets.

At the fort they were met by Sir Thomas. He had left Kilsmere the evening before their departure. William, who had decided his presence had not been needed, had given him leave to return to London. Helping Ariel dismount, Sir Thomas informed them the king awaited them in the hall.

Taking her belongings off her horse, Ariel pushed past Broc and walked into the hall. She heard Broc's heavy tread behind her. William met them at the entrance.

"There have been two chambers readied for you. I'll give you a half an hour to change and refresh yourselves then come to my chambers together."

Before either Ariel or Broc could voice any protest, William led them to their chambers. Ariel was ushered into her chamber first. Once she crossed the threshold the door firmly shut behind her.

Moving over to the bed she found a gown spread out on top of it. She next noticed the steaming bowl of water that sat on a table beside the bed. Cloths were piled neatly beside it. Ariel would have preferred a bath, but she would make do with the water she had been given.

Throwing her belongings on the bed, Ariel stripped out of her travel stained gown. She dipped a cloth into the warm water and quickly ran it over her body. She felt a little better now that some of the dirt had been sponged away.

Her hair now reached past her shoulders once again. She gathered it together and pulled it back with a piece of leather so it hung in a tail down her back. It needed washing, but it would have to wait.

The gown was made of light weight wool, dyed a pale yellow, which complimented Ariel's fair coloring. It was of much finer quality than the gown she had been given to wear at Kilsmere.

Slipping the gown over her head, Ariel found the size to be a perfect fit. Right down to the extra material that allowed for her expanding girth. After a check to make sure she was presentable for her interview with the king, she left the chamber and went to see William.

She knocked on the door and stepped through it. William wasn't alone. Much to her surprise Ariel saw a priest standing next to William. She turned to look questioningly at the king. He was up to something. Something Ariel was sure both she and Broc would not particularly like.

Moments later Broc entered the chamber. Seeing the tableau of William standing next to a priest with Ariel standing before them, it didn't take him long to figure out what the king had in mind. Wanting no part of it, Broc spun on his heel to leave, William stopped him before he could reach the door.

"I did not give you permission to leave."

Broc stopped in mid-stride. "Don't do this to me. If you are my friend, you will not make me go through with this."

William didn't relent. "I'm sorry. I cannot allow you to walk away from this. You already have one child who is illegitimate. This time you are able to prevent another from being labeled a bastard."

Broc whipped around to face William. "This child is not mine! I will not claim another man's child as my own."

Sighing, William turned to Ariel. "How far along are you?"

Not looking at Broc, she answered the king. "I am six months gone."

"You were a month gone when you were taken?"

"Aye, sire."

Broc interrupted. "She could be lying. If the child does not come in four months, she will only say she is late while all along that was really when the child was due."

William's face grew stern with impatience. "Are you saying before coming to London to annul your marriage you didn't in any way become intimate with Ariel?"

Broc flushed. "Aye...aye, I did. But that doesn't mean much. It was only one night."

Ariel shook her head in disbelief then put Broc in his place. "It only took one time for me to become pregnant with Colwyn. How do you explain that?"

Watching Broc open and close his mouth like a gasping fish, Ariel knew she had him backed into a corner. She could only hope he changed his mind about who fathered her child.

Chapter 38

"Be that as it may, I want this marriage to take place and I will do everything to see it done." William ended the discussion before it could progress any further.

Knowing there would be no swaying William from this course of action, Broc moved to Ariel's side. The priest started the ceremony that would bind them together for life.

The vows were exchanged with neither participant looking at the other. There was no love shining in their eyes as the words were said over them. What should have been a joyous occasion was nothing more than a task set before them to be completed and endured.

At the conclusion of the ceremony, Ariel received a quick peck on the cheek and Broc's unicorn ring on her finger to seal their vows. His services no longer needed, the priest bowed to William and quietly left the room. Broc and Ariel tried their hardest to ignore each other.

Unable to bear another minute of William's smug looks, Broc spoke to his friend. "If you have gotten all the enjoyment you can from this charade you concocted, I wish to leave now."

"You may go." Broc stalked to the door, but William delayed his departure. "There is one more thing. Don't try to seek an annulment, I will not allow it this time. I will brook no defiance from you concerning this matter."

Broc bowed to William. "As you command, sire. Just because I'm stuck with this marriage, it doesn't mean it will ever be consummated." He left, slamming the door behind him.

* * * *

Ariel kept her eyes averted away from William. She focused intently on the floor, but when an arm came around her shoulders she looked up to find the king standing beside her. She gave him a weak smile.

"I thank you for what you tried to do for me. I just don't think Broc will."

William flashed a smile. "He'll come around, Ariel. He loves you. Just give him time to figure that out and all will be well."

"I hope you're right. But I have a feeling it will be a very long time before Broc gets over this."

The king didn't try to change her prediction on that particular matter. "Is there anything I can do for you?"

"Aye, there is. First I would like to see my son and second, I would be in your debt if you could arrange an escort to take me back to Elmstead. I need to be with my father right now."

William seemed to understand because he quickly agreed to her requests. "Of course. I sent word to your father when we found you before leaving for Kilsmere. He stayed at Elmstead in the hopes you would be able to find your way home on your own."

"If I had been able to that is exactly what I would have done."

"The escort will be ready whenever you decide to leave."

"Thank you, sire. I would like to leave for Elmstead tomorrow. You can tell Broc, I'm sure you will see him before I do."

Ariel curtsied and walked out the door. She now had a husband who hated her. At least she still had Colwyn and her father. They would always be there for her.

* * * *

The reunion with Lily and Colwyn ended up being a tearful one. Ariel could not believe how much her son had grown during her absence. He was no longer a baby. If it possible, he looked even more like his father. Seeing Colwyn walk on his cubby legs, Ariel felt the loss of all the time spent away from him. But when her little boy toddled over to her and allowed Ariel to pick him up, it helped to ease some of the pain she felt.

Ariel spent the rest of the day with Lily and Colwyn. She ate her meals with them instead of going to the hall. Broc never made an appearance, which was just as well.

Once Colwyn was put to bed, Ariel and Lily took the opportunity to talk. With Colwyn not around to hear, Lily gently broached the subject of Ariel's disappearance.

"I can't tell you how happy I am to see you unharmed. When Broc told me Theodoric had made you a serf I feared the worst."

"Geoffrey treated me fairly. Theodoric probably expected him to abuse me. He would not be too happy to see I was not."

Lily glanced down at Ariel's stomach and smiled. "How does Broc feel about being a father again?"

Ariel shook her head at first unable to answer. "He's not very happy about it."

Lily seemed puzzled by her answer. "Whyever not? With you gone he tried to fill the void in Colwyn's life. He loves the boy, they became inseparable."

Ariel sighed and thought of how best to word her response to Lily. "I was a serf, Lily. Broc assumes Geoffrey made use of my body. He hasn't given me a chance to explain."

Lily's face flushed at Ariel's words. "Ah, I see. So Broc thinks the child is Geoffrey's. Did you not tell him you were with child when you were taken?"

"Of course, but he doesn't believe me." Ariel paused and stared at Lily. "How did you know I was already pregnant?"

"I live with you. I helped you with the washing and such. You didn't have your monthly flow that month. The last time was before Broc left and sought an annulment from Alwen. I had a feeling you were."

Ariel just shook her head. "As you can see your suspicions turned out to be correct. Now all you have to do is convince Broc. He will no longer listen to me. Especially now, since William forced him to do something he didn't want to do."

"What could be so bad that he will no longer speak to you?"

"After assuming the child was not his, he retracted his offer of marriage. So William took matters into his own hands. He had us married shortly after we arrived in London."

Lily sadly shook her head. "Oh, Ariel. I'm so sorry. I know that was not how you wished to be married. So I take it Broc is even madder than he was before."

Ariel nodded. "Very. After the ceremony he walked out and I haven't seen him since."

"What do you plan to do now?"

Shrugging, Ariel said, "There is nothing left to do but to go home to Elmstead. Father will at least be happy to see me."

"When do we leave?"

"William has arranged an escort. We will leave as early as possible on the morrow. The king said he would tell Broc where I went."

Seeing the heartache in Ariel's eyes, Lily gave Ariel a hug. "Maybe the separation is what Broc needs. Give him time to think things over. He's just jealous. His anger won't last long."

"Time will tell, Lily. Time will tell."

* * * *

The escort consisted of two guards with one unexpected surprise. Ranulf stood next to her horse waiting. When he saw Ariel walk into the yard, he threw his arms open wide. Needing no further invitation, she stepped into his embrace.

Ranulf pulled Ariel close and held her tightly against him. He seemed almost afraid to let her go, afraid she would disappear once again. Ariel let him hold her until Ranulf felt comfortable with letting go.

"I can't tell you how pleased I am to see you again, Ariel. When I arrived here late last night, William told me you had been found. He had to stop me from rushing to your chamber to see for myself."

"Have you been out searching for me all this time? On your own?"

"Aye, I couldn't sit here and do nothing."

Ariel smiled warmly at Ranulf. "You probably have heard I'm leaving for Elmstead today."

Ranulf nodded his head. "Aye, I think it's for the best. With the babe on the way you need to be where you are most comfortable."

Averting her eyes, Ariel shrugged her shoulders. "I guess."

With a finger under her chin, Ranulf made her look up at him. "William told me about Broc, I know everything. That is the reason why I asked to be part of your escort. I also plan to stay at Elmstead for however long you have need of me. You don't have to go through this alone."

"Broc will not be at pleased."

Ranulf waved her concerns away. "Do you think I care? You need a friend right now, someone to lean on for support. Think of me as your shoulder to cry on."

Ariel chuckled. "I can't say I will make much use of your shoulder, but I will probably have use for your sword arm. I have a feeling Broc will do all he can to make me angry, which means lots of sword practice."

Ranulf smiled in return. "Well then, my lady, I'm yours to do with as you wish. Now if you will allow me, I will assist you onto your horse. The rest of our party is ready to depart."

Realizing Lily and Colwyn already sat on a horse, Ariel let Ranulf help her mount up. Looking back at the hall she saw William standing at the entrance.

"All ready to leave I see."

"Aye, I'm most anxious to see my father."

William bowed his head. "Then I bid you adieu, my Lady Knight. You are welcome to come to court any time you wish."

"Thank you, sire. I'll send word when the babe is born. Until we meet again."

Kicking her horse into motion, Ariel surveyed the yard. There was no sign of Broc. She did not need him. She managed to have Colwyn without him. She could have this babe on her own as well. There were plenty of people at Elmstead who cared about her.

Chapter 39

Every afternoon since the messenger had come from London, Swein stood at the edge of the village waiting. He knew he looked foolish, but he couldn't help himself. His daughter was coming home. He needed to see her first before anybody else in the village.

Swein looked into the distance and saw a cloud of dust rising in the air. Blinking, he looked a second time, to make sure he had actually seen it instead of his mind playing tricks on him. The cloud didn't disappear under closer inspection.

With each minute that passed the cloud moved ever closer. When shapes could be discerned within, Swein recognized Ariel in the forefront of the group. His heart skipped a beat.

Her hair had grown long during her time away. Swein swallowed convulsively. Ariel looked so much like her mother; it hurt to look at her. The older Ariel became the more she resemble her dead mother. Waving at the riders, Swein caught her daughter's attention. Detaching herself from the rest of the group, Ariel cantered her horse over to where her father stood. In a cloud of dust, she eased herself from her horse's back and threw herself into Swein's arms.

Maybe it was from the familiar sensation of her father holding her, or the tiring days of travel, Ariel burst into tears. It was some minutes before her tears stopped. "I'm sorry, father. I don't know what came over me."

Placing his hand on his daughter's expanding waist, Swein felt the unmistakable feel of the child kicking. "Much of it probably comes from this little one. Your mother used to burst into tears at the slightest incidences when she was carrying you." The child gave another hearty kick, making Swein smile. "I presume the child is Broc's?"

"Aye."

Looking over the group of travelers who waited on the road, Swein noticed Broc was absent. Seeing Ariel shake her head, he motioned for Ranulf to take the others to the hall. Linking Ariel's arm through his, Swein led her to the meadow.

Picking one of the colorful flowers that grew in abundance, Swein sketched a bow and offered it to Ariel. "A flower for, my lady."

Laughing, Ariel accepted the bloom from her father. Closing her eyes, she breathed in its rich scent. "William calls me Lady Knight."

Swein smiled at her. "It suits you. How else is one supposed to address you respectfully? We can't go around calling you Sir Ariel, now can we?"

"Nay, but you can call me Ariel St. Ceneri."

Turning his back on Ariel, Swein bent down and picked up a stone. Before he answered, he threw it across the meadow. "So he married you before he abandoned you. That is what he did, right?"

"I guess you could put it that way. William didn't give him much choice in the matter though."

A silence stretched between them before Swein spoke again. "What happened?"

"Theodoric sold me to a Norman. Geoffrey is young and his wife, who he hadn't met, had not yet come to England. To make a long story short, Broc believes the child is not his."

Swein snorted. "I thought the lad was a lot smarter than that. Theodoric made you a serf. You lost all your rights from that point on until you were released. If you disobeyed this Geoffrey in any way he could have killed you if he wished."

Ariel started to walk. Swein followed beside her. "Be that as it may, Broc has no intention of forgiving me. He may be my husband, but he will never fill that role in my life."

"I had the hall rebuilt while you were gone, you can live there with me. With the new baby coming I will gladly have another chamber added."

Kissing her father on the cheek, Ariel said, "I love you, father. What would I do without you?"

* * * *

That evening the villagers had a celebration in honor of Ariel's return. Tables were set up out in the yard and everybody contributed food. When put together there was more than enough for all present. The fare was simple, but tasty.

There were kegs of ale and mead to help wash down the food. Swein feeling generous retrieved a keg of French wine Broc had stored in the main hall. His reasoned if Broc didn't deign to put in appearance, then his good wine could be appreciated in his place.

It didn't take long for everyone to hear the tale of her abduction. All Ariel had to do was tell the story to a couple of villagers and it spread like fire throughout the entire gathering. All agreed, Ariel being married to Broc was exactly what Elmstead needed.

It kept the thane on the land while making the Norman knight one of them. Not that anyone had much to complain about Broc. It was only before the marriage he was still considered an outsider. Ariel didn't have the heart to tell them Broc was not thrilled with the bond their marriage created.

Part way through the meal Colwyn fell asleep in Ariel's arms. She was surprised he had lasted as long as he had. The days of travel had worn him out. Seeing her charge had fallen asleep, Lily left her place at the table and went over to Ariel.

"Here give him to me. I'll put the young master to bed."

Ariel shook her head. "Nay, you stay and enjoy the festivities."

Not paying her any heed, Lily lifted Colwyn into her arms. "I will hear none of that. The villagers arranged this for you. It would not do for the guest of honor to leave so early. I do not mind staying with Colwyn."

"Don't worry, Lily will not be alone." Ranulf had come up to them while they had been talking. Lily blushed. Ariel nodded her head. There was no point in arguing.

Watching how close Lily and Ranulf walked together, Ariel shook her head. If she was correct in her thinking, her two friends would find companionship in each other, which pleased her immensely.

Turning back around, Ariel found the villagers' attention fixed on something near the yard. Craning her neck around, she strained to see what had caused everyone to grow so quiet. It would have to be something intriguing to put a stop to all the drink they had been consuming. Catching a glimpse of what held such fascination, Ariel quickly looked away. The object of all the attention was Broc. Without bothering to dismount, he walked his horse over to where she sat. From his superior height he looked down at her. Ariel glared back at him.

Standing, Swein went to confront Broc. "It's good to see you again, Broc. You have been missed. Let me take this opportunity to welcome you into the family."

Broc smirked. "I'm happy to be back at Elmstead. As to my marriage to your daughter, you should thank William. It was his decision to have me wed Ariel, not mine."

A gasp rippled through the villagers. Their loyalty to Broc was tenuous at best. His rejection of Ariel would not endear him to them. They would take Ariel's side before they ever would take his.

"What is done is done. You're now married to my daughter; can you not try and make the best of it?"

"I'm afraid that is beyond my capabilities."

Swein gave up any pretenses of civility and glared at Broc. "I know what has caused this change in your feelings for Ariel. My daughter has suffered enough these last few months. She should not be punished for something she had no control over. Since you can't abide being around Ariel, she will move into my hall."

Broc shook his head in denial. "I will not allow it. Ariel is now my property through marriage bonds. I will treat her however I deem fit. I can treat her like a serf and none could say me nay."

While he had been speaking, Broc hadn't notice the hostility that had come over the men of the village. These were the men who had followed Ariel to fight with the fryd. Being a Norman was just another notch against Broc. His last statement caused the men to move against Broc.

"I'm afraid, my lord, that will not be allowed. You are one against many. I would rethink your position before you make any moves toward my daughter."

The village men surrounded Broc's horse. The blacksmith, who was the largest man of the village, watched Broc intently. The situation was getting out of hand. With no other alternative avaliable, Broc backed down.

"I concede to your superior numbers. Ariel may live where she wishes, I will not interfere." Backing up his horse, Broc left the revealers to continue with their celebration.

Chapter 40

Two weeks went by after the celebration of Ariel's return and nothing had changed. Ariel lived with Colwyn and her father in the newly built hall. Meanwhile, Broc shared the main hall with Ranulf much to his displeasure. Ranulf wasn't a very good live-in companion. He ignored Broc whenever they met and spent most of the day at the other hall.

From the start Broc had been disgusted by Ranulf's presence at Elmstead, he figured Ranulf went to Ariel's hall just to be close to her. But when Lily could be seen more and more at his side, Broc began to realize the other knight's attentions were focused on the girl and not on his wife. Broc watched them with envy. This was how his relationship with Ariel should have started. He had done everything wrong.

When William had told him Ariel had gone home to Elmstead, Broc had decided to follow. He had left London the very next day. On the road he had had time to go over the events that led to his and Ariel's separation. Before reaching Elmstead he had promised himself to be more objective with Ariel. Her story did have a ring of truth to it, but Broc still couldn't bring himself to forgive her. The thought of her in another man's bed hurt him deeply. Picturing Ariel taking another into her body, the place where Broc had been the only one to have gone before, made his blood boil. Ariel was his and no one had the right to take from her what was for him alone.

Sighing, Broc looked down at the letter that lay before him on his desk. He had come to his chamber to read it in privacy. It was from his mother. His mother and father were coming to Elmstead.

While in London seeking an annulment, Broc had dispatched a letter to Normandy. In the letter he had briefly described his life in England and his good fortune in acquiring Elmstead. He had also mentioned his impending nuptials to Ariel. Having sent the letter, his parents now were coming to see their second son's new wife. They would arrive any day.

Putting the letter away, Broc decided to go and see his son. At least Ariel had not stopped him from being with Colwyn. When he had asked why she allowed it, she had only said that Colwyn should not be deprived of his father just because his parents didn't get along. Broc was grateful for that one small concession.

Thinking of his son brought a smile to his lips. Now that Colwyn had mastered walking, he now had started to run. He would take off in a burst of speed only to lose his balance and fall flat on his face, but that didn't stop him. Broc only had to put him back on his little feet and Colwyn would be off again.

His son was another thing Broc would have to explain to his parents. In his letter he had made no mention of Colwyn. He had felt it would have been better to inform his parents after his marriage to Ariel.

Reaching the smaller hall, Broc peered inside. No one seemed to be around. There was only one other place they could be—the practice field.

Every day Ariel could be found at the field crossing swords with Ranulf. She had flatly refused to stop when Broc had told her to leave off such strenuous activity. She had asked him why he cared considering he held onto his belief that the child was not his. He hadn't known what to say to that.

More worried Ariel would do damage to herself, Broc had gone to the village healer with his concerns. She had laid his fears to rest. She had assured him the exercise would keep Ariel strong for the delivery, making her time of trial go quicker. The woman had placed both hands on his arm and told him Ariel had done the same when she had carried Colwyn. If he had been here then, he would have realized she was always careful.

At a short distance away, Broc stood and watched Ariel. Her pregnancy did not hinder her movements at all, the rise and fall of her sword never faltered. Smiling to himself, Broc could see Ranulf give way to Ariel.

They fought without armor. Each hit was carefully placed so as not to harm their opponent. They went through the movements strictly for exercise and not to see who could bring the other down. The healer had been right. Ariel didn't take any unnecessary chances.

Broc had no idea how long he stood there enjoying the sight of his wife. It wasn't until he felt someone returning his stare, did he realize Ranulf and Ariel had finished with their practice. Ariel stood away from the others, silently staring. The urge to go to Ariel was almost too great, but the ghost of what she had done rose up between them. Unable to bear it anymore, Broc turned his back on her.

* * * *

Three days later Broc's parents arrived at Elmstead. Ariel was in the village with Colwyn at the time. Broc was working in fields with the villagers.

Ariel knew they were expected, Broc had briefly mentioned it to her the other day, but she hadn't realized they would arrive so soon. Seeing no way out of it, Ariel sent one of the village boys to fetch Broc and prepared herself to greet her parents by marriage. Adjusting Colwyn on her hip, she moved to stand in the middle of the path.

Lord Eustance St. Ceneri was a large man, his height a match for his son's. His hair, though streaked with grey, was the same tawny color that both Broc and Colwyn shared. The St. Ceneri males all seemed to have gold eyes. Right at that moment, a set of those said eyes looked down at Ariel. There was no mistaking this man as Broc's sire.

Broc's mother, Lady Mary, was quite beautiful. Even age had not dulled her looks. At first glance she didn't appear old enough to have a child Broc's age. Her skin was smooth with only a few laugh lines at the corner of her eyes. Her auburn hair was gathered into a single braid that hung down her back. Intelligent green eyes skipped from Ariel's face and then to Colwyn's. She seemed to be fixated with Colwyn.

Walking closer, Ariel smiled up at Broc's parents. "My lord, my lady, allow me to welcome you to Elmstead." The couple returned her smile.

Much to Ariel's surprise, Lady Mary dismounted and came to stand before her. Her eyes never left Colwyn. Ariel started to feel uncomfortable. Not knowing all that much about the St. Ceneris, she was unsure what to do next. Before Ariel could think of something else to say, Broc's mother reached out and took Colwyn from her arms.

At this point Broc had arrived to greet his parents. "Hello, mother."

Without taking her eyes off of Colwyn, his mother returned his greeting. "Broc. In your letter you failed to mention you had a son. If it was because you didn't feel confident enough to tell us he was illegitimate, you should have known better. It does not matter."

Brushing a kiss across his mother's cheek, Broc chuckled. "You always have a way of bringing everything out in the open, mother."

"Well you should have told us. Say hello to your father, dear."

Broc looked at his father. "Nice to see you, father."

Lord Eustance dismounted. After looping both sets of reins through his hand he went over to Broc. He clapped his son on the shoulder. "Your mother is quite right, this is our first grandchild. No matter he was born on the wrong side of the blanket, he's a part of our family. From the looks of him, the St. Ceneri blood runs strong through his veins."

Completely ignored and forgotten, Ariel watched the family reunion with distaste. It was bad enough Broc's parents saw through her. What really infuriated her was his behavior. He made no move to introduce her. If he wanted it that way, he could have it.

Clearing her throat loudly, Ariel interrupted. "Now that you're here, Broc, I will leave you to settle your parents in. Since our son seems content to be with your mother, you can watch Colwyn as well." Before Broc could refuse her, Ariel walked away.

Broc called after her. "Ariel, wait. Where are you going?"

Ariel threw over shoulder, "Where else do I go when I need to work off a little anger? To Ranulf, of course."

As she left, Ariel heard Broc say, "Don't worry, mother. That was Ariel, my wife."

His mother then replied, "Oh my, I didn't even think. Why did she not say anything?"

Ariel didn't wait around to hear what Broc's response would be.

Chapter 41

"This tale you have told us is fantastic and to be quite frank, hard to believe. I know there are women who are strong willed and independent, your mother can be included in their ranks, but I have never heard one take it as far as your Saxon wife," Broc's father said with some disbelief.

"On the contrary, I find it quite believable." This came from his mother. She sat in the middle of the hall floor playing with Colwyn.

"I'm glad to see at least one of you believe me, because it's true, all of it."

"Never mind your father, Broc. He needs to see the facts with his own eyes before he takes anything to heart. But I only have one question for you, how can you be so sure Ariel does not carry your next child?"

His mother's eyes seemed to bore right through him. Broc knew that look. He had seen it many times as he grew to adulthood. There would be no sidestepping away from her question. She would not allow it.

Broc sighed inwardly. "She went to another man's bed, Mother. I was only with her that one time."

A very unlady-like snort came from his mother in response to his comment. "That proves nothing. It only took one time for me to become pregnant with both you and your brother. The St. Ceneri men are known for their virility. How far along is she?"

"Six months."

His mother nodded her head. "She was forced to be a serf for five, it adds up. A woman knows these things. The child is most assuredly yours."

Broc could only shake his head. Once Lady Mary made a decision she stuck to it, no matter how others felt about it, but his mother was right about his father. He needed to see how correct Broc was in his tale.

"If you need further proof, father, then come and I will show you."

Not one to be left out of anything, Lady Mary quickly gathered Colwyn into her arms and followed the two men out the door.

The sound of clashing swords could be heard before the small group reached the practice field. At his mother's questioning look, Broc nodded his head. Elbowing ahead, Lady Mary arrived at the field before the men. She stood watching in utter amazement.

Ariel and Ranulf moved across the field with swords flashing. Unlike the other times Broc had watched them, Ariel was not taking it easy on Ranulf. Granted Ranulf let Ariel gain the upper hand, but he still had to fight to keep what ground he had. It didn't last long. With a savage thrust of her sword, Ariel ripped the sword out of Ranulf's hands.

Lady Mary cheered and Lord Eustance's jaw dropped open in astonishment. It was obvious his father had gotten the proof he had wanted.

* * * *

Alerted to the presence of others by the cheering, Ariel lowered her sword. She was surprised to see Broc's mother clapping her hands. She didn't seem like the same woman who had ignored her an hour before.

Unsure of what to expect, Ariel stood beside Ranulf making no move to go to Broc and his parents. Lady Mary took the initiative. Striding across the field, Lady Mary walked over to Ariel. She looked her up and down then with her free arm pulled Ariel close. "It's so very nice to finally meet you, my dear. Broc wrote to us about you. Our earlier meeting, accept my apology. Your son here overwhelmed me. He's our only grandchild, but from the look of you, our second will soon come into the world."

Ariel could only nod her head, she had been rendered speechless. Broc had to have told his parents all that they had gone through, but his mother had taken Ariel's side. She didn't know what to say.

Lady Mary laughed, making her eyes crinkle with amusement. "Have I shocked you, dear? That is something you will just have to get used to. I always speak my mind. Now, as to my son accepting the child you carry as his, he will see how wrong he is. The St. Ceneri gold eyes are very prevalent in the family. When this child is born with the same eyes your son has, Broc will realize what an ass he has been."

Without further ado, Lady Mary linked her arm through Ariel's and led her away. As they walked away, Lady Mary asked Ariel where her father might be.

* * * *

Swein hadn't been so entertained in a very long time. Mary St. Ceneri was a joy to watch. She kept the men in her family on their toes.

When Swein had first seen Broc's mother striding to his hall with Colwyn in one arm and her other linked through Ariel's arm, he was a little apprehensive. Taking Broc's almost violent reaction to Ariel into account, he didn't have much hope in the younger man's mother siding with Ariel. Broc was her son after all. So it was a nice surprise to find he had misjudged the Lady Mary.

The first thing she did was to leave Ariel's side and kiss his cheeks in welcome. She then said she was happy her son had married Ariel. Regardless of how her son felt, she formed her own opinions.

Putting Colwyn down so he could toddle about, Lady Mary put the hall under close scrutiny. It must have past muster, because she helped herself to a goblet of mead that sat on a table and took a seat on a bench. Ariel and Swein joined her.

"Ariel you live in this hall with your father and not with Broc?"

Ariel's face flushed as she nodded. "I know Broc is your son so you will find this hard to hear, but I couldn't live under the same roof with him."

The hall filled with Lady Mary's laughter. "I have lived with Broc's father for over thirty years. Broc is very much like his sire. I know exactly how you feel. There have been times during my marriage I would have gladly gone to live elsewhere. The St. Ceneri men are a stubborn lot. Once they make their minds up, whether they are right or wrong, it's extremely hard to sway them. Broc's older brother, Matthew, is the same way. The three of them get on famously of course, where as I irk them on occasion."

Ariel smiled at the older woman. "I thought you would shun me."

"Why should I? I must admit I envy you. Look at you, a woman who can handle a sword as well as any man, and a knight on top of it all. I would have loved to have seen Broc's face when he realized he had knighted a woman. If I was twenty years younger, I would be out on that field with you."

Cutting into the conversation, Swein said, "Ariel's mother would have been proud of her. But I'm sure she sees what her daughter has become."

Looking over at Swein, Lady Mary patted his hand. "What happened to your wife?"

Swein still found it painful to speak of his wife, even now more than two years after her passing. "Beth became ill one evening. Throughout the night her fever rose. The village healer tried everything she knew, but nothing seemed to help. By morning, she was gone."

Lady Mary shook her head in sympathy. "It must be hard to loose a loved one so unexpectedly."

"Aye, it is. I took her death very hard. I shut out the world, even Ariel for a time. When Ariel became pregnant with Colwyn, I pulled myself together. It was my turn to be the strong one."

"Obviously that is when my son came crashing into your lives."

Swein looked over at Ariel and nodded. It had been a turning point for both of them.

* * * *

It became decided everyone would partake the evening meal in the main hall. Ariel was not at all sure Broc would like the arrangement. She even went as far as to tell his mother that very thing, but Lady Mary would hear none of it.

At the appointed time, Swein, Ariel, Colwyn and Lily stepped through the hall doors. Lady Mary came and took Colwyn from Lily and told her to sit with Ranulf. It would seem Lady Mary's keen eyes missed nothing. She winked at Ariel as she gently pushed Lily in Ranulf's direction.

Her next act was to seat Ariel beside Broc at the head table. He instantly bristled at Ariel's intrusion. He would have risen to leave, but his mother placed a firm hand on his shoulder and pushed him back down into his chair.

With everyone seated, Lady Mary motioned to one of the serfs to being serving. Platters of food were placed on the table along with trenchers to hold it. Everyone was given a trencher, all except for Broc and Ariel. One trencher was placed between them, the intention quite clear. They were to share. Along with the trencher only one goblet was placed next to it.

Broc craned his neck to look down the table at his mother. She smiled sweetly at him. Ariel could see he was tempted to summon a serf to bring him another trencher when his eyes skipped over one of them. Lady Mary cleared her throat to gain his attention and shook her head. Broc sighed and made no move to have one of the serfs come over to him.

Tentatively, Ariel filled the trencher with food that sat on the table. There was roasted venison and pheasant. Another platter held boiled greens covered in a creamy sauce. Fresh bread rounded off the meal. Allowing for Broc's greater appetite, Ariel took large portions of all the fare offered.

Taking out his eating knife, Broc cut off chunks of meat and placed them in his mouth, he didn't offer any to Ariel. She had to cut her own between his mouthfuls. They both reached for the goblet at the same time. When their fingers met they drew back their hands as if they had touched a live coal. Grunting, Broc allowed her to drink first. To add insult to injury, he wiped the rim of the goblet with his sleeve before taking his drink.

For the sake of his parents, Ariel was willing to let it slide. Acting as if she had not seen what he had done, she continued to eat. When Broc didn't reach for more food, Ariel cautiously looked over at him. His attention seemed to be caught on an area near her lap.

Following his gaze, she realized Broc watched her stomach. The baby shifted around so much her stomach visibly moved with each kick it gave. So used to such activity, she had paid no heed to it.

Without thinking, Ariel took one of Broc's hands and placed it on her stomach. The baby obligingly gave a hearty kick, lifting his hand. The joy Ariel felt at having Broc share a moment with their unborn child burned to ashes under his stern scowl. His face contorted into a mask of rage.

In an instinctive gesture, Ariel released his hand. Broc quickly snatched it back. His eyes burned a brighter gold. His anger could be easily seen by everyone present in the room.

Feeling the full force of his temper directed at her, Ariel pushed back her chair and left the table. Giving Lady Mary an apologetic look, she hastily made her way out of the hall. She had tried to at least be civil to Broc while his parents were at Elmstead, but no more. That he could hate an innocent babe so, made her think he was not the man she had first thought him to be.

She crossed the yard and made her way through the village. Once inside the comforting walls of her father's hall, Ariel began to relax. The door crashed open behind her, shattering her feeling of contentment. She didn't need to turn around to see who had come through the door. Her body became instantly aware, no other but Broc could cause her to feel his presence in a room before she could see him.

Ariel pulled herself up to her full height and turned to face her enraged husband.

Chapter 42

"How dare you walk away from me? Especially in the middle of a meal my mother went to great lengths to arrange."

Not one to be outdone, Ariel equally raised her voice to yell back at Broc. "How dare you treat me like I'm not even in the room? Your mother's idea was for us to share a trencher, probably in the hopes your attitude would soften toward me. If I remember correctly, you taught me when a knight is in that situation, he is to cut the meat for the lady and offer her the choicest cuts. I could take umbrage with your conduct this evening."

Broc's anger seemed to dissipate. Bending at the waist, Broc bowed. "I'm sorry, you are correct. I will try not to insult you in the future."

He would have left then had Ariel not called out to him. "Broc, I need to know. Did you ever really love me?"

Gold eyes moved over Ariel's face. "Of course I did."

"Then why do you not believe me when I say the babe is yours? If you truly loved me, you would never have questioned my word."

Pain was etched on Broc's face. "I can't."

Ariel tried to push back the unshed tears that threatened to spill. "I still love you. How I feel will never change. I endured having you take two women to your bed. In that instance you made that choice to bed them. I wasn't given that freedom. My love didn't die for you. You have my heart. It's yours to do with as you wish. But let it be known here and now, I will fight you if I have to. My love for you will not make me weak."

Broc swept her form with his eyes once more. Without a word he silently left the hall.

* * * *

One month passed and then another. The hot summer days gave way to the cooler nights of autumn. It also became a busy time at Elmstead. The fields had to be harvested and winter stores had to be prepared. All did their part to insure the winter months would find the larders well stocked.

Ariel's time drew nearer. She no longer had the energy she once had, her added bulk made her tire easily. She still kept up her sword practice, but she had to limit the amount of time she spent doing it. Ranulf would only shake his head and tell her she should be resting. Every day Ariel would tell him she knew when it was time to call it quits and now was not the time.

After their heated discussion in her father's hall, Broc avoided Ariel whenever possible. The only thing that brought them together was their son. Ariel had stopped going to the main hall for her meals. Thankfully, Lady Mary made no more overtures to bring them together. Their marriage had become a farce.

Ranulf and Lily grew quite close over the passing months. One was hardly seen far from the other. Many times Ariel found Ranulf helping Lily care for Colwyn. Those times were few though, Ariel had immersed herself in the raising of her son.

At this time a priest came to Elmstead. The village was not considered large enough to have their own priest to minister to them, so they relied on the priests who traveled the countryside. At these times, marriages would be performed and children born in between visits would be baptized. So it was not surprising when Ranulf and Lily announced their intentions to wed shortly after the priest's arrival. Both Ariel and Broc were asked to act as witnesses.

The night before the ceremony, Ariel left Colwyn in Lady Mary's care and went to Lily's home. In her arms she carried a gown. It was a wedding present for her friend. Lily's mother and a couple of girls from the village were visiting the soon to be bride. Stepping up to the door to knock, Ariel heard a burst of laughter coming from within. They were probably giving Lily advice on her soon to be nuptials. Ariel regretted she had not received such treatment before she had wed Broc. Sighing, she knocked on the door and the voices fell silent.

Lily's mother, Edna, opened the door. When she saw Ariel standing there, she clucked and pulled her into the hut. "What are you doing, my lady? You should be resting, not walking around in the night."

"I'm fine. I came to give Lily something for the morrow."

Unfolding the gown, Ariel held it out to Lily. It was one of her best. The gown was a pale blue and had been made with the softest wool. When Lily didn't reach out to accept it, Ariel held it up against the other woman's chest to make sure it would fit her. Lily made no move to claim it.

"Take it, Lily. I want you to have it."

Lily shook her head in denial. "I can't accept this, Ariel."

"Why ever not? I have no use for it."

"It's too fine for the likes of me."

Slipping the gown over Lily's arm, Ariel smiled into her friend's face. "I will not take no for an answer. Every bride should have a beautiful gown on her wedding day. I brought it here tonight so you could make any alterations that may be needed. I want you to keep it."

With tears in her eyes, Lily hugged Ariel. "This means so much to me. I only wish you could have had what I will have, you deserve better."

"Forget about me and think of tomorrow. It marks the start of your new life with Ranulf. Now I will leave you ladies. I will see you in the main hall come the morn." Even before Ariel left the hut, the others had gathered around Lily to get a better look at the gown.

Once outside the night closed around her. The nights were definitely cooler. Wrapping her arms across her chest, Ariel wished she had brought a cloak along. Increasing her stride, she hurried in the direction of her father's hall.

Before she could reach it, a lone figure stepped out from the shadows. Not expecting anyone else to be about, a shiver of fear ran down her spine. The incident of being stolen away on another night came to the forefront of her mind. Thinking to escape the figure that stood before her in the dark, she took a couple steps back.

Ariel didn't see the rock that lay on the ground behind her. Catching her heel on it she stumbled, throwing herself off balance. A large male hand grabbed her by the arm and pulled her close. Startled, Ariel looked up to find a pair of gold eyes shining down at her. Broc kept his arm wrapped around her waist, holding her against him. It had been such a very long time since he had held her.

"Are you all right?"

"Thanks to you I am." Broc made no move to release her.

"That was a nice thing you did, giving Lily one of your gowns."

Ariel's brows drew together in puzzlement. "How did you know about the gown?"

"My mother sent me to tell you Colwyn had fallen asleep. She wanted to make sure it was all right for him to stay the night."

"So you followed me?"

Broc shrugged. "You had already left the hall before I arrived. I wanted to see what you were about."

"Now you know. Colwyn can stay in your hall. I would hate to wake him just to put him in his own bed. If you will excuse me, I would like to go inside. The night grows cold."

Ariel's body shook with the cold, but also from being in close proximity to Broc. She hoped he didn't realize it was not just the cold night air making her shiver.

"Here, I will walk you to the hall." Broc took off his cloak and placed it around her shoulders. It was warm from his body and his scent wafted over her with each step she took.

Once they reached their destination, Ariel pulled off the cloak and gave it back to Broc. Their fingers touched when the cloak passed between their hands. Expecting Broc to flinch at this brief contact, Ariel quickly pulled her hand back. There was no telling how Broc would react nowadays.

This time he didn't shun her like he had so many times in the past. Instead, he touched his fingers to her cheek and gently caressed it, all the while his eyes never left her face. His look was so wistful, Ariel almost begged him to forgive her. Broc didn't give her the chance.

Backing away, he said, "Until tomorrow. Have a good sleep."

Ariel watched Broc until he disappeared into the darkness. Was Broc finally softening towards her? She could only hope.

* * * *

The ceremony took place in the main hall with everyone in attendance. Ariel stood at Lily's side with Broc next to Ranulf while the happy couple exchanged their vows.

Lily was beautiful. The love she had for Ranulf made her radiant. The gown's length had been shortened. Ariel had known it wouldn't have taken much work to adjust the fit for Lily. Flowers from the meadow had been woven into the bride's hair.

When the ceremony reached the part where Ranulf spoke his vows, his eyes never left Lily's face. His voice rang out loud and clear throughout the hall for all to hear.

Ariel's eyes strayed over to Broc. He seemed to be listening intently to what the priest was saying. He must have sensed her watching him, because he turned his head and looked directly at her. Some unknown emotion flitted across his face. As quickly as it had come, it disappeared.

The couple sealed their vows with a kiss, which caused a cheer to be raised. Then one and all sat down to a feast that would last throughout the day and well into the night. Spirits ran high and the amount of ale, as well as mead, being consumed was rivaling the amount partaken at Ariel's homecoming.

Midway through the festivities a couple of villagers produced a drum and pipe. A space magically became cleared in the middle of the hall to allow couples to sway to the music.

When Lily and Ranulf decided to leave, they were met with some good-hearted ribbing. The bride's face flushed red at the explicit instructions the village men gave Ranulf. The groom assured the men their instructions were not needed.

Having sensed the excitement of the adults around him, Colwyn had taken to running around the hall. No one complained when he went from one to table to the next. For his efforts he was rewarded with a sweet. The dancing continued. Ariel happily sat next to her father, tapping her foot to the music. Colwyn had finally fallen asleep and had been put in Broc's bed. Now she was free to enjoy herself without having to chase after her son. Rubbing her aching back, Ariel watched the dancers. Broc was dancing with his mother. He had sat away from her all evening. At times Ariel felt him watching her, but every time she looked up he had already turned away.

The feast was still in full swing when Ariel decided she had had enough. Covering a yawn with her hand, she leaned close to her father and told him she was going to retire. Nodding, he helped her to stand.

Ariel made her way slowly to the back of the hall and went to Broc's chamber to collect Colwyn. It would be a shame to wake him, but she couldn't count on anyone hearing him if he cried. Quietly opening the door, she tip toed into the chamber.

Colwyn slept in the middle of his father's bed. His knees were drawn up under him with his bottom stuck up in the air. Ariel couldn't help but smile at him. How he slept through all the noise coming from the hall was beyond her.

Moving over to the bed, Ariel reached for Colwyn. Before she could lift him up she felt someone come up behind her, close enough for her to feel the heat from his body seep into hers. Broc had followed her into the chamber.

"Leave him, Ariel. He's sleeping peacefully."

"I wish to retire. Someone needs to be near in case Colwyn should awake."

"Then sleep here with him."

Ariel shook her head. "I couldn't do that. Where would you sleep?"

Broc waved her question away. "Don't worry about me, you're tired. Lie down and sleep. You look ready to drop where you're standing."

Stifling another yawn, Ariel knew Broc was right. "It's the babe. It drains me so, especially near the end. It was the same with Colwyn."

Taking her by the shoulders, Broc made Ariel sit down on the bed. He took off her slippers. Before he left, he brushed a quick kiss across her lips. Stunned, Ariel sat on the bed with her fingers pressed to her mouth. The feel of his lips on hers lingered. The sensation was still there when she finally allowed herself to lie down beside her sleeping son.

Chapter 43

A truce formed between Ariel and Broc. How it happened totally escaped Ariel. The morning after Ranulf's marriage to Lily, she had awakened to find Broc standing beside the bed, watching her sleep. No emotion showed on his face. Ariel couldn't tell if he was pleased or displeased with her. He just stood there, watching.

The sheets rustled beside her, making her aware of Colwyn's wakefulness. When he saw his father, he gurgled happily. In response, Broc bent over and picked Colwyn up. He immediately grimaced. "It would seem someone has a very wet bottom."

Lifting herself up on her elbows, Ariel struggled to get out of the bed. "Give him to me, I will change him."

Broc gently pushed her back down on the bed. "Rest. I had lots of practice when you were gone. Colwyn slept with me on a regular basis. Most mornings he woke up in this condition."

Opening the chest at the end of the bed, Broc pulled out a clean changing cloth. He then moved to a table that held a pitcher of water and soaked the cloth. Coming back to the bed, he lay Colwyn down and proceeded to change his son's bottom. Ariel was pleasantly surprised.

When Colwyn was once again dry, Broc picked him up. "I'll feed him, if my mother allows me to that is. Sleep as long as you wish, I will see you out in the hall after you've rested a bit more."

So the truce had begun. With Lily gone to London with Ranulf, Broc stepped in to help Ariel, though at times he had to fight his mother to gain his son's attention. It turned out Lord Eustance could be just as determined as his wife. For many times he would sneak Colwyn away from Ariel leaving the other two empty handed.

The three St. Ceneris provided Ariel and her father with a vast amount of entertainment. Swein would burst into laughter at the sight of Lord

Eustance holding Colwyn in his arms, trying to sneak past his wife before she noticed what he carried. Most of the time he would make it past her, but not all the time. When Lady Mary spotted him, he would hold Colwyn close and take off at a run. Lady Mary could be seen running through the village with her skirts hiked to her ankles chasing after her husband.

On one such occasion Broc was with Ariel. He laughed along with her at his parents antics. His arm snaked out and wrapped around her shoulders. He pulled Ariel up close against his side. It was the first time in a very long time he had held her close, displaying any kind of affection. But much to her disappointment he didn't hold her for very long. Broc stiffened and then withdrew from her.

Not wanting Broc to see how much she would have liked for him to hold her again, Ariel turned away to look for his parents. She noticed something had stopped their play. Looking past them she sucked in her breath with surprise. It also explained Broc's reaction. Two people were walking toward them from the direction of the main hall. It was Lisette and Geoffrey.

Ariel was happy to see them, but their presence at Elmstead would only destroy what little closeness she had found with Broc. She could only hope he would be able to forget the past, but it was obvious he was not willing to let it lie. He curled his lip in disgust and walked away.

Pasting on a smile, Ariel went to greet the new arrivals. Broc's parents had already introduced themselves. "Lisette, Geoffrey, I'm glad you decided to come."

Lisette kissed Ariel on the cheek. "I promised I would come when your time drew near."

Hesitantly, Geoffrey kissed her on the cheek as well. His eyes shifted to Lord Eustance. He looked as if he expected some retaliation brought on by his actions. Lady Mary's laugh reassured him all was well.

"Have no fear, young man. My husband and I do not share the same point of view that our son does."

"I must admit I was a little worried about how well our visit would be received. If Broc's leave-taking is any indication, I assume he still doesn't think too highly of me."

Ariel was not going to lie to Geoffrey. "He still believes the babe is yours and William did nothing to alleviate the problem. He forced Broc to marry me when we returned to London."

A look of pity crossed his face. "I'm so sorry, Ariel. I wish I had never laid eyes on Theodoric."

"Enough of this talk," Lady Mary interrupted, "there is no point in dwelling on what could have been. What is done is done. Have you met our grandson?" Before Lord Eustance could protest, Lady Mary took Colwyn from his arms.

Knowing his wife had managed to take Colwyn from him, Lord Eustance moved to reclaim his grandson, but Lady Mary was quicker. Stepping out of her husband's reach, she picked up her skirts and hurriedly walked away. Lord Eustance went after her. Lady Mary shrieked and took off at a run while her husband gave chase.

Seeing Lisette's and Geoffrey's shocked looks, she giggled. "Never mind them. They do this on a regular basis. It's a game they play. They take great joy in vying for the right to have Colwyn. You'll get used to it."

* * * *

The once fragile peace shattered with the de la Roches' arrival. Geoffrey and Lisette stayed with Ariel and her father. There was no question of them staying in the main hall. Whenever Broc came anywhere near Geoffrey he looked ready to kill him.

What little ground Ariel had managed to gain from Broc she now lost. He no longer came to see Colwyn, his mother and father had to bring his son to him. The looks Broc sent Ariel's way were far from warm. They were as frigid as a cold winter day. A week went by and Broc's facade of indifference never faltered. Her hopes of having a real marriage died a silent death.

* * * *

For late September the day was pleasant. It seemed summer was making one last valiant attempt to hold back the cool autumn weather, but it would be a losing battle. Broc was in the yard with his father, they each stood next to their horses as they prepared to leave. Bows and arrows hung from their saddles, Ariel assumed they were going hunting. Taking a deep breath she confronted Broc.

"I'd like a word with you, Broc."

Broc didn't bother to turn his head. "Can it not wait? I'm going hunting with my father."

"Nay." Looking over at Lord Eustance, Ariel said, "You don't mind if I borrow Broc for a moment?" Smiling he led his horse a short distance away.

With eyes that blazed, Broc turned on Ariel. "What can be so important you must interfere with my plans for the day?"

After being ignored for days, Ariel felt her anger flare to life. "It's important to me," she said sharply. "It has to do with your attitude toward me. I'm your wife. Could you at least give me a modicum of respect?"

"Not likely when you persist on having that man sleep under your roof."

"His wife is with him. What do you think is going on?"

"Oh I don't know, maybe he would like to sample your wares again."

A resounding crack echoed through the yard as Ariel's palm connected with Broc's cheek.

"How dare you insinuate I would break my marriage vows to you? If you think any man would find me appealing while I'm fat with your babe, you must be blind."

The imprint of her hand could be seen clearly on his face. Broc rubbed it absentmindedly. "He had you once, he may want you again."

"Unlike you." Ariel couldn't resist making that barbed remark. "You had me once, but now you avoid me at all costs. Fine, I give up. Have it your way. I only thought of Colwyn. When he's old enough to understand, you can explain to him why his father hates his mother so."

Ariel swung away from Broc. She wasn't going to waste anymore time on him. She was tired. Cramps had been plaguing her off and on since she woke up this morning. But as she took a step away from Broc, she felt a shooting pain race across her stomach. A moment later, there was a gush of warm liquid followed by another sharp pain. Unable to hold back, a moan escaped her lips. Clutching her stomach, Ariel gasped. The pains came fast, not giving her much time in between before another hit her.

After the third pain had hit, she noticed Broc standing in front of her with concern etched on his face. "Ariel?"

"The babe has decided now would be a good time for it to come into the world." Moaning, another pain hit her, this one stronger than the last.

Picking Ariel up in his arms, Broc yelled at his father. "Go to the village and get the healer. Find mother and tell her Ariel has need of her." Lord Eustance left at a run to carry out his tasks.

Broc kicked open the door to the smaller hall. Lady Mary sat inside visiting Lisette, Geoffrey and her father. Ever observant, Lady Mary quickly assessed the situation and took control. "Take her into her chamber. Geoffrey, go fetch the healer."

Broc shook his head. "No need, mother. I sent father for her."

"Good lad. Lisette, come with us, I will need your help."

Once in the chamber, Broc laid Ariel on her bed. Backing away, he allowed his mother to take his place. The two women started to remove Ariel's gown.

Ariel held out her hand and called to him. "Stay, I want you here. Please."

Broc backed away from her outstretched hand. "Don't ask this of me."

Ariel's eyes begged him silently. "Please."

"Nay."

A pain overtook Ariel causing her to gasp. "Then get out, I don't need you. I hate you." The last part she yelled at his back before he closed the door behind him.

Chapter 44

Giving a final push, Ariel felt her child slide from her body. The sound of a newborn's cries filled the chamber. Collapsing back on the pillows, she closed her eyes. Though her labor had not been long, she was glad to have it over with.

Ariel opened her eyes and found Lady Mary hovering nearby with a mewling bundle in her arms. "Here is your daughter, love. She's beautiful."

Accepting the bundle, Ariel stared down at the new life she had created. She was indeed perfect. Kissing the velvety soft cheek, she passed her daughter back to Lady Mary. "Take her to Broc. He needs to know how much of a fool he has been. You can also tell the high and mighty lord, I would rather walk over hot coals in bare feet before I have any intention of seeing him again."

It was no secret that Lady Mary was not at all pleased with her son's behavior either. She nodded her head in agreement. "With pleasure."

* * * *

Broc had finally stopped his pacing when the cries of a babe could be heard coming from Ariel's chamber. He now stood by the hearth. He watched his mother come out of the chamber with a well wrapped bundle in her arms. Broc began to feel uneasy. His mother was not happy and her anger seemed to be solely directed at him.

Without asking permission, Lady Mary placed the bundle in his arms. "It's a girl. Look at her."

Obediently, Broc looked down. The first thing he noticed was the tufts of blonde hair that appeared almost white, so much like Ariel's own. The little face tugged at his heart. Broc had never been this close to a newborn child. He was amazed at how small she seemed. Her hands were tiny with perfectly shaped fingers. Tentatively he touched a small fist, he watched as the hand opened and tightly clasped his finger. Broc smiled at the strength one so small could display.

The child's eyes had been closed, but Broc now saw they were wide open and looking up at him, he gasped. Gold eyes stared back at him. It had the same effect as having a fist slammed into his belly. Ariel hadn't been lying, this was his daughter.

Feeling knocked off kilter, he looked at his mother. "How fares Ariel?"

"She's fine. I have never seen a woman have such an easy time of it."

"Can I see her now?"

His mother shook her head. "Nay."

"Then when?"

"Ariel doesn't want to see you."

Broc could understand Ariel not wanting to see him, but it didn't make it hurt any less. "I know I was wrong."

"Aye, you were wrong, but that doesn't make it right either. What could you have been thinking? I'm afraid you pushed Ariel too far this time. You have lost her and maybe for good this time. To be honest, if it had been me, I would have had nothing to do with you long before now."

His mother meant every word. It was he who had been in the wrong. "I know how much of an ass I have been. There's no need to tell me, mother, but this is my daughter. She changes everything."

"How stupid can you be? You called Ariel a liar and insinuated she was a whore for allowing another man to take her. Would you have been happier if you found her beaten and broken?"

He wasn't very proud of himself at the moment. "Of course not. How I treated Ariel was unconscionable, I just couldn't seem to stop myself. Every time I picture Ariel in Geoffrey's arms my blood boils. I hate myself for it. I need to ask Ariel for forgiveness, to see if we can start over."

The baby started to squirm. Turning her head, she nuzzled Broc's chest with her open mouth. When she didn't find what she sought, she began to whimper.

"Give me the babe. I have to take her to Ariel. She needs to be fed."

Reluctantly, Broc handed his daughter to his mother. "Please talk to her. I never really stopped loving her, regardless of what I may have said. I want us to be a real family."

Sighing, Lady Mary nodded. "I will try, but don't expect much. At least wait until tomorrow. She just gave you a daughter, let her rest."

"Fine. One more thing. Do you know if Ariel has chosen a name for our daughter?"

His mother shook her head in denial. "She hasn't said anything about a name that I know of."

"Ask her if she wouldn't mind calling the baby Brianna."

Lovingly caressing Broc's cheek, his mother smiled. "It suits her. A pretty name for a pretty girl. I will suggest it to Ariel."

* * * *

The next day found Ariel up and out of bed. Her labor hadn't been too strenuous and the thought of lying in bed all day held no appeal. She also put away her gowns and again wore her tunics and trews.

Against her better judgment, Ariel had allowed Lady Mary to talk her into seeing Broc this day. Her mother-in-law could be a very convincing woman when she set her mind to it. What had finally brought Ariel around in the end had been Lady Mary telling her how guilty Broc felt over his past actions, and how he wanted to try and make a fresh start. Ariel had no intention of forgiving him that easily, but she was interested in seeing what Broc would do. He had yet to arrive.

Ariel spent a peaceful morning with her father and Colwyn. The baby had been asleep in her cradle near the hearth, but she now made fussing noises. When sucking could be heard coming from the cradle, Ariel decided her daughter was in need of feeding. She spent a great deal of time eating and keeping Ariel awake half the night.

Colwyn who had taken an instant liking to his sister, rushed over to the cradle. Placing his small hands on the side of it, he bent down and gurgled something to the baby. The new face above her distracted her for only a moment. When it became apparent Colwyn would not be feeding her, the baby let out a hearty wail. The stricken look on Colwyn's face made Ariel laugh. Holding out her arms, Ariel gathered Colwyn close when he came to her. Swein picked up his new granddaughter. Her cries stopped once she was held close.

Ariel kissed Colwyn. "Give your sister a few months then she will be able to play with you." As if he had understood, Colwyn clapped his hands.

Drawing air into her little lungs, the baby let loose with another ear splitting wail. Swein cringed. "I think you had better feed this one before she brings the hall down around us with her cries."

"Aye, she really does have a good set of lungs." Releasing Colwyn, she took the baby from her father. Swein took Colwyn by the hand and left Ariel alone.

Unlacing the collar of her tunic, Ariel pulled it down, releasing her breast. Eagerly the baby latched on and began to suck. Ariel allowed herself to relax as her head fell back against the back of her chair. The heat from the fire washed over her making her feel drowsy. Her eyes fluttered closed.

With a jerk she opened her eyes. She could have only slept for a few seconds, but surprisingly she found Broc standing in front of her. The baby still nursed at her breast.

"What are you doing here?"

Broc smiled at her. "You said I could come and speak with you today."

"I'm feeding the baby."

"I can see that."

Knowing Broc was being deliberately obtuse, trying to get a rise out of her, Ariel took a deep breath. "I want you to leave. You can come back when I have finished."

"I think not. I have never seen a woman nurse her child before."

There was no point in arguing with him for it would only upset the baby. "Stay if you want then, she's almost finished anyway." Which was true, the baby's sucking came in fits and spurts. Sleep would claim her soon.

"Did you have a chance to think about the name I suggested?" Broc's eyes seemed drawn to her breast. He stared at the sight of his daughter nursing. The baby's little hand lay on Ariel's breast.

"Aye, I did. Brianna is fine with me. I had no other name chosen."

"Then Brianna it is."

The silence stretched between them when they found nothing else to say to each other. Feeling uncomfortable, they both focused their attention on their daughter. Broc grabbed the chair opposite from Ariel and moved it so he sat a few inches from her knees. Leaning forward, he quietly watched Brianna.

With her belly full, Brianna released Ariel's nipple and dozed off.

Pulling her tunic closed, Ariel propped her daughter up into a sitting position and gently patted her back.

"Can I try?"

Finding no real reason to deny him, Ariel nodded her head. Placing the baby on Broc's knee, she placed his one hand on Brianna's chest so her chin rested on it. The other she placed on the small back.

Brianna looked so tiny held in Broc's large hands. Almost afraid he would hurt her, he lightly patted her back. Ariel chocked back a laugh, which caused Broc to look up at her.

"What's so funny?"

Suppressing a laugh, Ariel said, "You are. What do you think you will accomplish with that tapping?"

"I'm burping her."

"Well you had better put some strength behind those taps or you'll never move the gas."

Broc looked decidedly uneasy. "I don't want to hurt her."

"You won't. Here, I will show you."

Wrapping her fingers around Broc's wrist, Ariel moved his hand on and off Brianna's back. After she figured he had the hang of it, she let him continue while she still held his wrist. After a couple of good pats a loud belch escaped the baby's lips. At Broc's shocked look, Ariel laughed.

Joining in on the laughter, Broc stared up at Ariel. One moment he was laughing and the next the laughter fell away from his face. Seeing the flames of passion flicker in his gold eyes, Ariel released Broc's wrist. If things had been different she would have responded in kind. But the rejection she had received from him in the past held her back. Feeling uncomfortable under his intense gaze, she moved to take Brianna from him.

"Give her to me. I'll put her in her cradle. She'll sleep until her next feeding."

Relinquishing the baby, Broc followed Ariel to the cradle. Once Brianna as all tucked in, he grabbed Ariel around the waist. He turned her and pulled her up against his body.

"Now we can have our talk."

Placing her hands against his chest, Ariel shoved, hoping he would release her. He didn't. "Let me go and I will speak with you."

Broc pretended to think over her request then shook his head. "Nay, this way you can't walk away from me."

Not having the energy to fight with him right now, Ariel made no other overtures for her release. "Very well, speak."

"I know my behavior toward you has been unacceptable, but I hope you can overlook it. I wish for us to start over, make a fresh start."

Ariel stiffened in his arms. He could not be serious. After months of being treated as low as the mud on his boots, he wanted her to forget what had happened. It could not be done. The wounds were still too fresh.

"How can you expect me to let the past go so easily? You're asking me to do something I find impossible."

Not about to give up so quickly, Broc pushed on. "Why not? I'm willing to forget what passed between you and Geoffrey. It goes against the grain, but I will push it from my mind."

The audacity of the man knew no bounds. He really needed to be knocked down a notch or two. Ariel would happily oblige by giving Broc the sharp edge of her tongue, but first she could no longer stand the close contact of his body. Throwing all her weight behind it, Ariel shoved Broc with both hands on his chest. Caught off guard, he lost his balance and landed on his rump with a thud. If Ariel had not been so angry, she would have found the sight of Broc on the floor rubbing his abused backside amusing, but not this day.

"How generous of you to forgive me for something that never even happened. You can take your fresh start and go to hell."

Standing up, Broc looked at her intently. "What do you mean it never happened? You slept with Geoffrey."

"Aye, but not in that way. You've never given me a chance to explain. The first night he wanted sex, but when I stayed unresponsive he let me be. After that I just slept in the bed next to him. He wanted to protect me from his men. If they assumed we were having sex I would be safe from their advances."

Broc paled slightly. "It looks as if I have to apologize to Geoffrey as well as to you. I'm sorry. I just don't want to lose you."

"You already have. How can I trust you again after this? If I accept you back, what are the chances of you turning on me once more? The one time I needed your understanding and support you withheld it."

Broc looked at her sadly. "I would give anything to go back to that first day and change how I handled the situation. The right thing to do was for me to ignore the pain I felt and be there for you. Your pain had to have been the greater."

Sadly, Ariel shook her head in denial. "But you can't go back. The hurt has been done and I find myself unable to forget the pain you caused me. For the sake of my heart, I must keep you out."

Broc hung his head in defeat. "What about the children?"

"You know how I feel about that. They are as much yours as they are mine. I will not keep them from you. We may not have a relationship, but I would like us to share our children."

"I will take whatever you can give me."

Pressing a kiss to Ariel's forehead, Broc left the hall.

Chapter 45

A month passed and Lady Mary and Lord Eustance decided it was time for them to go back to their home in Normandy. Even though Broc's older brother was capable of filling in during Lord Eustance's absence, they both agreed they had been gone too long.

The day of their leave taking was a sad one. Tears weren't held back as Lady Mary and Ariel hugged each other good-bye. Sensing something was going on that involved his grandparents, Colwyn wrapped his arms and legs around Lord Eustance's leg and refused to let go. Taking a moment to play with his grandson one last time, Broc's father walked around the yard asking where Colwyn could be. This made Colwyn squeal with delight.

When their departure couldn't be delayed any longer, Broc pried Colwyn's arms from around his father's leg and swung him up onto his shoulders. Deciding sitting atop his father's shoulders was just as fun, Colwyn grabbed a handful of Broc's hair and commenced to hit him on the head. Broc winced with each blow his small son gave him as he bade his parents a fond farewell. The St. Ceneris made sure they received promises of a visit to their home in Normandy from Broc and Ariel before mounting their horses. Lady Mary even managed to convince Swein to visit as well.

A few days later, Lisette and Geoffrey made preparations for their departure. This farewell was a trifle more reserved. Since the birth of Brianna, Broc had grudgingly attempted to get along with Geoffrey. Surprisingly, they found a lot to like about each other.

There was a definite chill to the air and everyone was wrapped in heavy cloaks. When they spoke their breaths puffed out in clouds. Soon no one would want to be traveling for any long distances.

Lisette kissed both Ariel and Broc then moved to stand next to her husband. "Now I expect you both to come see us at Kilsmere, say in about seven months from now. That should be approximately when our first child will be born. I would really like you, Ariel, to be with me when my time comes."

Smiling, Ariel hugged Lisette. Out of the corner of her eye, she saw Broc shake Geoffrey's hand in congratulations. "I'm so happy for you, Lisette. I promise to come to Kilsmere, but be prepared where I go, husband and children follow."

"We have plenty of room, as well you know. You're all welcome to come."

Geoffrey assisted his wife onto her horse, and once more came to stand before Ariel and Broc. He seemed undecided about something. Taking a quick look over at Broc, he swooped down and gave Ariel a kiss. Just as fast, he stepped away and mounted his horse.

Watching them make their way through the village, Ariel couldn't shake the feeling that she was being left alone with Broc. She felt her blood pump at a faster pace, but she forced her body back under control before it could get out of hand.

"Is what you said to Lisette true?"

Startled, Ariel jumped at the sound of Broc's voice. He stood close behind her. Her body quickly responded to his nearness, making her heart race. "What...what I said?"

His breath gently stirred her hair with each word he spoke. "Aye. Where you go, you would take me along."

Ariel found it hard to think clearly with him so very close. "Of course," she stammered, "You are my husband. We may not share intimacies, but we still can be friends."

"Really?" Broc stepped even closer. He was now close enough for Ariel to feel the heat from his body radiating onto her back. "I hope we can be very close friends."

With her emotions running high, Ariel sought a way to discreetly move away from Broc. Before she had the chance to even try, a baby's indignant wail could be heard coming from the hall.

Broc chuckled. "It sounds as if our daughter is hungry. She does have a way of demanding your attention."

Already heading back in the direction of the hall, Ariel cringed at the sound of Brianna's crying. "That she does. It helps to have a good set of lungs as well. I'd better rescue my father from her before she renders him unable to hear."

Swein paced the floor with his granddaughter in his arms. As he walked he bounced her, trying to settle her. Brianna was having none of it and continued to cry all the louder. Ariel had to give her father credit though he was giving it his all, even going as far as to offer the squalling infant his finger to suck on. His attempts were met with no success.

Going to Swein, Ariel relieved him of her upset daughter and went to sit in the chair next to the hearth. In passing, she noticed Colwyn sitting on the floor with his small hands covering his ears trying to block out the sound of his sister's cries. Hastily unfastening her tunic, Ariel offered her breast to Brianna. Opening her mouth, the baby clamped down on her nipple and greedily sucked. The hall fell blessedly silent.

Not having a howling child in his arms to contend with any longer, Ariel saw Swein's body visibly begin to relax. "I'm glad you weren't too far away. I would hate to see what would have happened if you did not come back quickly. It seems as if your daughter has a slight temper."

The thought of her father trying to appease Brianna for any length of time when her belly was empty made Ariel laugh. At the sound, her daughter opened her eyes and paused in her sucking. When Ariel patted her back reassuringly, Brianna continued nursing.

"If you call Brianna's temper slight, father, I would hate to see what she would be like in a full blown temper."

Joining in the conversation, Broc said, "We will give her a sword once she is grown. Brianna is sure to be stiff competition for Colwyn."

Both Swein and Ariel exchanged glances then looked at Broc. He appeared to be quite serious. Ariel had to ask just to make sure. "Is that what you want, Broc? You would not be bothered if our daughter chose to take up the sword?"

"How could I be? Her mother is a knight, by my own hand I might add. It's in her blood. In fact, I will encourage her to take up the sword. I want her to be able to defend herself."

Knocked speechless by her husband's intentions, Ariel could only stare at him. Oblivious to her shocked expression, Broc sat on the floor with his son for some play time.

* * * *

A week later, Ranulf and Lily returned to Elmstead. They both made much of Brianna. Now with Lily wed, Ariel had not expected her to continue in her duties. But Lily would hear none of it. She said, until she had a child of her own to take care of, she would lend assistance to Ariel.

The baby was now settled into a daily routine, allowing Ariel to find more time for herself. Lily watched the children when Ariel wanted time to practice with her sword. Ranulf happyily partnered her once more. He said while he had been in London he had hardly picked up his sword and needed to get back into shape. There were times when Ranulf would decide to stay with Lily and play with the children. During those times, Broc would step in and cross swords with her, which pleased her.

Memories of the days spent training for her knighthood were fondly remembered. It was during those times Broc had been the closest to her. Those days she missed and Ariel was thrilled to be able to once more test herself against her husband.

Today she decided to forgo her usual practice. The day was warm for that time of year and the sun shone brightly. Thinking to take advantage of such good weather, Ariel headed for the meadow. She had not been there since her return from Kilsmere. Suffering under Broc's treatment, she hadn't wanted any reminders of what could have been.

With a deep breath, Ariel allowed the sounds of nature to wash over her. She could hear the birds singing in the trees and a gentle breeze pulled at her hair. The meadow was still her favorite place to go when she needed some time alone.

Her steps led her where they might until Ariel found herself heading in the direction of the pond. Like the meadow, the pond remained the same in an ever changing world. But today Ariel noticed a change had taken place, a hut stood near the water's edge. A few trees had been removed to accommodate the structure, making its presence seem isolated in a sea of trees. It gave the feeling of privacy.

Wanting to see more, Ariel skirted the pond and went over to the hut. At closer inspection she could see it had been built using the same design the villagers used, but much larger. Curious as to what other changes may have been done to the inside she grabbed the door handle and pushed it open.

Here was where the similarities to the villagers' huts ended. Instead of just hard packed dirt, fresh rushes covered every inch of the floor. The walls had been white washed. A small table, along with two chairs, sat in the middle of the room close to a fire pit. What drew her attention the most was the large bed sitting in the far corner of the room.

Along with being large, the bed was covered in beautifully made sheets, sun bleached to a perfect white. A thick pile of rich furs were spread atop the mattress. The overall appearance was of a lovers' retreat from the outside world.

Only one person who could have arranged for this hut to be built on this particular spot. It had to have been Broc. No other knew what had taken place here. She hadn't even told her father what had happened at the pond. Then, almost as if he had sensed her thoughts, Broc appeared at her side.

"Was this your doing?"

"Aye." Moving from her side, Broc went to the fire pit and placed some of the wood he carried inside it. "Do you like it?"

"It's lovely." Seeing Broc strike a flint, Ariel watched the spark turn into a small fire that licked greedily at the wood.

With the fire well established, Broc stood. His eyes held an intensity that made Ariel aware of her woman's body, especially when using that same look he moved his eyes up and down her body. She felt drawn to him.

"I'm glad you approve. Consider it a marriage present."

"How...why?" Ariel didn't understand why he would do this when their marriage was not a close one.

Broc smiled at her making her heart beat erratically. "As to how, I had some of the villagers build it while I stayed in London looking for you. My mother graciously furnished the inside. The bed was her doing. As to why, it's really quite simple. This place holds great meaning for me. Here is where I met and claimed my one true mate. Here is where I found the only woman I could ever give my heart to."

Hearing those words, Ariel felt a rush of desire so keen that it made any kind of thought near impossible. Her whole being focused on the man who stood before her. Losing herself in a set of blazing gold eyes, the outside world fell away leaving only the two of them in their own realm of existence.

Taking a step closer, Broc pulled Ariel hard up against his body. "I need you, Ariel. More than I have needed anything in my whole life. Don't reject me. I have suffered enough for my past actions. Give me some peace." He bent his head down to her. Broc let his lips hover a breath away from her mouth. "Let me."

Ariel could no more deny him then stop her heart from beating. For in denying Broc, she would be denying herself the pleasure only he could give. Sighing in acceptance, Ariel closed the short distance between their lips and wound her arms around Broc's neck. Groaning, he pulled her even closer. Her breasts flattened against his hard chest. She felt his heart beating at a rapid pace. She knew Broc felt her heart racing along with his.

The joining of their lips was fierce, holding none of the gentleness as it had in previous meetings. Neither of them had the patience for such wooing. Their hunger had been too long denied and shoved aside. Once unleashed their passion ran rampant. Lifting Ariel off her feet, Broc walked to the bed in two long strides. Laying her on the soft mattress, he then followed her down.

Chapter 46

Swords dropped to the floor with a thud as they hit the rushes. Clothes were flung in every which way in their haste to be free of them. Broc knew he was going too fast, especially since this would be Ariel's first time since giving birth. He hated himself for it, but he couldn't wait any longer. For too many nights he had been haunted with dreams of Ariel, with her held in his arms exactly like this.

Now that she lay beside him in all of her naked glory, he let his eyes skim over every inch of her body. For a woman who had recently given birth, her body was virtually unchanged. The only indication of her motherhood was a slightly rounded stomach and a faint brown line running from her navel to the curling hair that shielded her sex.

Claiming her lips once more, Broc kissed Ariel until she started to wriggle impatiently under him. Wanting more, he nibbled at her throat and down to her breasts. They were full and heavy with milk. Watching Ariel's face for any sign of resistance, Broc suckled at one of her breasts. She closed her eyes and pulled him closer.

Releasing her breast, Broc inched his way down her body and placed featherlight kisses against her skin as he went. In his dreams he had done this to Ariel over and over again. Slipping lower he spread her legs and tasted her. Ariel moaned as his tongue laved her clit. The taste of her drove him wild.

Ariel gasped as Broc used his tongue to push her desire to greater heights. A keening moan escaped her lips. Not wanting to push Ariel over the edge, Broc moved back up her body and kissed her. He needed her hands on him. Taking hold of one of her hands he led it down to that part of his body that craved her touch the most—his throbbing cock. Closing her hand around him, Broc showed her what he liked as he moved her hand up and down his length. He released her hand when she squeezed his cock and pushed down on him. Broc groaned. He knew he couldn't take too much of this, he was already on the verge of exploding. Unable to wait any longer he pulled her hand away from his body, slid between her legs and joined their bodies in one thrust.

At the feel of Ariel's hot slick opening closing around him, Broc groaned in ecstasy. Knowing there would be another opportunity to love her again at a much slower pace, Broc pulled almost out of her body and then rammed back into her. He couldn't slow the pace down, and from the way Ariel clawed at his back, he knew she didn't mind. Ariel wrapped her legs around his waist, taking him in deeper. Moving so his cock rubbed her clit has he entered her, Broc pushed Ariel over the edge. Her climax claimed her as her hot channel squeezed around his cock. It pushed him into an intense release. Ramming home one more time, Broc groaned.

Once his breathing returned to normal, Broc rolled onto his back and pulled Ariel until she snuggled up against his side. He cushioned her head on his chest. Pushing the white blonde hair aside, Broc kissed Ariel's forehead. "Does this mean you have forgiven me?"

Ariel smiled against his chest. "I suppose I best. Every time we make love, I end up with child. You better make an honest woman out of me."

"Let's hope this joining doesn't bear any fruit. I would like to have you to myself for a little while."

"Aye, that would be nice. We always seem to have obstacles put between us."

Growing serious, Broc lightly rubbed the pad of this thumb across Ariel's bottom lip. "Nothing will tear us apart again, ever. I give my solemn word. You are my wife, the love I have for you will never die. I only hope you can learn to love me like you did before. That would be my greatest wish."

Going up on one elbow, Ariel kissed him lovingly. "I love you, Broc. My feelings for you never changed. Aye, you hurt me, but I'm willing to forget. My life would not be complete without you by my side. I need you, always."

Pulling her head down, Broc thoroughly kissed her leaving her breathless. With a groan he pulled away and slipped out of the bed.

Ariel frowned. "Where are you going?"

Donning his tunic and trews, Broc searched for his boots. Finding them under the table, he went and sat down on the edge of the bed and pulled them on. "We need more wood. What little I brought will not last us throughout the rest of the day. I will return, don't worry about that." He flashed a cocky grin.

Ariel returned his knowing grin. "You want to stay here all day?"

"Of course, I haven't had you to myself for a very long time. I intend to make the most of it while I can."

"What about Brianna? She will need to be fed."

"When I get the wood, I will stop by the hall and tell Lily to bring her here when she grows hungry. Relax. It will not take me long. I'm not through with you yet, not by a long shot."

* * * *

With Broc gone, Ariel lay back down on the pillows and pulled the covers up. She felt drained and satiated, but happy, very happy. Happier than she had been for quite some time. A smile formed on her lips as she allowed herself to drift off to sleep.

The door creaked open a short time later, Ariel didn't stir. Figuring Broc had returned from his errands, she waited for him to slip back into the bed beside her. So with some surprise, Ariel felt the cold steel blade of a dagger pressed against her throat. Wrenched fully awake, she opened her eyes to see a face she had hoped never to look at again.

Theodoric sat on the edge of the bed and smiled maliciously down at her. "Did you think you could so easily escape from the plans I painstakingly made for you? If you did, then you were mistaken. Now I will remove the dagger from your throat, please don't give me cause to use it. Get dressed like a good girl."

Once more Ariel found herself in a situation she was powerless to prevent. With Theodoric's hard eyes watching her every move, she hurriedly pulled on her clothes. Bending down to retrieve a stray boot, her eye caught the sparkle of a gem stone. Her sword lay half under the bed with the hilt easily within reach of her hand. Giving Theodoric a furtive look, Ariel lunged for the sword.

Pain shot through her head as Theodoric grabbed a handful of her hair and roughly pulled her out of reach of the sword. "Now, Ariel, did you think

I would allow you to gain possession of your sword? Remember, I've watched you on the practice field. I would be a fool to allow that to happen. I don't seek my death by your hand."

Yanking on her hair, Theodoric brought her to her feet. Her eyes watered with pain. Ariel pulled her cloak around herself and followed the older man out the door. He seemed to have a destination in mind, because Theodoric unhesitatingly led Ariel deeper into the forest.

Ariel felt a wave of sickening panic wash over her. In the forest they would be much harder to track. Their passage through the woods would go almost undetected. Her only chance was Broc's ability to track them from the hut. Hoping to leave some sort of sign of their passing, she dragged her feet and brushed up against trees breaking off leaves and branches.

Deep inside the forest the air seemed cooler. Very little sunlight managed to penetrate the thick cover of foliage that rose high about their heads. It gave the impression that the day was further along than it truly was.

With a jerk on her hair, Theodoric came to a halt. Just as quickly, he released her hair and pulled her hands behind her back. He then proceeded to bind them together with a piece of cord he carried with him. Searching the shadows to make sure none had followed, Theodoric wiped at the sweat that trickled down his face. "It would appear we are alone, for now. But I will feel better when we have reached the deepest part of the forest."

Taking hold of her arm, he once more dragged Ariel through the bush. With her hands bound behind her, she had trouble keeping her balance over the rough terrain. Theodoric took no notice. When she would begin to fall, he would only pull her up onto her feet and push her ever deeper into the forest.

Finally, after what seemed like hours, Theodoric stopped their travel. His breath came in pants and sweat dampened his hair as well as his tunic. Ariel guessed this was probably the most walking her captor had done in quite some time. His soft body gave testimony to his easy life.

Looking around her, Ariel realized Theodoric had to have been here before. He had set up a makeshift camp. A small lean-to type shelter sat off to one side in the natural clearing. A ring of stones filled with ash gave her the suspicion this man had been here for more than one day.

Forcing her to sit down with her back against a large tree, her captor took a few steps away. Theodoric reached for a saddle bag and pulled out a length of rope. He walked back to her. He wrapped the rope around her chest and the tree trunk binding her tightly to it. Unable to move, she knew she would have to wait for another opportunity to escape to come her way.

* * * *

Stepping with a light heart and feeling a small amount of anticipation, Broc moved hurriedly across the meadow. In his arms he carried the needed wood. The others who had been at the hall where not too surprised to hear of his and Ariel's reconciliation. Swein had clapped him on the back saying Ariel had needed the time to see what she had been missing out on. She wasn't a stupid girl. She knew when to hold onto something of great value.

Broc had been knocked speechless at his father-in-law's words. He had thought Swein didn't think too highly of him, but this speech told him otherwise. It came as a surprise to find himself held in such regard by his wife's father, considering Broc had taken Elmstead away from the man. Broc had said as much to Swein. The older man had chuckled. He had said he was getting too old to run Elmstead anyway. Swein made it quite clear he preferred to pass the responsibilities onto a much younger set of shoulders. He had no complaints with Broc's ability in running the land.

Now with the pond in sight, Broc broke off his musings and lengthened his stride. The thought of Ariel lying naked in the bed was all the motivation he needed to hurry.

Seeing the door to the hut standing open, Broc came up short. Something wasn't right. A sense of unease washed over him. A feeling of Ariel being in trouble overwhelmed him the more he looked at the open door.

Broc dropped the wood and ran into the hut. As he had feared, Ariel was nowhere to be seen. A quick inspection proved his uneasiness had not been unfounded. He knew she wouldn't have left willingly on her own. What they had shared told Broc he hadn't been wrong in his thinking. Ariel had accepted him back into her life as well as into her body.

Moving about the room he searched for any kind of sign, something that could have caused Ariel to leave. All he found was her sword half hidden under the bed. Broc had all the proof he needed, his suspicions had been correct. Ariel would never have left her sword behind. A knight's sword was as much a part of him as was his sword arm. A knight would feel lost without his sword hanging at his side. The same would be true for Ariel as it was for him.

Finding no other clue as to what had befallen Ariel, Broc searched the outside of the hut. It was then he noticed the scuffed footprints that led to the back of the hut. He followed them and found others that headed into the forest. The prints in the fore were large, a man's boot possibly, the other set had to be Ariel's.

Needing nothing else to persuade him Ariel had indeed been taken without her consent, Broc started to run back to the hall. The day was fading fast and soon it would be too dark to see the trail Ariel had left for them to follow. Time was of the essence. If they didn't move fast his wife could very well be taken from him once again. This time he may not be so lucky in finding her, she could very well be gone from his life for good.

Chapter 47

Night descended leaving Ariel cold and stiff. Theodoric had tied her to a tree that wasn't even close to the fire. Her lightweight cloak didn't offer much in the way of warmth, especially on a frosty night such as this. She shivered uncontrollably.

Shifting around she tried to find a more comfortable position, which was impossible given the circumstances. Her hands were numb and her breasts ached with too much milk, another reason why she needed to return to her daughter. Ariel could just picture Brianna screaming with hunger. That thought alone made her feel all the more anxious to be with her.

Her movements drew Theodoric's attention. Stepping away from the fire, he came to stand above her. He smiled. There was no warmth in it. Ariel silently wished him to hell. "How is my lady holding out? Cold? Good, we wouldn't like you to forget your place, now would we?"

"Why are you doing this to me?"

Theodoric chuckled, but no mirth was in the sound he made. "You haven't figured it out yet? It's quite simply really. I dislike being denied the pleasure of seeing Broc suffer. He gave Alwen a grievous insult by annulling their marriage."

"You know Broc will come for me." At least Ariel hoped that was true, but the fading light made her doubt Broc would be able to find her.

"He will not find you. The forest at night can be your enemy, or in my case, a friend. Broc doesn't know this forest very well, he will become lost very easily and by morning we will be gone."

"What are going to do with me?"

"I haven't decided as of yet. For now, I will keep you with me. Having you separated from your new daughter should cause Broc some upset."

Ariel felt her blood turn to ice in her veins. This man knew too much about her family. She had to wonder how long he had been watching them.

If he didn't succeed here, would he go after her children next? The blood drained out of her face just thinking of what could happen to those two innocents.

Theodoric watched her face grow white. He laughed, making him sound deranged. Ariel cringed at the sound, which caused Theodoric to laugh all the louder. She could still hear him laughing even after he returned to the fire.

* * * *

Torches held high, Broc, Swein, and Ranulf slowly made their way through the thick forest. It was decidedly getting harder to see. Broc, who led the small group, lost the trail on a number of occasions. Once that happened they would have to backtrack until they picked it up again, which caused unwanted delays. It also did nothing to calm Broc's already strained nerves.

The deeper they penetrated the forest, the more of a struggle it became to walk. Branches seemed to claw at their clothes and hair. Fallen tree limbs, or whole trees, had to be stepped or climbed over. In the dark Broc would sometimes miss seeing them, causing him trip or come up short in surprise.

Losing the trail for what seemed like the hundredth time, Broc took his frustration out on the trees surrounding him. Taking out his sword he savagely swung the blade, causing leaves and bark to fly into the air. Stepping forward, Swein moved around him, catching the younger man's arm in a grip he could not easily ignore.

"Enough Broc. I think it's time to call it quits for the night. It's just too dark to see clearly. We can return on the morrow."

Pulling his arm out of Swein's grasp, Broc shook his head. "Nay, Ariel will be out of reach by then. I'll continue on. If you and Ranulf wish to return to the hall, you both may go, but I'm staying."

Looking at Ranulf, Swein saw him give a quick nod of his head. "We will stay with you. It would not sit well with me to leave Ariel unfound throughout the night."

Sheathing his sword, Broc lifted his torch above his head and went in search of Ariel's trail once again. The faint markings were their only link to where she could possibly be. As luck would have it they had not strayed too far off the trail. Picking it up once more the three men continued on with their quest.

A short time later Ranulf stopped in mid-stride and sniffed the air. The others hadn't noticed Ranulf had lagged behind, so giving a shout to draw their attention he called them back. "Wait, I think I hear something. And I think I smell smoke."

Swein and Broc rushed back to the spot where Ranulf stood motionless, listening intently. Standing perfectly still, they both strained to hear what Ranulf had heard.

Smiling, Swein whispered. "Voices, coming from over there." He pointed to a spot in front of them.

Broc agreed. "Aye. How far in that direction, we will have to see. I suggest we split up. Try to form a circle around whoever they are. I think we're only dealing with one man."

Swein looked at Broc, searching the younger man's face. "I have a feeling you know who it is."

"Aye. Who else has been a bane of my existence for the last little while? Theodoric. This is something that slimy bug would do, it reeks of his scheming."

"You're probably right, he tried this once before. The man likes to hide in the shadows."

"Not this day. His petty grudges end here and now. He isn't going to get away with this, not this time."

Swein nodded his head in agreement. "Theodoric has to pay the price for his underhanded ways. Once we have him surrounded he should be easy to subdue. If he fights us, I'll take great pleasure in forcing him to comply with our wishes."

On silent feet, the three men stealthily made their way across the forest floor. Their footsteps were muffled by the cover of fallen leaves. Just before they reached the small clearing, Broc spied the flames of a fire flickering between the trees. He motioned to the others to circle the camp as he inched forward to take a closer look at what awaited them.

Broc smiled, he had been correct in his thinking. Theodoric sat on a log before a small fire, acting as if he had nothing to fear. The man was overconfident. Quickly scanning the area with his keen eyes, he found no other men lurking about. The only other person in the clearing was Ariel, bound to a tree off to his right. That sight alone gave Broc enough reason to exact some form of retribution from Theodoric's hide. She appeared to be unharmed, but the sight of her tied like an animal made Broc see red. He would have to make sure to pay Theodoric back in kind.

Praying the other two men had had enough time to move into position Broc stood and rushed the camp. Letting loose an ear splitting war cry, he went after Theodoric. Swein and Ranulf could be heard crashing through the woods a few seconds later from opposite sides of the camp. There was nowhere Theodoric could run. He was theirs.

* * * *

The cold and lack of food made her sleepy. She closed her eyes, no longer fighting the drowsiness. Ariel figured no harm would be done if she let her body rest for a little while. There was not much else she could do to better her situation, being bound to a tree as she was.

In a blink of an eye all hell broke loose. One moment all was peaceful and the next, the night became filled with battle cries and men crashing through the trees. Before Ariel could rouse herself completely, her ropes had been cut away from her chest. With a dagger held at her throat, Theodoric held her before him as a shield.

Seeing the face of her beloved, Ariel felt confident enough to smile at Broc. Theodoric's plans would be foiled now, she would be saved. Her husband had come to free her.

Snarling, Broc stalked Theodoric into the middle of the small camp. Swein and Ranulf took up positions around the other man and closed in on him. There was no other route he could use to escape, he was boxed in and well he knew it.

Broc took a menacing step toward him. That action only caused Theodoric to press the blade closer against Ariel's neck. Broc froze as a trickle of blood welled up to run beneath the blade of the dagger.

"Release Ariel, you're outnumbered. Neither one of us will allow you to take her. It's over. Give me the dagger and no harm will befall you."

"I think not Norman," Theodoric snarled at Broc. "Who is to say I will not slit your wife's pretty throat."

"If you do, I will personally make sure you take your last breath shortly thereafter. Enough of this. Let Ariel go. Don't make this any harder than it has to be."

Theodoric was obviously well beyond being able to see the situation in a sane way, for instead of surrendering, he tried to bolt. Dragging Ariel with him, Theodoric started to move between Ranulf and Swein. Fear for Ariel made them hold back from moving against the other man. The dagger shook in his hand and was liable to hit the vulnerable vein in Ariel's neck. A desperate man was known to do just about anything to escape what fate had dealt him.

Ariel saw the frustration on Broc's face as Theodoric pulled her away. She knew he wouldn't take the chance of any harm befalling her. If she wanted to get out of this mess, she would have to help herself. Now was not the time though, Theodoric was too agitated and he would be unpredictable.

Once more Ariel found herself dragged through the dark forest. This time he blundered his way past the trees with no set destination in mind. His only thought was to escape Ariel's rescue party. When the small clearing disappeared from sight and Ariel could no longer see Broc, she heard him cry out her name in anguish. Tears pricked the back of her eyes. *Would the fates not let them ever be together? Was it their destiny to always find each other and then be cruelly torn apart again?*

The dagger bit sharply into her neck when Theodoric stumbled over an exposed tree root. Ariel hissed in pain. The dagger never wavered from her skin. Theodoric had centered all his attention on the sounds coming from a short distance behind them, not caring what damage his dagger inflicted upon Ariel.

Knowing Broc, her father and Ranulf were responsible for the sounds echoing through the trees, Ariel tried another tactic. If she could manage to make Theodoric talk to her, maybe he would become distracted enough for Broc to make a move. Clearing her throat, Ariel made her first attempt to draw Theodoric out.

"You know Broc will never let you get away. You're only delaying the inevitable."

Theodoric remained stoically silent. Ariel wasn't even sure he had heard her speak. She would have to think of something to say that he couldn't ignore. Something that would incite him to anger. She knew she would be taking a big chance. Instead of voicing his anger, Theodoric could very well lash out at her, but that was the chance she would have to take. Ariel wasn't going to allow him to have control over her life again. He could very well make her life a living hell.

"Give up, Theodoric. Broc is the much better man. Do you actually think you can get away from him so easily?"

That seemed to do the trick. Theodoric's face flushed red. His grip on her arm tightened causing Ariel to wince in pain. The dagger pressed closer still, but Theodoric didn't stop their ever forward movement.

"You think that bastard of a Norman is better than me? If it wasn't for his kind coming to our shores, I would still hold sway over you. They took everything away that once belonged to me."

Theodoric pulled her close to his face and laughed. "Don't you understand? Your sojourn as a serf was revenge for my daughter. This time, I do this for me as well. These greedy, grasping Normans think we Saxons will just blindly allow them to run our lives without a fight. Well, I intend to make one particular Norman feel my sting. Broc St. Ceneri will rue the day he had the presumption to take one of my holdings as his."

Ariel, in a small way, could sympathize with Theodoric. His loss of status was much greater than what her father and she had taken from them, but that did not give him the right to disrupt her life. Broc may be a Norman, the enemy, but Ariel still loved him despite that fact.

"Your plan has failed, you have been found out. Broc will find you."

Theodoric increased his pace. "I'm afraid you are wrong. This situation has definitely turned for the better—for me."

Looking in the direction Theodoric headed, Ariel felt her hopes of rescue sink. Somehow he had managed to bring them to the other side of the forest. The trees were already thinning out.

Bursting through the tree line, Theodoric whistled a signal. In response, Godwin and Hugh stepped out into the open. Ariel groaned to herself. Her two nemeses would have to be here.

"Go get the horses. We have to leave, now."

Never one to question his lord's commands, Hugh went to do as he had been bidden. The few minutes it took to collect the mounts had Theodoric constantly looking at the edge of the forest. He moved restlessly from one foot to the other. He knew Broc and the others could not be too far behind.

Hugh led three horses over to where Theodoric stood waiting. Godwin mounted one and Hugh mounted another. Theodoric grabbed the reins of his own mount. Releasing Ariel's arm, he dropped the dagger from her neck. With a shove he tried to force her to mount the horse, Ariel fought him. She could not allow him to leave with her in tow.

An instant later Broc, Ranulf, and her father crashed out of the forest. Theodoric once more pulled Ariel in front of him and placed the dagger at her throat.

Signaling to his two henchmen, Theodoric sent Hugh and Godwin to rid him of his assailants. When both Broc and Ranulf pulled their swords out of their scabbards, Hugh and Godwin turned their mounts and beat a hasty retreat. Theodoric hurled insults at their backs.

Now that his guards had deserted him, Theodoric faced the three enraged men alone. He was cornered and well he knew it. His desperation showed plainly on his face, but he was not ready to admit defeat. As Broc took a step closer, Theodoric moved the dagger threateningly against Ariel's throat. Having taken all she could of being used as a pawn in someone else's attempt to regain control, Ariel decided this would end here and now.

She used a trick Osbern had taught her long ago. She let herself relax, which forced Theodoric to hold her full weight. The unexpected move caused him to stumble and shift the dagger away from her neck as he reached to catch her in both arms. With the dagger removed from her neck, Ariel twisted in Theodoric's hold and kicked out, hitting him between the legs. Cupping his manhood, he groaned in pain and slowly slid to the ground.

Ranulf pounced on him. Motioning to Swein, he had the older man remove Ariel's bindings and give them to him. With more force than was necessary, Ranulf wrenched Theodoric's hands behind his back. The cord that had bound Ariel's hands together now bound Theodoric's.

Rubbing the numbness from her hands, Ariel crossed the short distance that separated them and threw herself into Broc's welcoming embrace. The tension she had felt while being Theodoric's captive slowly drained out of her body.

Broc crushed Ariel to him. That had been too close of a call for both of them. Squeezing his wife again, he heard her grunt in pain. Holding her away from his chest, Broc searched for any sign that Ariel was injured. "What's wrong? Where did he hurt you?"

"I'm fine." Broc paid her no heed and began to move his hands over her body trying to locate the source of pain. "I'm fine, really. Theodoric didn't harm me, it's just I have been gone too long from our daughter. I'll find relief once she has had a good nursing."

Broc looked down at Ariel's breasts, seeing the two wet spots that darkened the material of her tunic. "Then we had best get you back to the hall with all due haste. One of the women from the village who has a child of her own agreed to feed Brianna, but I'm sure our daughter will be happy to relieve you of some of your milk."

Looking over the top of Ariel's head, Broc asked, "Ranulf, Swein, can you manage to bring our prisoner back on your own?"

Swein nodded. "Aye, go ahead. Theodoric will give us no more problems. Go tend to my granddaughter, Ariel. We will be along shortly."

Needing no more encouragement, Broc clasped Ariel's hand in his and started the arduous journey back to the hall.

* * * *

Once more in the comfortable surroundings of the main hall, Ariel woke Brianna and put her daughter to her breast. As Brianna took her fill, Ariel felt the pressure in her breasts dissipate. She couldn't hold back her sigh of relief.

With the pain alleviated, Ariel set about satisfying her baser needs. Lily, overjoyed to see Ariel not the worse for wear from her ordeal, took it upon herself to take care of her. Once she decided Ariel had had enough to eat and drink, Lily prepared a bath in Broc's chamber for her.

Sinking into the warm water, Ariel felt the remaining stiffness leave her body. Luxuriating in the bath's warmth after being out in the cold for so long, she sank even further down into the water and rested her head on the rim of the tub. A moment later Broc stepped into the chamber.

Removing his sword, he rolled up his sleeves and moved to the tub. Fishing the wash cloth out of the water, he proceeded to soap Ariel's body. When the cloth moved to more intimate spots, Ariel laughingly swatted Broc's hand away.

"Control yourself, my lord. There will be time enough later to indulge in that particular pleasure. Now tell me, what has become of our guest?"

Letting the cloth slip from his fingers, Broc went to stand at Ariel's back and began to massage the tense muscles on the top of her shoulders and neck. "Theodoric will have to be taken to London. William will take great pleasure in meting out his justice on that man. William has developed an extreme dislike for him."

"So, where did you put him?"

"He's in one of the empty huts in the village. The men of the village demanded Theodoric be placed under their care until he goes to the king. If I recall correctly, your friend the blacksmith took the first watch."

Ariel giggled. "By the time Theodoric leaves he will only be too happy to face William. The villagers will not go easy on him. Their dislike for Theodoric is a match for William's own."

"I quite agree. Now if my Lady Knight would permit, I'm going to take you out of that bath and show you how much I love you."

Bending down, Broc scooped Ariel out of the tub and still dripping wet, placed her on the bed. Ariel gloried in the feel of Broc's weight on top of her as her husband joined her on the mattress. Allowing the pleasure only Broc could give her wash over her senses, Ariel held him close to her. Nothing would separate them again. Tonight would mark the beginning of a new life together.

The last coherent thought she had before succumbing to their lovemaking, was how much her life had changed since first meeting this Norman knight. Some of the changes were for the better and some were definitely for the worse. If by some fate Ariel had the ability to go back to that spring day, she wouldn't change what happened. Now with the future so bright before them, Ariel only hoped life would provide more adventures for a knight and his Lady Knight. What else could she ask for?

LADY KNIGHT

THE END

WWW.MARISACHENERY.COM

ABOUT THE AUTHOR

Marisa Chenery was always a lover of books, but after reading her first historical romance novel, she found herself hooked. Having inherited a love for the written word, she soon started writing her own novels.

After trying her hand at writing historicals, she now also writes paranormals. Marisa lives in Ontario, Canada with her husband and four children. She would love to hear from you, so stop by her website and send her an email while you're there.

Siren Publishing, Inc.
www.SirenPublishing.com

CPSIA information can be obtained at www.ICGtesting.com
Printed in the USA
BVOW05s1033110314

347293BV00018B/997/P